SHADOW OF DEATH

The prick of a needle woke me. Lamps were lit, making the man above me waver in shadows when he straightened with an empty syringe in his hand.

"Ah, you're awake, Miss St. George," he said smoothly. "I've given you something to help you rest easy."

It was Dr. Dijon, and there were matters I wished to discuss with him. "How is Carlie? What . . ." I began, but the room and the doctor began to circle around my head. I struggled frantically to remain conscious, but darkness rolled over me like a giant wave.

Grotesque shapes wavered in a menacing circle from which there was no escape. My feet . . . my feet were still there, but they would only move with difficulty. I ran in an exaggerated slow motion toward an opening in the circle. I tried to scream, but had no voice. I was tired, so very tired.

I knew that I had to fight. I couldn't give in to the overwhelming desire to sink into unconsciousness. With a monumental effort, I struggled to sit up in my bed.

I reached out, clawing desperately at the sheets. But just as I felt the cold floor beneath my bare feet, the dark shadow of Dr. Dijon loomed over me once more, and I knew that I was lost . . .

SHADOW MANSION

BY LEE CALIF

ZEBRA BOOKS
KENSINGTON PUBLISHING CORP.

ZEBRA BOOKS

are published by

Kensington Publishing Corp.
475 Park Avenue South
New York, NY 10016

First printing: December 1985

Printed in the United States of America

Chapter One

Diedre's shrieks woke me. My eyelids were heavy, reluctant to open as I hovered between worlds. At last I forced myself to roll onto my back, and through sleep-clogged lashes saw strange shadows dancing on the ceiling. Through the cries of terror and pain filling the room came a crackling noise, and then I tried to return to the real world.

Turning my head, I saw her. Diedre danced with eerie contortions in front of the open stove, arms slapping wildly at herself even as she screamed in agony. Her mouth contorted and her eyes squeezed shut, and then she vainly tried to rid herself of her burning nightgown.

A nightmare? I was still in the grip of my interrupted dreams, too groggy to accept the reality of what I was seeing. It was a nightmare!

Flames shot upward to her hair, framing her pixie face in a halo of destruction. Panic changed her screams to a keening wail as she beat frantically at her relentless pursuer. Black streaks appeared on her face, and when the fire claimed an eyebrow a sound issued from her mouth like no sound I'd heard before.

Scrambling from bed, I reached her in a trice, but she danced away from me. She fell against the curtains and I ran to her to beat at the flames, feeling the scorching heat sear my hands. Tears blurred my vision as pain registered, but I still tore relentlessly at her gown.

Then our room filled with people and their cries added to the din. Someone plucked me bodily from the holocaust, and I looked up to see Sarah, our floor housemother. One of her arms circled my waist, while the other hand beat out the flames that had started their crackling journey up my sleeve. Her voice was shocked as she gasped, "Oh, my dear . . . my dear . . ." and then her words were lost as her voice turned into a moan.

I wrenched free from her so I could see Diedre. Horror filled me when I saw a blackened figure protruding from a smoldering blanket. Smothered flames licked weakly at Diedre's chin before they flickered out. Hands pulled blazing curtains from the window, while others beat at the smoking coverlet. The smoke made me cough as merciful tears blinded me once again.

The clang of fire engines sounded in the distance. They grew louder as the horses galloped clatteringly over the cobblestones in front of Miss Brigham's school, then came to a halt amid shouting firemen. The firefighters in the room gaspingly worked their way out, in no way reluctant to give way for professionals.

Sarah dragged me into the hall, wincing at the clamor of girlish shrieks and screams. Masculine voices mingled in the bedlam when the firemen reached the second floor where Diedre and I had our room, and we made way for them and the equipment they brought with them.

Then I tried to free myself. "Diedre . . ." I stammered. My hands burned as though still on fire, but I had to see Diedre. Tears covered my face even as Sarah's voice came urgently to my ears.

"Diedre is not on fire anymore, Shadow. Hush, now!" She half-carried me to her own room and deposited me on the bed, then examined my hands. "Oh, my!" She looked up as one of the other girls paused in the doorway. "Get me some lard, Fanny. Quick!"

Carefully, so as not to touch my hands, Sarah pulled covers over me. I realized then that I was shivering in the cruel coldness of her room. "Where's D-Di-Diedre?" I asked, my teeth chattering in the zero temperature.

Fanny returned with the lard bucket in record time, and Sarah brought a handful of its contents to smear over my reddened hands. "Diedre's probably in Miss Brigham's room," she said briskly. "The doctor should be here any minute."

Her touch was light, but I winced from the pain. Try as I would, I couldn't stop the tears that welled from my eyes. "I want my father," I wailed. "Please get my father!"

Miss Brigham heard my words as she entered. "We've sent for your father, Shadow," she said. "He should be here soon, so stop this crying." Her face found my hands and she winced, then resolutely brought her face under control. "That lard will make your hands stop hurting soon, I'm sure. Come, Shadow, brace up."

Hiccupping sobs brought shudders when I tried to stifle my grief. "Diedre? H-how is sh-she? Please tell me!"

Sarah and Miss Brigham exchanged glances before Miss Brigham answered. "The doctor just arrived. He'll take care of Diedre and I'm sure she'll be all right. You are both good, strong girls."

She glanced around when a fireman stuck his head in the doorway. "Fire's out, ma'am," he said, and at her nod, left.

Miss Brigham turned back to me. "I'll bring your father up as soon as he arrives, Shadow. The doctor will come look at your hands when he finishes with Diedre, so compose yourself, my dear." She bustled out, ordering the other girls to return to their rooms as she went.

I shuddered, thinking of poor Diedre's blackened little face in my last glimpse of her. She was twelve, two years my junior, and my dearest friend among the girls at Miss Brigham's school. We had shared a room for more than a year—a younger sister I dearly loved. A chill raced up my spine and a vague sense of great loss brought a hollow feeling inside me.

"Will you rest now while I go help Miss Brigham?" Sarah asked gently. "You're all right now, aren't you?"

I nodded, sniffling, then tucked my nose under the covers for warmth. My hands burned dreadfully, so I left them on top of the covers in the icy cold and tried to ignore the hurt.

Snow stuck to the windowpane, blotting out the

darkness of the night. Wind howled dismally around the gables, rattled the glass, and even moved the curtains inside. The storm had grown to blizzard proportions since I had been wakened. Would my father come, despite the freezing temperature? I hope so, I thought desperately. Oh, I hope so!

Fresh tears trickled down my cheeks as I lay waiting. If only I had a mother to comfort me. Mother . . . Carmelita . . . oh, Carmelita . . . I need you, I need you! Alone in the dimly lit room, the fourteen years that comprised my life passed before me. . . .

My mother had died on the day I was born— October 8, 1858—so I missed knowing the beautiful Carmelita de la Cruz y Cuadro. A picture of her hung in a locket around my neck, and through the years I had studied it often. It was a charm that had dispelled the feelings of loneliness that many times had tortured my soul.

Carmelita's dark eyes laughed at me from the picture. The proud lift to her head under its covering of lustrous dark curls proclaimed an imperious background. Could her long-ago ancestry include a haughty Roman empress? Or perhaps a stately Egyptian queen? How had she come to marry the stern Englishman who was Edward St. George? I imagined her as warm and happy, and he was as cold and unsmiling as a man could be. Had he always been that way, or had he changed so much after his loss?

My father had named me Shadow because I was all that Carmelita had left behind. He refused to discuss her with me—or anything else, for that matter—so I had only my imagination to draw on when I speculated how life would be had my mother lived. Did a child fare better with both parents? Surely my mother would have kept me close to her heart. Of that I was sure, of that I *had* to be sure.

Aproned nannies and housekeepers were my first companions. They were so much alike, I had trouble remembering their names. All were courteous, most were kind, but none of them gave me warmth and love such as a mother would give . . . and a father? Under usual circumstances, didn't fathers love their children as much as mothers? One of my nannies told me why I was called Shadow, but it was not until I was sent to boarding school that I realized how strange a name it was.

At first, the girls at Miss Brigham's had taunted me because of it, and I crumbled into shameful tears. But then my pride made me rally. After all, I was part of Carmelita, and the blood of the conquistadores ran through our veins, perhaps even that of ancient royalty. Raising my head in haughty imitation of her portrait, I sallied forth to conquer my small world. Never would I allow anyone to daunt me.

Before long I had made friends of my classmates, and they accepted me and my name. The older girls plagued me a while longer, but as we grew knowledgeable about social position and prestige, their badgering faded. My father was a man of wealth, as well as a member of New York's aristocracy. As his daughter, I was eminently acceptable—to everybody but him.

Edward St. George preferred me out of his sight. Before I was sent to school I was usually in bed before he came home, and he never entered my room to kiss me goodnight or for any other reason. Only occasionally would I see him before he left the house in the morning, and that was only a glimpse. I breakfasted with my current nanny. When I entered Miss Brigham's boarding school, things did not change. On visiting days, when the other girls' parents hovered over them, I was alone. Until the time I was twelve, I stayed in my room on parents' day and wept in private.

Then one sunny day when the carriages began to arrive, my conquistadore blood stiffened my spine in anger at my father's cavalier treatment. I pressed a kiss on my mother's portrait before tilting the banner of my chin and sallying forth. This time I had only my own hurt feelings to conquer, and they were nothing I would permit anyone to see.

As I watched the day's activities from the background, I discovered how much more difficult it is to quell an enemy within than something outside yourself. Adoring mothers and fathers lavished presents and attention on their daughters, making me even more aware of my lonely state. Tears pushed hotly at my eyes, but I batted my lashes, forcing my thoughts to other matters and forbidding these shameful signs to descend to my cheeks.

Riding lessons at the academy began at age sixteen, and on parents' day the older girls showed off by donning their riding habits and mounting staid old mares who spent most of their time in the school stables munching hay. The girls sat precariously on the slippery side-saddles while the mares plodded around a spacious ring of sawdust. Anxious grooms hovered at the edges, ready to dash forward in the event someone needed rescuing.

11

It looked like fun, and I was having no fun at all. Tears pushed up through my throat despite my desperate swallowing and threatened to force their way into my eyes in overwhelming force. I slipped into the tack room where I could cry without making a spectacle of myself. Sobs shook me as I leaned against the rough wall and gave myself to the grief inside.

When the storm subsided and I looked around, a shy stableboy stood watching me. We stared at each other, and then he pulled a handkerchief from his pocket and daubed gently at the tears rolling down my face.

"Want to go for a ride?" he asked softly.

I stared, uncomprehending.

"The horse cars," he said patiently. "Want to go with me? I was about to leave when I heard you."

"I-I d-don't dare," I stammered. "Miss Brigham would get angry."

"Not if she doesn't know."

"I'll have to get a coat."

His dark eyes laughed at me . . . like Carmelita's . . . and suddenly I wasn't crying anymore.

"It's spring, missy, and warm outside, but I'll go borrow one for you." He disappeared, but soon returned with a coat I recognized as belonging to one of the serving girls.

"Come on," he coaxed, "they won't even miss you."

That was true, I knew, and my twelve-year-old heart lightened as I rose and let him help me into the alien garment. It was of rougher cloth than I had ever worn, but it fit passably well. Snugging it around me, I followed him out the back door into the street.

Wherever I had gone heretofore, I had ridden in my

father's elegant carriage, always attended by a nanny or a groom beside the dignified coachman. The thought of riding on one of the clanging horse cars crowded with people I didn't know filled me with excitement. In my loneliness I had daydreamed of having adventures, and surely now I was having one.

We took only a few steps before I stopped in dismay. "I have no money! And I don't even know your name!"

He turned to look at me. "My name is Juan. What's yours?"

"Shadow St. George," I answered, waiting for the disbelief and scorn I was sure would follow.

"Shadow," he said softly. "That's nice. Well, Shadow St. George, I have money." He jingled the change in his pocket. "Now can we go?"

We rode the cars that day, and I saw a New York I hadn't known existed. People crowded elbow-to-elbow and jostled each other boarding and leaving through the narrow doors, at times calling greetings to friends they recognized or grumbling angrily as they were shoved by someone in the crowd. Juan held my hand and warded off strangers, and we soon leaped on and off with the agility of longtime riders. The patient horses ignored pedestrians and other carriages dodging around them, only flicking their tails when flies settled on their broad rumps.

I learned that Juan had been a stable boy at Miss Brigham's school for the past two years. He had been orphaned then, and although he was only two years my senior, had been forced to seek employment in order to live. His people were poor and left nothing when they died. One of the many epidemics had swept the tenements, carrying them along on its tide. A momentary sadness flicked across Juan's face as he told me this, but then he shrugged philosophically and grinned at me again.

Juan's last name was Monterro—Spanish, as had been Carmelita's. My head pounded as I wondered if, in some remote way, he could possibly be related to my mother . . . but then I knew that was silly. Just because he was Spanish and she was Spanish didn't mean they were relatives. His eyes were dark brown, like Carmelita's, while mine were blue like my father's, but we both had dark, almost black hair, as did the picture resting at my throat. And he exuded warmth and friendship and even admiration, to such an extent that I felt more alive than ever before.

We wandered through markets piled high with produce, and when the smell of fresh-baked bread made me ravenous, Juan bought a loaf to divide between us.

The harbor beckoned when we neared the southernmost point of Manhattan Island. We strolled down cobblestoned South Street, crisscrossed by the bowsprits of the tall ships rocking in the gentle tide, masts and rigging creaking overhead, folded sails stirring in the breeze. Vagrant men hunched over scruffy belongings right in the piles of the wharves, angry eyes daring the world to so much as touch. Vendors peddled coffee, baked beans, and "rice pudding, a penny a portion," the delicious smells wafting through the air until they were overwhelmed by the atmosphere.

The air reeked of dried codfish, molasses, and rum. Gulls shrieked overhead, angering sailers who were targeted with their errant droppings. Out on the water billowing sails bellied windward on schooners entering and leaving the busy harbor. The sails reminded me of dancers at the ballet as they dipped and rose at the whim of the seas. We passed by shops where chandlers sold nautical maps and ship's hardware to men with rolling gaits and wind-reddened faces. Fragrant smells rose from the pipes some of them smoked, and I wondered how it would feel to clench a small furnace in your teeth and have your head beclouded in fumes.

My nose wrinkled at rotting fish odors, but then I took a deep breath as the salty smell of the sea pushed them away. My eyes widened in wonder at the strange people milling around the docks. Stocking-capped sailors entered and left a row of saloons we passed, and Juan pulled me almost to a run until they were left behind. Dark-visaged men, hunched over as though carrying a load, tramped resolutely along. Some were accompanied by stout, bundled-up women scurrying beside them with their arms full of odd-shaped parcels. Their faces had a weathered quality much like the men they followed, and I wondered if it was because they stayed on the beaches so much watching for their men to return.

Then I saw my first Chinese! Slight of form and with eyes at a slant, a yellowish tinge to his face, and flapping, balloonlike trousers. I gaped like any peasant. Juan gave a tug at my sleeve and my feet followed him, but my eyes stayed glued to the pigtail the man wore under a round flat hat.

"That's a Chinaman!" I whispered excitedly.

"So it is," Juan agreed. "There are lots of them around here. They come in the hold of every ship that unloads."

Even as he spoke I noticed several more pigtails bobbing in the crowd, but then my interest was caught by something else.

"What's that?" I demanded.

Juan pulled at my hand, but I refused to move.

"It's a church," he explained.

"On the *water*?"

He nodded. "They built it on an old ferryboat so it'd be near where the sailors land." He grinned. "Sort of a fight between the saloons and the Episcopalians over who gets them first."

It seemed I would never see everything there was to see, and then I noticed the sun was sinking. Panic filled me as I clutched Juan's sleeve.

"I have to get back! Miss Brigham will find out I'm gone!"

"No, she won't," he answered. We raced laughing for the nearest horse car.

It was near dark when we reached the school. Juan showed me how to get into the basement before he took my borrowed coat and returned to the stables. I fled up the stairs, then paused to allow my breathing to become normal. A quick peek showed me a deserted hall, so I knew supper was being served. After shaking the wrinkles from my skirt and patting my hair to smoothness, I walked sedately to my seat at table.

"You are late, Shadow," Miss Brigham said sternly. "Just because we had visitors today is no reason to relax our deportment. Where have you been?"

"I'm sorry Miss Brigham," I said meekly. "I had no visitor, as you know, so I napped. I'm afraid I

16

overslept." I trembled at the lie, wondering if God would strike me dead. When the fatal bolt didn't appear, I released my held-in breath while I looked anxiously at the headmistress.

She frowned and fussed with her napkin, but I knew she felt sorry for me when I alone had no parent on the day the other girls were overwhelmed by theirs, so she let the matter drop.

Juan's position as stable boy at the school was a lowly one. Grooms attended the young ladies and their horses, while Juan was one of several boys who merely cleaned stalls and polished the saddles and other tack, or carried feed to the mangers. If Miss Brigham had known we were friends, Juan would have been sacked immediately.

With the help of a few confederates in the years that followed, we were able to keep our friendship secret. It was comforting to know Juan was always there. On parents' day, when it could be managed, we ran through the city like any tenement children, and I lost the dreaded feeling of aloneness that had haunted my life.

Diedre had come to Miss Brigham's school a little over a year before, grief stricken at her mother's passing. When the other girls began their usual hazing of a new student, I stepped between them, feeling a strong sympathy for the unhappy little girl. She looked like a fragile doll with shining golden hair, light blue eyes, and a heart-shaped mouth. Her heartbreak had left her vulnerable, and she attached herself to me in her need. We became roommates at my request.

Although she had lost her mother, her father apparently adored her, for he came each visitors' day to see her. She became my most willing conspirator in helping me escape for a few hours to roam the city with Juan, then shared the gifts she'd received that day with me when I returned. In turn, I related the wonders I had seen that day, mostly so her eyes would crinkle in laughter as we traded our experiences.

My thoughts were interrupted when Dr. Williams came into the room carrying his little black bag. He shivered, then glanced at Sarah behind him. "How can you stand sleeping in such a frigid place?"

"I prefer it," she said primly. "It's healthy. Besides," she added, "it precludes the possibility of a fire while I'm sleeping."

The terrible sight of Diedre in flames drifted into my memory, and once more I began to cry, too weary to suppress it.

"Here, here," Dr. Williams said jovially, "we can't have this." He patted my head, then examined my grease-smeared hands. "These will heal in no time, and you'll be fine."

"H-how is D-Diedre? Will she be all right?" A dreadful fear filled me as I questioned him. Diedre's face—how could anything heal her burning, blackened features?

"Bring a basin of hot water, Sarah," he said.

When she had left, he studied my face before he spoke. "Diedre is hurt quite badly. You were very brave to try to help her as you did, but she will need all our prayers and help from God if she is to recover."

Sarah carried a steaming basin into the room and placed it on the table beside the bed.

"Not there, Sarah," Dr. Williams said. "Hold it so

I can bathe Shadow's hands."

The hot water stung my burns and brought more tears, but this time I ignored them. Dr. Williams was gentle in letting the grease melt from my wrists and hands. After drying them on soft flannel, he covered both my hands with a soothing salve, then bandaged them.

Miss Brigham entered, and I strained to see if my father was behind her. She saw my look and shook her head.

"The messenger has returned, Shadow, and I'm afraid your father cannot come tonight. He sent word hoping for your speedy recovery, but he is busy tonight and will not be here."

My heart plunged as she gave the message. Complete despair filled me. I knew my father must not love me, but if he wouldn't come when I was hurt, he must hate me!

I closed my eyes, feigning sleep until I was alone, then cried into my pillow until no more tears would come.

Chapter Two

Sleep would not come, despite the fact that Sarah had built a small fire in the little stove to warm the room. I lay miserably awake, wishing there were some way I could talk to Juan, but knowing there was none. He had become like a beloved older brother, and I knew he could comfort me, but there was no way I could get to the nearby stable now. I yearned for sleep to erase my thoughts, but to no avail.

When dawn began to lighten the window I heard whispers and footsteps and the rustling of skirts in the hall. Evidently I was not alone in my wakefulness.

Sarah came at the usual time of rising. On seeing my eyes open, she smiled in a trembly way. "Do you feel well enough to come to breakfast, Shadow?"

"Oh, yes, I'd like to get dressed, please." It would be a relief to talk to the other girls and not be plagued by my unhappy thoughts. "How is Diedre this morning?"

Sarah chewed nervously on her lower lip while tears filled her pale eyes. She averted her face as she whispered, "Diedre died during the night."

I stared, unable to comprehend what she was saying. Diedre couldn't be dead! She was small for her age, but so full of life! It had taken a while before she had shaken off the gloom caused by her mother's passing, but since then she had been merry and always ready for fun. The bright blond hair curled in ringlets around her pixie face, framing laughter and joy in everything she did. Diedre dead? How could Diedre be dead?

Something inside me shriveled when I realized the meaning of Sarah's words, just as a part of me had died the night before when I heard my father's cold message. Well, I would not cry! I would never cry again, I decided. Nothing worse could happen.

Squaring my shoulders, I took a deep breath as I looked at my bandaged hands. "Will you dress me, Sarah? I'm afraid I can't manage."

Her face was scandalized at my acceptance of her news in such calm fashion, but she brought my clothing from the closet in the wrecked room and helped me into them. Her lips were pursed as she combed my hair and buttoned buttons, but she said never a word.

Later that day Diedre's father descended the stairs behind a small coffin carried between two men. We had spent the day in hushed solemnity, the other girls discussing the previous night's calamity in whispers. At the sight of the procession, most of them burst into tears, but I sat dully, wishing Diedre alive. Her father's face was bloated with grief, and sorrow showed in his drooped shoulders as he plodded along. Would *my* father care if I were in her place?

I wanted to forget my father, but somehow I

couldn't. I still loved him, still wanted him to love me, even though there was a hopelessness inside me that hadn't been there before.

My hands healed, as Dr. Williams had predicted, and the burns left no scars that were visible. The damaged room was repaired, but by then I was settled with another roommate and didn't have to return to it.

At the first opportunity I slipped out to see Juan. I just looked at him, unable to speak.

"People die every day," he said with his sixteen-year-old wisdom. "Diedre wouldn't have wanted to live all scarred up, would she?" His eyes were sympathetic and his voice gentle.

"I suppose not," I said slowly. "She must have gotten cold during the night and opened the door of the stove for heat."

"Nobody ever gets cold in Heaven," Juan said in a matter-of-fact tone. "Diedre is most likely happy up there."

I *hope* so, I thought fervently. Shudders crossed my back. "Fire is horrible!" I burst out. Never again would I run with Juan at the sound of the fire gong to see the horses thunder past pulling the gleaming red fire wagon. We had thought it such a glorious sight, but now I knew it meant disaster somewhere. Now I knew it meant things and perhaps people were turning into charred shapes that in no way resembled what they'd been. I would never forget the sounds I'd heard while Diedre was burning to death.

Life at Miss Brigham's resumed with normal dullness when traces of the fire were erased from sight. It took a while, but then the hurt of Diedre's death softened to an occasional pang when one of the girls mentioned her name, or when I woke from a nightmare built around fire. In either case, I allowed no one to see my feelings. I became known as a stoic who refused to cry, no matter the cause.

At rare intervals when special occasions warranted, my father allowed me to return to our house on the corner of Thirty-second Street and Fifth Avenue. These were short visits, never prolonged beyond the time the event dictated. The house was large and elegant, but strangers served as butler, cook, and housekeeper, and although they were always deferential and polite, there was no warmth in the way they treated me. The furnishings were quite sumptuous and the fireplaces were kept burning, but to me there was a chill that would not be dispelled.

My father was charming to guests who visited, but as soon as they left, he returned to his frozen shell and seemed hardly able to look at me. I tried in every way I could to interest him, but he kept me at arm's length. I had long since forgiven him for his absence on the night of the fire, and my love for him returned with such desperation that I was sure he would some day realize he loved me, too. But it didn't happen.

Just after I turned seventeen, Miss Brigham called me to her office, and from the look on her face I knew she had dire news. "Shadow . . . my dear," she said, "you must be brave." Her hand went to her bosom, as though to keep her heart inside. "I don't know how to say this," she whispered, then straightened. "Oh, my dear, your father is dead!"

My heart plummeted into my stomach as I stared at her. Now I can never make him love me, I thought wildly. Tears I had thought banished rose to choke me. Carmelita . . . Carmelita, help me, I prayed. Oh, Mother, help me! Then, as though at a trumpet blast, my conquistadore blood thickened and I straightened. Swallowing my rising bile, I composed my face into a noncommittal mask.

"Don't you understand, my dear?" Miss Brigham asked impatiently. She waited, expecting me to have hysterics, or faint, as a well-bred girl should.

"Yes, Miss Brigham, I understand," I answered mechanically. I wanted to be gone, to be alone with my devastation.

A frown wrinkled her brow as she shook her head in exasperation. "I don't think you understand, Shadow. You are to leave school. Mr. Arbuthnot, your father's solicitor, is waiting for you in the parlor. Your father is dead, child."

I nodded. "May I be excused?" I murmured.

She lowered her head in sympathy and turned away.

I left the room, and when I was sure I was unobserved, slipped out to the stables.

Once again I leaned against the rough wall and shed tears. Torrents flowed as I sobbed for Edward St. George. My tormented father had loved my mother so much he couldn't bear the sight of me. Was it because I looked so like her? Had he banished me so I would not remind him of what he had lost?

He blamed me for Carmelita's death, I knew, but how could I be guilty? No one can control life, especially before it has begun. Many a time I had wished she were alive and I had never been born, but by now I knew wishes were mostly futile. Wishes were childish things, and now I would have to be an adult and leave them behind.

"You going to bawl all day?"

I looked around to see Juan standing in the shadows.

"My-my f-father is dead and I must leave school," I stammered. This time I had a kerchief of my own to use.

A stricken look crossed his face. "Leave? Why?" Then, belatedly, he remembered. "Oh . . . I'm sorry about your father," he said awkwardly.

"My handkerchief is soaked," I said, sniffing dolefully. He offered me his, and after the damage was partially repaired, I rose. "My father's solicitor is waiting for me, so I'd better go."

"Where are you going? Will you still live in New York?" he asked, his dark eyes more anxious than I had ever seen them.

"I don't know, Juan. Perhaps I'll be sent to another school. I really don't know." I returned his handkerchief and left him standing alone.

My thoughts were dismal. Edward St. George was dead and I had no father. But had I had one before? Oh, yes, he had provided for me handsomely. The school I attended was the best and most expensive in New York, and my wardrobe was always the finest. He had never been stingy with money—only with himself. The other girls' fathers were businessmen, but they *made* time for their daughters. Why hadn't mine made time for me?

When I reached the parlor, Mr. Arbuthnot was waiting. He sighed mournfully as he told me I was now in his charge. "You are temporarily my ward, Miss St. George, and I shall do my best to take care of your interests. Your father was a fine man . . . a fine man." His voice died away as the door opened.

Miss Brigham came in, followed by Sarah.

"Your bags are packed, Miss Shadow," Sarah said kindly. "I don't think I've overlooked anything." She patted my shoulder. "I'm so sorry about your father. . . ."

I forced a smile, wondering why Miss Brigham's charges automatically became a "Miss" when they reached the age of sixteen.

"Thank you for everything, Sarah . . . Miss Brigham." Quickly, I left the room, followed by Mr. Arbuthnot and the maids who fell in behind carrying my luggage.

The carriage deposited us at the house I could never think of as home. In my room I found mourning clothes prepared for me, sewn by hand and to my size, so someone had been preparing ahead for my father's demise. The maids unpacked my luggage, tending to my needs with sorrowful faces befitting a house in mourning, tiptoeing around as though trying not to disturb the master.

On the day of his funeral my father lay in state, surrounded by waxen-looking flowers smelling of perfumes other than their own. I stood beside his bedecked coffin and no tears would come. The black veil that covered my face served me well, for the dowagers who clustered around would have been shocked indeed at my callousness. I sniffed and dabbed at my nose beneath the veil at intervals. My grief was no affair of theirs, but I would keep up appearances for the sake of my father. Murmured condolences were given by the friends of Edward St. George, and I nodded and used my black chiffon handkerchief.

My father's face was waxen and cold, but when I had seen him alive it had had little more expression. His eyes had always been steely when they looked at me, even when I was a child clamoring for his affection. How could I love someone so much who didn't know he loved me? He *had* loved me, for I was part of Carmelita. *He had just never realized it.*

The day after the funeral, Mr. Arbuthnot called me to the study and informed me that he was to administer my father's estate.

"You are an extremely wealthy young lady, Miss Shadow St. George—or will be when you reach the age of twenty-one, or have a husband," he said solemnly. "Until then, you will be the ward of your father's sister, the Countess Chauvanne, and her husband, the count."

"Aunt Elizabeth?" I asked timidly. I'd heard of the aunt who had married a French count and now ruled society in San Francisco, but I had never met her. She had a daughter a year or two older than I, a cousin I had never seen.

When Edward St. George had married a Spanish girl young enough to be his daughter the rest of the St. Georges had eliminated him from their calling lists. Even after her death the coolness had persisted, but then it was on Edward's part, and he refused his place in the family. Now Elizabeth, his sister, was the only surviving member.

"Does she want me?" I asked curiously.

Mr. Arbuthnot's astonished face confronted me. "What has that to do with it? Your father named her in his will. You are her kin, and therefore her responsibility until you come of age."

"Can't I just stay here?"

We were in the study of my father's house, and although I had never been happy here, at least it was familiar. New York was my home, and Juan lived in New York. What would I have in the wilderness of the West?

The solicitor opened his briefcase and shuffled papers before his gaze rose to meet mine.

"Of course you can't stay here! You need a wiser head to finish molding you into maturity." He shook his head fussily. "Young people need guidance," he muttered, "although most of them are sure they know everything."

"But if I have so much money, can't you hire someone to be my guardian? I much prefer to say here." I stood my ground, mostly because the thought of staying with hostile relatives terrified me.

"Impossible! I have already arranged for the sale of this house." He sat back and thoughtfully tapped his pen against his teeth. "Your aunt has received the news of her brother's death by now. As soon as I hear from her I'll arrange your passage to San Francisco."

"By train?" As my mind toyed with the idea, I began to feel a faint excitement. Juan had shown me the New York Central, which ran underground from Forty-second to One Hundredth Streets, but he had never had enough money for tickets. Since I was given no pocket money, we could only marvel at the cars as they entered the station and stood puffing while passengers poured from the doors.

We had looked upward to the elevated train as it rumbled along, but it blew out smoke and cinders and looked terribly unsafe. And was there not the danger of its plunging from the rails down onto the street? Juan and I had decided we never wanted to ride it.

"Of course, by train," Mr. Arbuthnot said decisively. "The railroad goes all the way to the West Coast now." He returned to his paper shuffling and I to my thoughts of the coming trip.

I had been only eleven years old when the Union Pacific met the Central Pacific in Utah near Promontory, but I remembered the wild rejoicing that had shaken New York. I hadn't known *why* it was of such major importance, but since everybody celebrated the event, we girls at Miss Brigham's had joined in. The idea of a spike made of pure gold being used to fasten the joining tracks had sparked my imagination, and I had since learned enough history to realize what a major step it was to bring one end of the country into closer contact with the other. In the years since this great happening, railroad travel had become commonplace, but not to me.

Wild tales were heard in New York about San Francisco, and to me it seemed terribly far away. One gentleman who had visited my father at a celebration I'd been allowed to attend had been to this exotic city, and, according to him, the streets really were paved with gold. He had been somewhat in his cups at the time he told of his adventures in California, so surrounding guests had nodded politely, then turning amused faces toward other targets. The thing I remembered best was his saying how very long it took to get there.

"Isn't it a dreadfully long trip, Mr. Arbuthnot?" I asked. "I mean, doesn't it take a fearfully long time to go clear across the country?"

He laid down the pen he was using and removed his glasses. "Well, yes," he said with a sigh, "it takes at least a week and sometimes more, depending on the weather and other conditions." He peered across the desk at me. "I've arranged for Sarah to accompany you." Picking up his spectacles, he fussily began to clean them. "Miss Brigham says she is dependable, and she says you are quite reliable, so if I make arrangements with the conductor to watch over both of you, you'll surely be safe."

"Oh, I'm not afraid, Mr. Arbuthnot." I sighed. "It's just strange to think of going that far from New York."

"Yes, yes," he mumbled, then, almost to himself, "I thought you modern young people were ready to fly off anywhere at a moment's notice."

I smiled at his words, remembering the junkets Juan and I had taken from one end of the city to the other. Would Miss Brigham have thought me so "reliable" had she known? Somehow I doubted it.

The dressmaker who had fashioned my mourning clothes arrived the next morning to fit other garments to my satisfaction, and I discovered that Mr. Arbuthnot had ordered them. It pleased me that he would think of such things, and I found out later that he'd called at Miss Brigham's school when my father became seriously ill and had had Sarah give him the proper size measurements so my funeral garments would fit. It was fitting to have a new wardrobe to begin my new life, but I was surprised at the lavishness of the one being provided for me. Miss Brigham had insisted that her charges wear unfrivolous garments, so I was doubly pleased by the frills and bows on these. I was to have an outfit for every occasion, and several for some.

Aimlessly, I wandered around the big house for the next few days until cook and butler had their day off and the housekeeper left for an afternoon of shopping. Then I slipped out and made my way to Miss Brigham's stable.

"Juan?" The barn was dark after the brightness outside, and my eyes were slow to adjust.

"I'm here," he said, appearing before me with a delighted smile lighting up his dark face. "Are you coming back to school?"

"Oh, no . . . I can't. I just came to say good-bye, Juan. I'm to go to my aunt's home in San Francisco as soon as Mr. Arbuthnot hears from her."

"San Francisco!" he exploded. "That's all the way 'cross country!"

"I know." By now I was used to the idea and even looked forward to the experience. "I wish you could come along."

The smile had left his face, to be replaced by a bleakness I had never seen. He stared at me, his shoulders slumping.

"You'll never come back," he said tonelessly.

"Oh, yes, I will, Juan. When I'm twenty-one I'm to receive my money, and then I'll come back to New York." I omitted the husband Mr. Arbuthnot had mentioned, for to me the idea was too ridiculous to consider.

"Four years!" His jaws clenched, and he swallowed before he said hopelessly, "You'll forget all about me by then."

"No, I won't, Juan. You're the best friend I've had

while I've been growing up. We'll always be friends, won't we?" He said nothing, so I continued. "I just came to say good-bye and to let you know where I'll be. I'll write to you."

"Oh, sure," he muttered.

"Well, aren't you going to wish me luck? That's a long way to go, you know. Mr. Arbuthnot is sending Sarah along and says he'll tell the conductor to look out for us."

Astonishment took the place of the bleakness. "You mean you're going all the way to California with just an old woman?" His eyes blazed. "Your father's solicitor must be mad!"

His vehemence surprised me into a giggle. "Oh, no! Miss Brigham told him Sarah was dependable and I was reliable."

"You're a baby," he said softly, "and if anyone hurts you, I'll kill him!"

He turned and walked across the stable and back while I noticed for the first time how his shoulders had broadened and his stride lengthened since our first romp on the horse cars. We had been such constant companions that I had not realized Juan was changing from a boy to a man.

His hands grasped my arms, and a faint shock went through me. It was the first time he had touched me, other than holding my hand to guide me through traffic, and his grip was strong. His eyes seemed to plead for something, but he said nothing.

I broke loose. "You're hurting. I have to go now, Juan. Aren't you going to say good-bye?"

He nodded. "Good-bye, Shadow." Then he bent a little and I felt his lips brush my forehead.

The gesture flustered me. I giggled nervously as I bid him adieu. I stumbled on the wooden walk we had skimmed over so often, then fled back to the big house to arrive safely before the housekeeper returned to find me gone. As I caught my breath I wondered why I felt so strange. It was only Juan.

Mr. Arbuthnot came shortly to advise me he'd gotten a wire from my aunt and had made the arrangements he'd mentioned. Within the week Sarah and I were taken to the Grand Union Depot, and Mr. Arbuthnot saw that we were settled in the finest car the New York Central Railroad offered.

The huge station was a beehive of activity and leave-taking. So much was going on, my eyes seemed unable to open wide enough to take it all in, and my head turned this way and that so I would not miss anything.

"Don't gawk, Miss Shadow," Sarah admonished. "There'll be plenty of sights to see after we get started." She smiled to remove the sting, and I had never seen her look so excited.

Then the whistle blew a loud blast and steam belched from the stack. With a pounding heart I settled back in my seat as we began the journey that would take me to my new home.

Chapter Three

Steam from the engine's stack billowed backward around the train, much as though we were traveling through the clouds. It was accompanied by fine cinders that seeped in the window cracks and covered us with a gritty dust that made my skin itch. The crowded station diminished with distance and soon disappeared as we rolled on. Before long we were out in the country, with only telegraph poles watching like gaunt sentinels as we passed. I tried counting them, but soon this pastime made me dizzy and I left the lonely masts to their unending vigil.

We stopped at each small town to disgorge a passenger or two and take on any who were waiting. The arrival of a train was still an event that caused great excitement among the villagers. Small children ran excitedly along the tracks, waving at the engineer and any passengers who would return their salutes. Adults came to watch, their eyes eager and usually a little wistful, as though they wished they could come along.

There were several immigrant cars behind the palace car we occupied. I knew they were crowded by the number of faces pressed against the small windows when we stopped for meals. Sarah and I, together with the other passengers in our car, were escorted grandly by the conductor to dine in a fine home or restaurant, but the immigrants made do with what they'd brought along, unless they were lucky enough to have money. Then they could dart out of the train to haggle with the hovering vendors before they scooted back with their prizes.

"Do they have enough to eat, Sarah?" I asked as we returned from a sumptuous meal at one of our stops.

She sniffed before answering, "They are not our concern, Miss Shadow. A lady does not notice such lowly persons."

Although she'd had a good position at the school, I was sure she had once been poor, and I wondered how she could be so callous to people in such need. I'd seen a child gnawing on a bone like a puppy, and my heart went out to these pioneers hardy enough to set out on their journey to the unknown.

True, I, too, was going into the unknown, but I was going in luxury to meet relatives who lived in even more sumptuousness, not into the harsh surroundings the emigrants faced. While the other girls at Miss Brigham's were realizing the world of the rich, Juan had shown me the world of the poor, and it wasn't a gentle one. I had seen ragged old women fighting over tossed-out produce behind the markets, and men begging for a few coins from passers-by who mostly ignored them.

The cars the immigrants occupied on the train were

bleak. Made of wood like long, narrow coffins, they contained hard wooden benches on either side of a narrow aisle. None were long enough to comfortably accommodate even a child, but at night this was where the passengers slept. Adults and children alike were forced to arrange themselves either on the benches or the floor for their night's rest. Most had brought rough blankets, but some had to huddle between their blanketed companions through the long, chill nights, and these were probably grateful for the crowded state.

Our lot was not nearly so harsh. We sat on plush-covered seats during the day. When the train stopped at night, Sarah and I were ushered out with the other passengers in our car and housed in a hotel, if the town boasted one, or else in private homes arranged for our convenience by the railroad officials. When we returned well-rested in the morning, haggard faces peered enviously from the small windows of the immigrant cars. I felt guilty for having fared so much better than they. At night basins of warm water were provided so we could get rid of the gritty soot, but the immigrants were fortunate if they had enough cold water to drink. As each day passed their faces became more begrimed from the eternal cinders.

In Chicago we transferred to a Pullman car, and I slept on a train at night for the first time. It was strange to see the porter transform our daytime seats into a bed, then pull out a shelf overhead that became another. The mattresses were thin, but surprisingly comfortable, or perhaps being able to stretch out after a long day of sitting upright made them feel so.

"Miss Shadow," Sarah said firmly, "sleeping here

practically in the open is quite dangerous, I'm sure." She sniffed in disapproval. "However, you'll be safe enough in the upper berth, if you prefer to sleep alone, or beside me in the lower berth, if you wish to sleep next to the window."

I chose the upper berth, and each night went to sleep rocked by the swaying train and lulled by clicking wheels until the train pulled to its nightly halt. Then all was quiet until the dawn hours when we resumed our journey. We took turns making our morning toilette in a tiny room, but again we were given hot water in a small basin, so life was not too rigorous.

Now we had a dining car on the train with us. The meals served were not fancy, but they were nourishing. They also relieved the monotony of the journey, and by now any diversion that interrupted the monotonous view passing by our windows was a welcome one.

We met the other passengers. Sarah stayed haughtily aloof as she thought befitted a true lady, but I was glad of the opportunity to talk to someone else when I had the chance. Most were from my father's class of people, and probably quite wealthy, but I had learned social communication and we got along quite well.

The flat country passed outside my window until I thought to go mad from the sameness of the scenery. A sense of abandonment and desolation built up inside me as the realization of my orphan status came home with dreadful clarity. Would my aunt be happy to see me, or would she consider me a nuisance? Fears circled in my head, and there was nothing of interest to remove them.

In Omaha we pulled into a huge brick station and

had to remove our belongings once again to transfer to a Union Pacific car. A grinning porter tried to make friends with Sarah by telling her we were in the "Cow Shed," at which she raised her nose even higher. She was going to dismiss him without a tip until my shocked face made her reconsider.

Just outside Omaha three cowboys saw our train and galloped alongside shouting as they waved their wide-brimmed hats. They spied me at the window and held their horses to a pace equaling the train's, grinning in high good nature. One bowed extravagantly from his pitching saddle, and I felt a blush spread up my throat as I hastily averted my eyes.

"Pull the shade, Miss Shadow!" Sarah reached over even as she spoke and indignantly twitched the covering over the window. "Those terrible men!"

"Really, Sarah!" I was embarrassed, but determined not to let the gaunt woman dictate my actions. "I'm seventeen now, remember." And then I added, "I thought we were to see the countryside and learn about our country on this trip."

Her inevitable sniff preceded her words. "See the countryside, yes. *Not* let rude men stare at you as they were doing." Her gaze ran pointedly over my corseted figure. "You're a young lady now, not some street hoyden."

I closed my eyes so she would stop chattering, but her words turned my thoughts to Juan. Street hoyden, indeed! Was that what I had been when we wandered the streets of New York together?

The seat grew harder, and I stirred uncomfortably as I thought longingly of running along the docks beside my old companion. Now our only exercise was a stiff walk through the aisle of the car. Sarah frowned if she had to follow me to the comfort station too many times, so I kept my trips to a minimum.

How I would like to canter on one of Miss Brigham's fat old mares! When I had reached sixteen, my riding lessons had begun. I was properly fitted with a riding habit, learning to gather it gracefully in one arm to keep it from tripping me as I walked to the stable. Then a groom would lead one of the horses to where I waited and another assisted me into the side-saddle. After I made sure my hat was settled firmly in place, a nod at the grooms made them step back to let the old mare amble around the sawdust oval.

We were not supposed to kick our horse, since a gentle clucking of the tongue would quicken her pace. However, my long skirts hid my feet, and once away from the grooms, an occasional nudge against the fat flanks started a genteel cantering gait that delighted my sense of adventure. That was as far as I dared go, for had my mount broken into a gallop, the grooms would have immediately grabbed her bridle and the ride would have been over. I would glimpse Juan's laughing face peering from a stable window, but I kept my eyes turned decorously ahead as befitted a young lady of my station.

The call of a candy butcher entering our car brought me back to the present. The wares they hawked were often stale and always bad for complexions, but it was another way to pass the time, and Sarah was inordinately fond of chocolate in any form.

He stopped beside our seat when Sarah held up her hand. She went about the delightful pastime of selecting one of the gooey confections displayed on the tray. My eyes glanced at the goodies before they rose to the butcher's face, and then my heart missed a beat. The strap from the tray circled Juan's neck, and his brown eyes held suppressed laughter at the startled look on my face.

My gasp of surprise brought Sarah's attention from the candies. "What's wrong, Miss Shadow?"

Juan shook his head warningly, and I subsided into my seat, willing my face to keep its usual composure. "Nothing, Sarah." My hand went to my chest in a vague patting motion. "Something in our lunch must have disagreed with me." I fanned my handkerchief in the approved fashion of a lady having the vapors. "I'll be fine, really."

Her look was doubtful, but she returned to the selection. When my eyes met Juan's, he again shook his head, then focused his attention on Sarah.

"What would you like, Miss Shadow?" Sarah asked after she made her choice. Her face turned expectantly toward me.

"Nothing just now, Sarah, thank you."

She handed Juan a coin in dismissal, then gave herself to the delight she had purchased. I watched Juan's broad shoulders as he walked away and wondered how he had managed to be aboard the train we were on. Even more, my thoughts centered on how I could make an opportunity to talk to him. Sarah was attached to me as firmly as any shadow, I thought, then laughed ruefully at myself for making a pun on my own name.

As I mulled over the problem, the train overtook and passed a long string of covered wagons plodding across the plains. The dust that swirled around them was horrendous, and my own throat ached as I imagined how the women seated on the wagons must be suffering. There were children with them, making me recall the child I'd seen chewing on a bone. I was ashamed when I remembered my petty irritation with the cinders that seeped into our car from time to time, soiling my handkerchief when I wiped my gritty face.

The rolling plains passed tediously outside the window, broken only by occasional scatterings of buffalo or a lone rider in the distance. I had wondered if we would encounter Indians, but by now the sight of a train was commonplace, so I supposed it was of no more interest to these wild cavalrymen of the plains.

The next morning I was still determined to talk to Juan. I even considered doing the daring act in front of Sarah, if necessary. Fate took a hand, however, and when the candy butcher's call sounded, Sarah was away on an emergency trip to the comfort station.

When Juan reached our seat, he squatted on his heels and ostensibly offered me the selection on his tray.

"Juan! How did you ever get here?" I asked excitedly.

"Sh-h." He glanced around to see if the other passengers had heard. His voice was barely above a whisper as he answered. "I was on the immigrant train, but I only had money enough for a ticket to Chicago. I got this job, but I'll have to find another at Ogden."

"But why, Juan? Why did you leave Miss Brigham's?" I whispered. "What will you do in California?"

41

His eyes sparkled mischievously. "I didn't have anybody to ride the horse cars with me anymore, so I thought it was time to better myself. Maybe I'll strike gold, or become a gambler. California is the land of opportunity." He smiled as he handed me a confection. "Here, have one."

Absently, I took a bite, and then a terrible thought came to me. "What if you can't find another job on the train in Ogden? What then?"

He shrugged, then saw Sarah coming down the aisle and rose. "I'll make it some way."

Sarah's sniff was audible as she moved Juan backward with one hand and sat stiffly on the seat between us. She glanced at the confection in my hand, then fished in her purse for a coin. Her cold, "That'll be all," accompanied the money she laid on Juan's tray.

When he left, she said, "Miss Shadow, it is not proper for a young lady to converse with tradespeople."

"Yes, Sarah," I answered demurely. My lonesome desolation was gone now that I knew Juan was on the train, and San Francisco was not nearly so fearsome now. Nothing very dreadful could happen to me with him nearby, of that I was confident.

I sighed, wondering why it was such a terrible sin for people to talk to each other. How simple life would be if we were all of equal station. Then Sarah could dole out enough money for Juan's ticket so he could join us on our trip. But I knew such a thing was utterly impossible, and I sighed again.

"Aren't you feeling well Miss Shadow?" Sarah asked, eyeing the candy still in my hand.

"I'm just tired, Sarah." I offered her the sweet. "I

don't know why I took this—would you care for it? I'm really not hungry."

She accepted it, but wrapped it carefully in a clean handkerchief. "We're almost to Ogden, so we'd best prepare to transfer again." Her sharp gaze covered my face. "You do look peaked. I wonder if there's a doctor on the train."

"Oh, really, Sarah, I'm fine." I forced a smile. "It just seems as though we've been sitting in these seats for an eternity."

The train slowed to a stop before a group of plain wooden buildings. Ogden's station was somewhat shabby in appearance and sadly in need of repairs. The rough, bearded men swarming around the platform did nothing to add to its appearance. They were gruffly jovial, spitting a stream of tobacco juice to punctuate each remark they made. Once again Sarah twitched the shade over the window while we waited for the conductor to come for us.

Snow was falling and a sharp wind brought a shiver as our guide led us to a Silver Palace Sleeping Car and stowed our belongings. I looked frantically around for Juan, but caught no glimpse of him. Had he once more found room in the immigrant cars? If he were to find employment on the train, he would have to be quick. Our new engine was panting in readiness to be gone.

The wheels began to turn while the snow swirled more thickly against the windows. At each opening of the door, I turned to see who had come in, until Sarah began to lecture me on proper decorum for young ladies. With each chug of the engine the desolation inside me grew, pushing a lump into my throat. Had

43

Juan been left behind?

As time passed, I was sure he had. No candy butcher came with a tray; neither was there a diner on our train now. When it was time for a meal, we stopped at wayside kitchen stations. Even though I gawked around in defiance of Sarah's frowns and lectures, there was no sign of Juan.

The food was plainer than any I'd tasted, and usually ill-prepared. Place settings were made up of mismatched pieces of china and common knives and forks. Water in the oftimes chipped glasses was cloudy and had a sort of muddy taste.

The immigrant cars were not so crowded now. Many of the travelers had gotten out along the way when they thought opportunity beckoned. The remaining immigrants crowded around the back door of the kitchens and either begged or bought food to carry on the train. It made me wonder wistfully if Juan ever went hungry, and somehow made the terrible food taste even worse and become infinitely harder to swallow.

Then we were in the foothills of the Sierra Nevada, and a change came at last to the scenery. The chug of the engine grew slower on the gradual gradient, sometimes straining in such a way as to make me wonder if it would reach the top of the hill. But helper engines were added after our progress slowed to a crawl, and we picked up speed.

One morning I woke after the train was on its way and I could see only dim illumination outside. When I peered through the window, we were passing under a narrow wooden shed. By the time Sarah and I had dressed, it was dark outside and I realized we were going through a tunnel that seemed to have no end.

When at last we came again into the sun I caught a glimpse of gleaming blue water below us before the wooden sheds returned. When the sunlight flashed again and we were out in the open, the train slowed, then came to a panting halt.

With an imperious hand, Sarah hailed the conductor. "Is something wrong?" she asked, a tremor in her voice giving away her nervousness.

"No, ma'am," the conductor said as he touched his cap. "We're just waiting for the bucker snowplows to clear the track. There are stretches along the way not sheltered by sheds." With a courteous nod he again touched the bill of his cap and moved away.

I looked out on a winter wonderland of blue, blue water framed by pristinely white snow. Huge trees made giant punctuation marks to accent the magnificence. Everything was so . . . so *big*, and so clean and wide open—not crowded and dingy like New York. Even the sun sparkled more brightly as it kissed the water to dazzle my eastern eyes. Several deer who'd been drinking at the water's edge raised their heads in our direction, then unhurriedly turned and wandered back to where the forest became more dense.

Then we were on the downslope. Pine-forested ravines beside foaming torrents of water slid by in fast succession. After the monotony of the great plains, the mountains were a riot of action and excitement. A pair of brown bears must have been startled when the train appeared, for all that could be seen of them was two fast-moving dark rumps going up a slope into the trees that were everywhere. Then we passed over wooden trestles above rushing water so far down it

45

took my breath away.

"We stop in Sacramento, ladies."

I glanced around as the conductor paused beside us.

He nodded toward the window. "That's the American River, and from here it's only four miles on to our stop."

We rattled across an iron bridge with lacy girders awkwardly straddling the rushing river. The train whistle blew, sounding eerily lonesome as its long moaning drifted into space. It echoed the dread inside me as we neared the end of our journey.

Edward St. George's cold face wafted frowningly in and out of my thoughts. Would the relatives he had so estranged welcome his orphaned daughter? Or would they see in me only the Spanish girl who had taken him from them?

The stop for a meal in Sacramento passed in a blur as my mind worried about the future. I dragged my feet, childishly imagining that by doing so I would slow things down. But in no time at all, we were back on the train and on our way to the Oakland Pier.

Forlornly, I still searched each face I saw, hoping against hope that some magic had brought Juan along. He could take care of himself, of that I was sure, but the thought of his being cold and perhaps hungry while he was stranded in some outlandish way station was one I didn't want to dwell on. The gaunt woman beside me was a traveling companion, but no friend, and right now that was what I needed the most.

We were rolling into a more populated area, and I saw a motley assortment of Indians and Chinese trotting through the streets beside heavily booted and bearded men, dodging carriages as whips cracked to urge horses on through the narrow lanes. Rutted thoroughfares gave precarious footing to the animals and much jouncing to the occupants. One had his head stuck out of a window and was shaking his fist at the driver on the box. Shanties and tents had been erected wherever whim and space allowed, but as we rolled along they were soon replaced by buildings of a more permanent construction. Then we were in a bustling city that went about its business while the train chugged through.

A blue stretch of water showed, and I watched it roll toward us as we passed along Seventh Street to the edge of San Francisco Bay. An immense shed arched over the train when it pulled into Oakland Long Wharf. We had come to the end of a long train ride, one that seemed infinitely longer than the week it had taken.

The conductor came to escort us on our way, this time to a double-ended ferry boat with *Oakland* painted on it for identification. We had come through winter in the mountains into a land of summer, and my clothing grew uncomfortably warm. Then the chill air of the sea wafted ashore and I was glad the layers of clothing were around me. After we boarded the ferry I almost wished for more.

The sun was sinking into glorious colors that bathed the city across the bay with a rosy glow. I breathed deeply of the salty air, wondering if so much beauty was a favorable omen of things to come. Perhaps my new home would be warm and pleasant and nothing to dread.

With many toots of its whistle, the ferry splashed majestically toward San Francisco, adroitly wending its way through the many vessels dotting the water. Echoing hoots answered the *Oakland*'s like a symphony of deep-throated birds against overtones from paddles churning their frothy wake. Plumes of rich smoke billowed into air scoured clean by breezes from the sea.

Excitement began to fill me as I craned my neck to see the shore we were nearing. A huge wooden building with a low, squatty clock tower on top dominated the scene. Then the ferry swung around to back into the slip, blotting the city from view.

Forgetting my decorum, I ran swiftly around the deck to see the docking. Suddenly, to my horror, my toe caught in a coiled rope, sending me plunging head foremost toward the deck.

Before I sprawled ungracefully against the planking, hands caught my waist and I was swung up and cradled against a rough, woolen-clad chest. My hat fell forward over my eyes.

A chuckle preceded a well-bred English voice, which said, "Just what sort of flying fish have I captured?"

I struggled to free myself from the encircling arms, but without success. When I finally managed to push my hat back so I could see, surprise kept me staring wide-eyed at the tanned, laughing face bent close to mine. Had Edward St. George been born again?

The man who held me looked like a young edition of my dead father, making my chaotic thoughts circle wildly against belief. The blue eyes were so familiar, and yet not really. They were laughing, and Edward

St. George had never laughed, especially at me. The blond hair, so like my father's, was tumbled in a way his had never been. The woodsy, tobacco-smell my captor exuded was alien compared to the well-groomed bottled odor of barbering so familiar to my childhood. Of course this rowdy was not Edward St. George!

"Put me down!" I demanded, but my voice quavered.

"Why?" The question came teasingly, as though he were amused at some small child.

"How dare you!" This time I put more assurance into my protest, but my struggles still produced no results. A glance over his shoulder showed Sarah rounding the wheelhouse. "My companion is coming, sir, and you'd better put me down this moment!"

His gaze followed mine, and then he looked down at me with the same mischievous grin. "I'd better take my reward before the old dragon gets here," he said, and his mouth came down to cover mine.

The fine hairs of his mustache tickled as I felt his lips caress me before he stood me carefully on my feet. I gasped, then remembered to stare haughtily at his impudence. "Well!" I gasped, then, "Well!" again.

Sarah's outraged face came between us. "You should be horsewhipped, sir!" she said angrily. "How dare you take advantage of this child?"

"Sorry, ma'am," he drawled. "I'm afraid I forgot myself." His eyes were still merry, but he bowed gravely to Sarah and then me. "Your servant, ladies," he murmured, then turned and disappeared into the wheelhouse.

"Well . . . I never!" Sarah exclaimed. "Are you all

49

right, Miss Shadow?" She examined me closely as she straightened my hat. "That will teach you not to run off as you did," she said tartly. "Oh, I really don't know why we were sent to this barbaric world. It's . . ." she struggled for a word, "it's *uncivilized!*"

Her words penetrated my consciousness, but I was still dazed from my first kiss. Some of my classmates had spoken daringly of surreptitious kisses they'd received at crowded balls, but I had never before been kissed by a man—not even my father!

The silky mustache had felt so strange . . . and the warm lips that had passed fleetingly over my mouth were at once shocking and at the same time most oddly thrilling. I touched my lips, but they felt the same as they had before. Bemusedly, I shook my head and made sure my hat was settled properly before I looked around.

The world shimmered in a silvery haze around me as the drawbridge lowered to the dock. My feet scarcely touched the planks as Sarah and I walked off the ferry, followed by two porters bearing our baggage.

Chapter Four

Ahead, a liveried man stood watching us disembark. He came toward us, removing his billed cap, and his gaze flicked over Sarah before settling on me. "Miss St. George?"

"Yes."

Sarah was not to be ignored. She stepped up beside me. "I am Miss St. George's guardian for the present. Who are you?"

He replaced his cap, grinning companionably. "I'm Count Chauvanne's coachman, Mrs. . . .?"

Sarah's sniff showed her disdain. "It's miss," she said tartly. "Miss Sarah Murphy." She waved toward the porters. "Please take charge of these men and our luggage."

He nodded. "The carriage is over here. If you'll please accompany me . . .?" He glanced at the porters. "You men bring the bags along."

Forcing my thoughts from the incident on the ferry, I walked out of the station with Sarah to an elegant English brougham drawn by two magnificent white horses. Our guide opened the door and assisted us inside, then went to instruct the men on placing the luggage in the boot, tipping them before returning to us.

"My name is Tom Jordan, ladies. If you want anything, please sing out."

"One moment, if you please," Sarah said imperiously. "Why did not Count Chauvanne come himself?" She glanced at me. "After all, this *is* his niece!"

"Yes, ma'am," Tom answered. "The count and countess had a prior engagement this evening, one they could not cancel. They told me to see that you got settled." His smile was cheerful. "They'll be around tomorrow."

He climbed to a seat in front of our compartment and clucked at the horses while the carriage moved out.

"Impudent clod," Sarah muttered wrathfully. "What sort of people are these to have such dreadfully ill-mannered servants? Disgraceful!"

I was still a little light-headed, and I laughed, remembering the frozen-faced men who drove my father's carriage with never a smile.

"We're 'out West' now, Sarah. People here are different from New Yorkers. Mr. Arbuthnot told me these were a 'new breed.'" I chuckled again, remembering his worried remonstrances when he told me about the wildness of the people who had come to make their homes here.

Sarah grumbled indignantly, her feathers still ruffled, but I turned to look at the city. Rosy sunset bathed the conglomeration of shacks and shanties that mingled with more substantial emporiums. We jolted over uneven cobblestones, weaving through other traffic, and often traveling abreast of a horse car, much like the ones in New York. A difference was the small open car trundling behind, and I thought what fun it would be to ride in one.

Streets rose on steeper hills than seemed possible. One in particular seemed to be headed for the sky. A clanging cable car chugged upward, pulled by some unseen giant hand. If the hand had let go, the car filled with people would have plunged down the hill and probably into the sea, but no one seemed concerned.

Our carriage swayed precariously as Tom pulled the horses aside to make way for a light rig with lathered horses whose driver shouted to get by. Sarah and I grabbed for the swinging straps on either side, and the incident was enough to start anew Sarah's monologue against the disgraceful population.

Throngs of people crowded the street, dodging through the stream of vehicles as though their lives depended on getting to the other side. It was a motley group that included sailors and Chinese, begrimed and booted men, and slow-walking, shabbily dressed women with young bodies and old faces. Evidently the wealthy of the city rode prudently in their carriages, foregoing the dangers of the streets.

Tall-masted schooners rode the gently swelling waves as they tugged at lines attached to the wharves. The same mixture of humanity eddied around the docks that I had seen in New York, save that the coolies were in more abundance here. I wondered if they had come all the way across country, then decided they had probably crawled from the holds of ships coming in from the wide ocean that slapped at the shores of their homelands. The sloped eyes and dangling pigtails still fascinated me, but I had learned a measure of decorum and no longer gawked openly at their oddity.

A sea of milling people brought our carriage to a halt. Sound came in waves as they shrieked and roared like animals in a zoo. Sarah pulled me roughly away from the window when shots rang out nearby, but I jerked away from her hands so I could see what was going on. Then I wished I hadn't.

A kicking, strangling man was hoisted by a rope around his neck to one of the iron lampposts scattered along the thoroughfare. His tongue protruded from his protesting mouth and his eyes stuck out like frantic beacons from a ghastly white face. His arms flailed wildly and his hands made futile gestures to loosen the tightening rope. The crowd below him roared their bloodthirsty anger, and I wondered what it was that could bring human beings to such a state.

Sickness rose within me, but I was held as though mesmerized. There were as many women in the bawdy horde as men, and they were the most horrible. Their eyes glittered as their shrill cries of " 'ang 'im!'" rose to a crescendo.

Some of the men drew guns to fire into the air. Others shouted and cursed and shook clenched fists at the unfortunate victim. A hairy face peered into our carriage and broke the spell that held me.

With a cry, I turned to Sarah and buried my face in her bodice. Tom Jordan's voice rose above the bedlam, shouting to make way for our carriage to move ahead. The crack of his long whip brought cries of pain from those it touched, the imprecations promising him a short life.

Sarah clutched me to her breast and I heard her mutter, "Oh, saints above . . . they're turning the air purple!" Then she clapped her hands over my ears to shield me from the language, but the sounds seeped through her fingers.

The thudding of hooves coming like a stampede brought me away from Sarah's comforting arms when curiosity again overcame aversion in me. A band of mounted men thundered down the street while the crowd milled, trying to escape. Behind the horsemen half a dozen men in gray pounded along on foot waving huge pistols in the air. They wore long frock coats over like-colored pants, but their hats were a strange assortment, ranging from derbies to silk top hats.

By the time the star-bedecked posse arrived, followed by the running members of the San Francisco police, the shrieking mob had disappeared into the nearby saloons and shanties lining the dingy alleys. Whistles were blown and general confusion prevailed, but the culprits were safely away in the labyrinth of the city's underworld.

The dangling figure swung alone in the breeze. His hands hung limply at his sides, pointing to his downturned toes. His head hung at an angle that could only mean he had a broken neck. I shuddered, realizing this bundle had once been a man . . . and only minutes ago. My father's dying was a thing of sadness and grief, but this . . . this was *death* . . . a death of such horror and violence as I had never imagined.

With a jolt, our carriage moved ahead out of sight of the bundle of rags draped from the post. Even now dusk was covering the scene with a merciful curtain to obscure the terrible sight. We rattled at a clip that jounced Sarah and me around like rag dolls on the seat. Then the carriage halted and the only sound was that of the horses' uneasy snorts and the jingle of harness hardware clinking against their panting sides.

Tom Jordan opened the door and peered in at us. "Ladies . . . are you all right?" His face was white in the shadows.

"What was that?" I gasped before Sarah could stop me.

"Never mind," Sarah said firmly as she righted her tipsy hat. "Take us to the Chauvanne home at once!"

The coachman inspected each of us, then settled on me. "It was the vigilantes, miss. I hope it didn't frighten you too badly."

"Why did they hang that man?" I knew my question was unseemly, but I ignored Sarah's hand on my arm. "What had he done?"

"I don't know, Miss St. George," Tom said gently. "I'm only sorry you had to see such a thing."

"But why would they do something so horrible. And who are the 'vigilantes'?" I persisted.

"That is enough!" Sarah said icily. "You will please get this carriage in motion at once!" She glared commandingly at Tom Jordan.

"Yes ma'am," he answered, then, with a nod to each of us, he closed the door.

We proceeded at a sedate pace in the soft dusk. One look at Sarah's face warned me against further questions about the execution we had witnessed, so I turned again to the passing city.

"Look, Sarah, they're lighting the lamps!"

A little old man scurried along with a long pole in his hand. He used it like a fairy wand to touch each gaslight into life. The flickering illumination grew brighter as the sun disappeared into the ocean and dusky fog crept in from the sea.

Damp, salty air swirled into the carriage making me shiver. The buildings grew fewer, then vanished completely. The cobblestones were left behind as the carriage came into open country, and we rocked along the dirt road much as I imagined a boat on the water would sway and roll.

The image of the hanging man flashed before me and I shuddered again. Try as I would to push it from my thoughts, it persisted. Would his tortured face never leave my memory?

Now that the excitement was gone, I felt only sickness. Was I going to disgrace myself by being ill? I swallowed the bile that rose in my throat. It rose again, but I forced it back. The process seemed to go on for an eternity before Tom's shout drifted backward on the wind and we passed through the wide iron gates held open by a gnomelike man who waved at Tom before he tugged the gates closed behind us.

The carriage pulled up with a flourish before an ornate building of imposing size. A wide veranda circled its girth under towers pointing skyward in swirls of fog. A horn wailed eerily in the distance. The dank smell of the sea hung heavy on the air.

A wide front door was opened by a Chinese boy in an immaculate white coat. Behind, a stout little aproned woman peered over his shoulder.

"Come in, come in," she called, beaming with delight as Sarah and I climbed the steps to the veranda. "Welcome . . . oh, it's so good to see you at last!"

"Is that David, Bertha?" an impatient voice from within demanded.

Before an answer could be given, a tall, elegantly gowned blond-haired girl pushed the little woman aside.

"Who is it, Chung?" she asked petulantly.

The boy moved aside so she could see better.

"Oh, it isn't David!" she exclaimed, and turned to flounce away.

"Miss Julia, I think your cousin has arrived," the woman said gently.

With an exasperated sigh, the younger woman swung around. "Yes, of course," she said. Her gaze took in my travel-dusted clothing. "You must be . . . Shadow? Is that your name?"

I nodded. "And you must be Julia," I said shyly. She was so coolly elegant and shiningly clean, I was terribly aware of my dishevelment.

An imperious wave of her hand dismissed us. "Take them to their rooms, Bertha, so they can freshen themselves."

She turned impatiently to enter the doorway to what was evidently a dining room, then paused. "Tell me the moment David arrives, Bertha." Without a backward glance, she was gone.

Sarah's indignant breathing made her seem about to explode. "Well, I never!" she exclaimed. "Miss Shadow, perhaps we had better leave."

"Oh, no, don't even think about leaving," the

58

woman said, her eyes widening in agitation. "The master and mistress would never forgive me . . . they gave orders I was to see you were made welcome and comfortable. I'm the housekeeper." She smiled apologetically. "Miss Julia is waiting for her fiancé to arrive, and I'm afraid he's late. She really isn't angry with you, you know." She sighed. "Young people are so impatient."

Then her attention returned to us. "You must be tired to death," she declared, "what with coming such a long, long way. Are you hungry? Or would you prefer to freshen up first?"

Her glance went beyond us. "Chung, bring their bags to the second floor." The smile that was turned on us was meant to be reassuring. "The third floor is used for the servants and the old countess, so there aren't too many steps to your rooms." She paused, then said gently, "You look peaked, miss."

I had winced at her saying we must be tired to death. Never again would I use the word "death" in any casual way. But now I forced a smile. "I'm fine . . . just a bit tired, I suppose." Then we were bustled up the stairs.

Sarah's face was prim with disapproval and her eyes still mirrored shock, but her lips were clamped firmly shut.

Our guide chattered merrily on. "I'm Mrs. Darwell," she said. "Bertha Darwell." She looked expectantly at Sarah.

Sarah would not relent, however, so Bertha turned away, beckoning to two maids coming down the upper hallway we had reached. "Bring hot water for the ladies, girls." She opened a door. "The tub has already been brought in, since I was sure you'd be wanting a bath first thing. This is your room, Miss Shadow."

She smiled at my sudden glance. "Oh, yes, we've been expecting you, and talking about you," she said gaily. "Do you mind if the servants call you Miss Shadow? We address your cousin as Miss Julia, you know."

"Of course," I answered. This motherly little woman was a chatterbox, but rather comforting to have around. She helped push our recent nightmare into the realm of unreality.

Bertha looked around as the Chinese boy entered. "Put the luggage here, Chung."

He nodded politely.

"This is our houseboy, Miss Shadow," Bertha said.

I smiled as he bowed shyly, then quickly left.

Bertha turned to Sarah. "Now, your room is just next door. What *is* your name?"

"Miss Murphy," Sarah said haughtily.

"Well, come along, Miss Murphy." She led Sarah toward the open door, then paused. "The maids will bring the water shortly. They'll help you bathe and unpack for you."

I wondered about the "old countess" she had mentioned, then forgot her as I gazed around the luxurious room. I thought that it should be called the sea room, because of its color. Pale green satin draperies were pulled over huge windows. The carpet was deep-piled, of same color, and softer than I had known a carpet could be. The bedspread and pillow covers matched the draperies. Flickering lamplight gave the impression it was all billowing, like the waves

60

outside.

At regular intervals, horns mourned woefully some-where outside. I shuddered, wondering if they were wailing for the dead man, then forced myself to think of other things. A peek out a window showed only fog and darkness, so I couldn't satisfy my curiosity as to how close the ocean was to the house. It must be at no great distance for the horns to sound so clearly.

A noise behind me brought my attention from the mysterious sea to the everyday matter of maids bring-ing my bathwater. I had noted the zinc-lined wooden tub placed carefully on old newspapers near the satin-covered bed, and now I watched while each maid emptied two pails of water into it as the steam rose around their heads.

Miss Brigham's school was noted for the cleanliness of its pupils, but we had been allowed full baths only once each week, and then we bathed in water warmed only by an overnight stand beside the stove. We had been taught to wash with maximum efficiency in a minimum of time, and the event was more of a chore than a pleasure. The homemade soap we used often refused to lather, and when it did there was a slight burning, drying sensation when we rubbed it on, and it always smelled somewhat rancid. We all made haste to splash ourself sufficiently to count as a bath, then used the Turkish rubber to warm ourselves before we caught cold.

Now I watched a maid pour liquid from a small vial into the steaming water. A delicious scent of fresh lemons and some sort of perfume wafted through the room.

Then she turned to me with a smile. "May I help

you undress, Miss Shadow?"

I came from my reverie with a start. "Oh! No . . . thank you, uh . . . I'm sorry, I'm afraid I don't know your name."

"I'm Carlie Jordan, Miss Shadow." She curtsied. "Tom Jordan is my father."

Then I noticed the resemblance between her and the man who had driven us here. "I'm happy to meet you, Carlie."

The hot water in the tub looked wonderful. No matter how I'd tried, grit from our ride on the train still brought an itchy feeling, and I was sure it had dulled my hair. My clothing felt grimy and unkempt, and I was anxious to shed it all.

One of the other maids and her companion had finished hanging my gowns in the closet and were waiting, so I smiled at them. "Thank you. I'll be able to manage alone now. If you'll place the towel and soap within reach of the tub, I believe I'd like to soak for a while."

My words startled me, for never had a bath been anything more than a trial to get over as quickly as possible. But the scented water was as enticing now as a soft bed was at night, and I was eager to immerse myself in it.

Carlie motioned the maids out, then pulled a low stool beside the tub to hold towel and soap. With another smile and curtsy, she left and closed the door behind her.

I began to peel off the innumerable pieces of clothing, feeling freer than a bird when I had loosened the tight corset and dropped it on the pile. Then, wanton as any trollop, I stepped naked into the warm

62

water and sank into its scented depths with a contented sigh.

Giggles threatened to overcome me as I dabbled my fingers in the water and felt the soft ripples caress my body. How sensual! And how disapproving Miss Brigham would be if she could see me now!

I picked up the soap and sniffed it. The odor of fresh lemon reminiscent of new-baked pie came tantalizingly to my nose. Splashing it in the water brought soft bubbles of suds around my hand. With a blissful sigh, I began to rub the soap on my neck and shoulders.

When I was clean, I lay back and let the heady fragrance swirl around me while idle thoughts drifted through my mind. Where was Juan? Would he have to stay in the dreary plains for a time before he made his way to California? That he would eventually work his way west was for sure, but that he could find me in this vast territory was not so sure. I sighed. Perhaps my future was all in the hands of capricious fate.

The hanged man tried to force his way to the front of my mind, but I deposed his image with the one of the stranger on the ferry. Who was he?

My eyes closed with the remembrance of the kiss he'd brushed across my mouth. My first kiss, and that from a man who looked so startlingly like my father! Only the silky mustache was different. I had thought a mustache was a prickly thing and often wondered how men could stand them, but this one was soft and smooth to the touch. And his lips . . . how warm they'd felt . . . and what a strange feeling had filled me at the touch. Time stood still as I lay remembering his kiss, but then guiltily, I jerked my thoughts away from such a sinful happening. Or tried to. A tingle still remained where his arms had clasped me to him, but I forced myself to other matters.

Was my cousin Julia's manner an indication of how my Aunt Elizabeth and her husband felt about me? It was hard to think of them as a count and countess of a foreign country, for my experience was limited mostly to Americans. My cousin's rudeness had hurt my feelings, and if her parents were like her, what kind of life would I have? I would just have to make them like me.

This was such a large house—larger than my father's. Idly, I wondered how many rooms it had and what they must look like. The "old countess"—who was she? Mr. Arbuthnot had mentioned only my aunt, uncle, and cousin. Was the mother of Count Chauvanne also living here? And why would she be on the third floor with the servants?

Then I dismissed my vague wonderings, and with a contented wriggle, gave myself to the comfort of the warm water.

Chapter Five

Sarah bustled in while I lay soaking in delicious dreaminess. Her sniff opened my eyes. She frowned, picking up the towel. "Get out of that tub at once, Miss Shadow! You'll shrivel away to a prune." Her face was stern. "Such decadence," she muttered. "Barbarians!"

I saw nothing either decadent or barbaric about the wonderful feeling of that hot bath, but when I held my hands before me, I saw the fingers were indeed wrinkled and whiter than usual. I rose from my fragrant pool and let Sarah blot the moisture away with one of the soft towels, then rub until I thought my skin would be removed.

"Now get dressed, Miss Shadow," she said. "I have ordered supper prepared for us. It should be on the table by now."

She handed me a clean shirt and bloomers, then the long supporters that hung from my shoulders like suspenders to hold up the long white hose. Sighing, I put on the white corset and grasped the bedpost. By now I knew Sarah would pull the strings until I could scarcely breathe.

At the sight of the short wool petticoat, I shook my head. "It's warm, Sarah, and I won't need that."

"Wear it, Miss Shadow," she said sternly. "The night air is chill this close to the water."

It was no use arguing with her, so I let her add the woolen petticoat before she slipped a long white ruffled underskirt over my head. Then I tied the wire bustle around my waist and stood patiently while Sarah selected a gown from the crowded closet. She chose a deliciously soft one with a high neck and long sleeves. When she had slipped it over my head, I smoothed it around my hips, saw that it draped nicely over the bustle, then looked at myself in the mirror.

The gown was a pale, glowing pink, contrasting attractively with my dark hair. Steam from the water had brought soft curls forward to frame my face. My eyes seemed to have grown bluer since my arrival, or perhaps the steam had deepened their color even as it had brightened the color in my cheeks.

"Vanity is a sin, Miss Shadow," Sarah reminded me.

I turned from the mirror with a rebellious toss of my head. Why was everything a sin when a young person did it? I'd seen some of the girls' mothers prink for half an hour before the mirror in Miss Brigham's hall before their hats were settled to their satisfaction, and no one had ever indicated by even a look that *they* were doing anything wrong.

"All right, Sarah . . . I'm ready," I said resignedly, then added, "and I'm hungry!"

We swept into the broad hall and descended the stairs. Voices drifted from the open door of the dining room as Bertha bustled from the kitchen to greet us.

"We'll have our supper now," Sarah announced firmly.

"Of course, Miss Murphy." The housekeeper glanced toward the dining room, a worried frown on her face. "Will you mind terribly being served in the morning room, Miss Murphy . . . Miss Shadow? I'm afraid Miss Julia and Mr. David are having words over their meal."

An angry female voice sounded in querulous complaint to substantiate Bertha's statement. Then a male voice answered, seeming to try to placate the young lady. Was my cousin always so irritable? Her shocking discourtesy at our earlier meeting rankled when I recalled her unkindness. Would I have to do battle because of my name all over again?

"We would prefer it," Sarah said grimly. "I shall be glad to deliver you to the Chauvannes, Miss Shadow, and be gone. However, the strangeness of our reception will be reported to Mr. Arbuthnot, of that you can be sure."

"Yes, Sarah," I murmured.

Desolation replaced the happiness I had felt in the soothing bath. Once more I was terribly aware of my orphan status and my dependence on relatives I did not know. Carmelita's locket lay warmly against my skin under the high neck of my gown. I wondered how often I would have to call on my mother's spirit and my conquistadore blood to uphold me in the days ahead. Then I raised my head in defiance. No one would ever daunt me again . . . no one!

Bertha led us to a smaller dining room at the rear of the house. Here the booming beat of waves was even louder than it had been in my room, but my curiosity as to the nearness of the shore was left unsatisfied when a peek between the drapery panels showed only blackness. This room must have been designed to supply a spectacular morning view with breakfast, I decided.

"The countess will be quite angry when she hears of Miss Julia's rudeness," Bertha said quietly. "Please sit down, Miss Shadow, Miss Murphy." She glanced at a hovering maid. "Bring silver and napkins," she bade. "I'll serve the food myself. You've both had a tiring day, I know, and perhaps a good meal will revive your spirits." She bustled her way out of the room, while Sarah sat in rigid silence.

When Sarah was sure we were alone, she spoke. "Miss Shadow, I don't think I should leave you with these people." She frowned as she fidgeted with the silver. "I can't imagine what they are thinking about. Your cousin is alone with a man! A nineteen-year-old girl is in that room by herself with a man!" Her scandalized eyes stared at me.

"Didn't Bertha say they were engaged?"

Sarah's snort was vehement. "Engaged—not married! A well-bred young lady is never left alone with any man who is not her husband! It just isn't done!"

"Perhaps customs are different out here, Sarah," I ventured. "People seem to be friendlier and more casual—at least, most of them," I amended.

"Humph! *Manners* are most assuredly different out here!" Sarah exclaimed, and then she sighed in indecision. "I *must* return to Miss Brigham's school, but I'm dreadfully fearful about leaving you with these people." She sighed again. "I do wish I could speak to Mr. Arbuthnot about this. If your father were still alive, I know he would not approve of this environment for you. These . . . barbarians . . . will totally ruin Miss Brigham's teachings, and what's worse, might even change you into one of them. Oh, my dear . . . I just don't know what to do!"

"I'll be all right, Sarah, and as for doing anything . . . well, I'm afraid it's too late. Before I left, Mr. Arbuthnot told me he'd made arrangements to sell my father's house, and by now my money has been transferred to the care of my aunt and uncle, so I'll have to abide by their wishes, whatever happens. My father surely made investigations before he willed me to the care of his sister. He must have known how the Chauvannes lived, don't you think?"

Before she could answer, Bertha returned with platters of food, and I patted Sarah's arm. "Let's eat, Sarah. I'm sure everything will be fine." I hoped what I was saying was true, but I was nowhere so confident inside.

Sarah nodded, but her usual hearty appetite had left her. While I ate heartily, she merely pushed food around on her plate. I felt unusual sympathy for this martinet who worried about me, and I rather dreaded the moment of her departure.

Sarah had made arrangements to board a train in Oakland the following afternoon, and now her boring trip would be further complicated with worries about my future. Determinedly, I brightened, trying to ease her mind about my welfare.

I wondered wistfully if Juan had been able to follow us to California, or would he perhaps be forced to return to New York and his job at Miss Brigham's?

And if he did get to California, how could he possibly find me? This dreaded thought was always in the back of my mind, for California seemed but a huge wilderness in which people could become lost to view forever. Suddenly I felt as small as a cricket in the brawling hugeness of the country around me. I wanted to be back in my room at Miss Brigham's, knowing Juan was safely in the stables.

"Have you finished eating, Miss Shadow?"

Sarah's voice broke into my musings as I realized I, too, was merely pushing food around my plate with the fork. Forcing my lips to smile, I nodded, murmuring, "Yes, Sarah."

"Then perhaps we'd both better get a good night's rest. I declare, I do dread spending more terrible nights on that awful train." Her usually erect shoulders sagged tiredly. "I'll be so happy to be back in my room at Brigham School!"

She had echoed my thoughts, but my father's will had dictated my future, and here was where it lay. I sighed as we walked from the bright room into the softly lit hallway. So be it, then.

Julia nearly bumped into me as she came from the dining room. "Oh!" Her startled exclamation interrupted the flow of conversation aimed at her companion. Her hand flew to her bosom in surprise, and I felt a blush start up my throat when I saw how low the neck of her gown was cut.

A man in evening wear followed Julia, then stopped behind her. My gaze went from the starched white shirtfront to his face, and the flooding warmth of my blush crowded into my face when I saw the laughing blue eyes of the man who had kissed me on the ferry!

I heard Sarah's outraged gasp behind me.

"Good evening, ladies," he said gravely. He glanced at Julia. "Perhaps you should introduce us, my dear."

I could not tear my eyes from his face. It was like seeing Edward St. George come back to life, only in a younger state. The room began to swirl around me, and I felt myself sway as voices came as though from far away.

"This is my cousin and her maid," Julia said. Dimly, I heard her careless laugh. "Her name is Shadow—can you imagine? Shadow St. George."

They moved with the slow, exaggerated motions of mimes while I struggled to free myself from the giddiness I felt.

Julia's careless voice carried to my ears. "This is my fiancé, Shadow. David Roberts."

He glided toward me through rapidly thickening mist and raised my hand to his lips. "I'm very happy to meet you," he said. His blue eyes burned into me while the room faded into blackness. He was reaching for me as I sank into unconsciousness in merciful oblivion . . .

The harshness of smelling salts nearly strangled me. Sarah bent over, waving a vial to and fro under my nose. Weakly, I pushed her hand away, noting that I was lying on a satin swooning couch in the dim room. Behind Sarah, Bertha Darwell clucked like a distracted hen.

"Are you all right, Miss Shadow?" Sarah asked, her voice sharp with worry. "That man should be shot!"

"But what did he do, Miss Murphy?" Bertha

71

asked. "What did he do?"

"Where is he?" I asked weakly. A stabbing head-ache made me blink when I sat up.

Sarah's capable hands smoothed my gown while she answered, "They've gone, and good riddance! Whatever came over you, Miss Shadow? I've never known you to faint."

"But what did he *do*?" Bertha wailed. "I didn't see him do anything but kiss her hand!"

Sarah frowned, helping me rise even as she straight-ened her back. "We do not wish to talk about it, Mrs. Darwell," she said coldly. "Come, Miss Shadow, I'll help you to your room. You must rest now."

With her arm around me, I walked woodenly up the stairs. I felt like a silly fool, much too embarrassed by my weakness to discuss it. Where were you, Carme-lita? My silent question brought no response.

Sarah undressed me as though I were once again a child, dropping the long nightgown over my head and helping me into bed. She drew the covers up to my chin and tucked them in, but her lips were clamped shut, so conversation was unnecessary.

I wanted to enter the world of sleep until my head stopped hurting. Perhaps then I could quiet the foolish thoughts about my father's return from the dead. David Roberts was *not* Edward St. George! He was a brash, obnoxious . . . *fiancé*! And Julia was welcome to him, for two such unpleasant people deserved each other. With that final thought, I de-cided to push them both from my mind.

Then why couldn't I sleep? Why did I still feel those soft, silky hairs tickling my nose while warm lips caressed my mouth? I flounced restlessly from one side of the bed to the other, loosening the covers Sarah had tucked so snugly around me.

At last I dozed, and Carmelita drifted into my thoughts like a vision of peace. She twirled gracefully across a polished floor, this time forgoing the wild flamenco I usually imagined her dancing. Her trim figure above the voluminous skirt swayed seductively as she held out her arms in welcome. Edward St. George came across the floor in evening dress, and this time he was smiling! His arm went around her tiny waist even as he bent down to kiss her. Then they began to waltz in graceful swoops and turns, looking at each other like lovers. For the first time, I saw my parents together, as sleep drew me deeper into its depths.

Chapter Six

When I woke, it was because Carlie had pulled the draperies aside to let the morning sun come in. She turned from the window, smiling when she saw I was awake.

"Good morning, Miss Shadow," she said. "Do you wish to have breakfast in bed?"

I stared at her. Never in my life had I eaten anything in bed. Miss Brigham had warned us sternly about crumbs drawing bugs, so even when we slipped goodies into our pockets to eat later, it never once occurred to us to wait until bedtime to eat them.

"Er . . . no, thanks," I murmured, wondering if she had asked Sarah the same question. "Is Miss Murphy up?"

"I think she's dressing now," Carlie said cheerfully. "One of the other girls went to wake her. I'm to be your maid, Miss Shadow. What would you like me to do?"

"Brush my hair," I decided. Today I would wash it, but after my week on the train, a good brushing would bring back the gloss cinders had dimmed.

Carlie brought the hairbrush and began gently pulling it through my hair. "Your hair is beautiful, Miss Shadow, and I love its natural curl."

"Thank you, Carlie." I sat dreamily content while her ministrations went on. Then as I came more fully awake, events of the day came to mind. "Who is David Roberts?" I asked, carefully keeping my voice casual.

"Miss Julia's fiancé."

Impatiently, I shook my head. "I know that! What does he do? Where does he come from?"

"Oh, I see." Carlie stood back to view her work, then resumed brushing. "He's a rancher. He has a big cattle ranch down the coast a ways, and a great big hacienda. He's thought to be very wealthy."

"Isn't he terribly young to have all that? Where did he come from?"

Carlie laughed. "He came from the East, like almost everyone out here did. And I don't think he's as young as he looks. I heard he was twenty-nine years old."

"Has he lived here long?" I felt a little guilty as I questioned her. If Sarah were here she'd lecture me about gossiping with the help, but they were always the ones who knew everything about everybody.

"I think he came out here while he was still a lad," she answered. Once again her brushing stopped, while she combed loose hairs from the bristles. "When he was nineteen or so, they tell me, he came into quite a bit of money. He probably had rich parents." She sighed, resuming her chore. "I wish my parents were wealthy."

Our eyes met in the mirror. "Being rich doesn't

mean you'll be happy, Carlie. Does your father love you?"

Her eyes widened in surprise. "Of course! Mum does, too, but she's poorly since the last baby." She frowned as she continued. "Money . . . at least a little more of it, would make their lives much nicer." Then her manner grew brisk as she laid the brush aside. "There you are, Miss Shadow. My, but you're pretty! Now, would you like to get dressed?"

"Yes, Carlie."

I went through the dressing ritual, this time culminating with a morning gown that was cool and airy. A deep shade of pink underskirt was overlaid with one of a lighter shell color. Tiny bows gathered fullness as they hovered up and down the skirt like resting butterflies. I twirled across the room, much as Carmelita had danced in my dreams, and was preening in front of the mirror when Sarah came in.

"Good morning, my dear. It's time to go down to breakfast," she said, frowning, and I knew she was disapproving of my vanity again.

"Then let's go, Sarah!" I stretched my arms, smiling at her. "Isn't it a beautiful morning?"

We walked down the long hall, and suddenly she stopped. "I don't know, Miss Shadow. I still feel guilty when I think of leaving you with these people." She glanced around to be sure no one was in earshot. "I don't think their morals are quite what they should be. Their own daughter must have very little supervision, so why would they take proper care of you? And when a dreadful occurrence such as we saw just after we arrived can happen right on the street, there must be very little protection from the law in this terrible country." She shook her head. "I just don't know. . . ."

"Oh, Sarah, you haven't met Count and Countess Chauvanne yet. Perhaps there are extenuating circumstances to their leaving my cousin and her fiancé unattended for just a short time. They are probably very pillars of respectability." I refrained from mentioning the vigilante happening so as not to upset her even more.

"Humph . . . I certainly hope so. I can't imagine what Miss Brigham would think of all these goings-on." Her pinched nose rose higher. "It will be a relief to return to a world of high standards such as hers."

We descended the stairs as my thoughts returned to my old school. If it hadn't been for Juan, my childhood would have been unbearably dull. Where was he? And then I forgot him as David Roberts pushed his way into my thoughts. Had he brought Julia home and then left, or had he stayed the night?

"Your cheeks are quite flushed, my dear. You haven't gotten a fever, have you?" Sarah asked, her worried eyes scanning my face.

I realized a guilty blush had crept up my face, and tried to push my thoughts onto more acceptable topics. "I'm quite all right, Sarah. It seems a little warm in here, but I suppose I'm excited, too. I hope Aunt Elizabeth likes me."

We walked into the dining room just as Bertha Darwell turned from the table.

"Miss Shadow!" she exclaimed with a smile. "You look fine this morning. I was just telling your aunt what a turn you gave us last night."

My aunt and uncle were already at table. Steam

rose from the cups before them, and half-eaten croissants gave evidence that breakfast was in progress.

Uncertainly, I smiled. "Last night was unfortunate, I'm afraid." The blond-haired woman raised elegant eyebrows as I continued. "I was overtired from the trip, I suppose."

"So you are Shadow," my aunt murmured. She turned to the tall, elegantly dressed man who had risen. "Sit down, Ferd. This is our niece, Shadow St. George." Her elaborately coiffed head turned again in my direction. "Sit down, dear, and tell Bertha what you wish to eat." Her gaze flicked to Sarah. "Miss . . . Murphy, is it? Bertha will help you get what you want in the kitchen."

Indignation pinched Sarah's face at my aunt's unkind words. I put my hand on her arm so she would stay. "I'm afraid you don't understand, Aunt Elizabeth. This is Sarah Murphy. She came with me as my companion and temporary guardian—not my maid." My chin rose. "She isn't used to eating with servants, you know."

The count bowed slightly as he pulled out a chair and looked at Sarah. "There is plenty of room for everybody, my dear. Miss Murphy, will you seat yourself here?"

The countess passed a diamond-bedecked hand wearily across her brow. "What a to-do about nothing! And so early in the day." She took a sip from a dainty cup. "I'm sure I don't care who sits where. And Shadow . . . *please* don't call me *Aunt* Elizabeth. It sounds so . . . so old. You may call me Countess, if you like, or Elizabeth, as Julia does. That reminds me . . . Bertha, is Miss Julia up yet?"

78

"No, ma'am." She smoothed her already tidy apron. "We thought perhaps she'd like to sleep late this morning."

"Oh, dear," the countess murmured. "Did those naughty children stay out terribly late again?" Then she turned to her husband. "Ferd, do hurry up their marriage. I think it's high time Julia had a husband."

The count shrugged his shoulders in resignation. "You can't hurry up a marriage that hasn't been proposed yet."

A look of irritation crossed my aunt's face. "Of course it's been proposed!" she said sharply. "They're engaged, aren't they?"

"Well . . . David gave her a ring, of course. But I don't think he's asked her to set a date yet." He smothered a yawn. "One doesn't hurry these things, my dear. David will arrange things when he's ready."

"Nonsense!" she said sharply. Then her glance fell on Sarah. "But we mustn't inflict our family problems on our guests. Was your trip simply dreadful, Shadow?"

"Not really, Au . . . er, Countess." I had thought of her as Aunt Elizabeth all during the journey, but now I would have to get used to another name. "It was just tiresome sitting for such a long time. The scenery was monotonous at first, but then it was beautiful coming over the mountains. There was so much to see, and it was so magnificent. . . ."

She nodded, returning to her croissant.

Chung walked so softly I didn't realize he'd entered until he put plates of ham and eggs before Sarah and me. I couldn't help staring in fascination at the pigtail bobbing against his neck. I'd only seen them at a

79

distance before, and this was so close.

My aunt's eyes opened in surprise at the ample helpings. "Young people have terribly good appetites, I know," she said, then arched her eyebrows inquiringly at Sarah. "I simply can't bear food this early."

"Sarah is returning to New York this afternoon, Countess." The smile I gave Sarah was meant to be reassuring. "We discovered during our trip that we'd best eat well when the food was good." My eyes were drawn to Chung's back as he exited the room.

"Have you never seen a Chinese before?" my aunt asked impatiently. "Really, Shadow, you must not stare so."

"I'm sorry, Countess," I said. "Of course, I've seen Asians before, but I didn't know they were used as servants." Her reprimand stung, for I knew I deserved it.

She patted her mouth with her napkin. "I keep forgetting how terribly conservative my dear brother was in his tastes. Except in the wife he chose," she added. "Everyone who is anyone has a houseboy. Chung was young enough to train properly when we got him, so he's better than most."

Her glance fell on Sarah. "You're leaving us today, then?" she asked indifferently. "Well, I shall have to thank Mr. Arbuthnot for finding such a reliable person to bring my niece across the wilds of the interior." She turned to her husband. "Ferd, arrange with Tom to take Miss . . . er, Murphy to the wharf whenever she wishes."

Sarah had said nothing, but I knew she still seethed over being classed as a maid, and my sympathies went out to her. I, too, knew how it felt to be humiliated.

My father had taught me well.

"Would you like me to go with you as far as the wharf, Sarah? You've been very kind, and I shall miss you, you know."

Her face softened somewhat. "No, Miss Shadow, it won't be necessary. You should rest today." She nodded conspiratorially. "You'll need your strength for other things."

She straightened her shoulders as she addressed my aunt. "Countess Chauvanne, Shadow has been reared in a God-fearing atmosphere. She has been taught social graces and manners, as well as the three R's, and she has also been schooled in her duty toward her elders. It is unfortunate that her father died when he did, but that was something nobody could foretell or change. She has been sheltered, as all well-bred young ladies should be, and chaperoned in mixed company. I hope you will duplicate this treatment in future, so she will continue to grow and be as socially acceptable as she is today." Her eyes were fond when she glanced at me. "Miss Brigham and I are quite proud of our young charge."

Surprised laughter tinkled from my aunt. "Really," she murmured. "Do you think we are savages, Miss Murphy?"

"No, madam, I do not," Sarah answered. "However, your daughter was left alone in a room with a young man last evening while they were dining, and of that I do not approve." Her lips clamped in the stubborn line I knew so well.

Laughter vanished from the countess' face. "My daughter has an impeccable character, Miss Murphy. She dined with her fiance alone, that is true, but there are always servants in this house. Her reputation has never been compromised."

"I would like to speak to you alone before I leave, Countess Chauvanne. There are things I think you should know," Sarah said primly.

My aunt rose. "I do not think that will be necessary, Miss Murphy. I never listen to gossip of any kind from anybody. From now on my niece will be in our care, and I assure you there is nothing that need trouble you about her future. Please give Mr. Arbuthnot my regards when you return to New York. I shall contact him myself if I have need of his services. So now I will bid you good-bye and safe journey." She turned away and swept regally from the room.

Count Chauvanne shrugged philosophically and hurried after his wife. "Wait, Elizabeth," he called.

Sarah sputtered as she watched them leave. "Now I *know* this is no place for you, child! Oh, dear, I wish there were some way I could discuss this matter with Miss Brigham before I leave."

"I'll be all right, Sarah," I said soothingly. "I really don't think you should tell her about the incident on the ferry. After all, Mr. Roberts didn't know I was Julia's cousin."

"His conduct was utterly outrageous," Sarah fumed. "The countess should know what sort of person her daughter is engaged to marry. A roving eye only gets worse once the knot is tied, and no daughter of mine would ever be allowed to involve herself with a man of that stripe."

"Now, Sarah . . . you know Miss Brigham never approved of gossip, so perhaps my aunt is of better character than you imagine." Guiltily, I thought of my questions to Carlie, then decided the blessing of knowledge overcame the sin of gossiping.

A look of vexation crossed Sarah's face. "Miss Shadow, you must promise me you'll avoid that man and never let him near you again." She shuddered. "He's evil! I can feel his sinfulness, and you must be careful of him. He had the audacity to touch you! He actually dared hold you, and he kissed you! I . . . I *never*!" she sputtered to a close.

We had finished our meal, so I rose and tried to soothe her. "Please, Sarah . . . shall we walk a bit around the grounds? Soon you'll be confined to a Pullman car again, and there's not much chance to exercise there. Besides, I'd like to see what it looks like outside, wouldn't you? Then you can describe this house to Miss Brigham."

I sent Chung to tell Carlie we needed light shawls. Sunshine warmed the day, but chill from the night's fog still lingered.

When Carlie brought them, she smiled cheerfully, saying, "The best place to begin from is the morning room where you ate supper last night. Doors open onto the lawn and you can walk right out into the garden area."

We followed her down the hall, while I wondered why my aunt and uncle chose the dining room for breakfast instead of the airy room facing the sea. This morning from the windows you could see the waves splashing on the shore, and it was but a short distance below the house.

"Madam Countess says the ocean makes her bilious in the morning," Carlie confided. "I love it, and I'm sure you will, too, Miss Shadow. It usually smells sort of fishy, but then the breeze brings other odors to mix with it, and it's like a salty stew."

"Is this the ocean, Carlie? I thought this was part of San Francisco Bay."

Carlie shook her head. "This is the Pacific Ocean, Miss Shadow. The bay is across the way."

She opened wide glass doors leading to a flat area paved with broad slabs of stone. Sarah followed me through, and then we both stopped to stare at the vista before us.

Behind the mansion the ground sloped downward until it reached a sandy beach. White-capped waves romped in to break and scatter against the shore. A short distance seaward, rocky fingers pointed heavenward while the waves rushed by, splashing them in their race to the land. Beyond the rocks there was only water. It stretched as far as the eye could see, disappearing into a misty horizon.

"Isn't it beautiful, Sarah?"

She shivered, pulling her shawl more tightly around her. "It looks terribly wet," she said flatly.

I led the way around the huge house toward the front. Ivy climbed in thick ribbons of green to the roof. The bright sun sparkled against white paint and spotless windows, radiating warmth that increased as the house came between us and the chill ocean.

Towering trees—which I eventually found out were eucalyptus—shaded velvet-green grass accentuated by brightly blooming flowers. November in California was a far cry from November in New York.

A gravel driveway led from the veranda to the wide iron gates. The hunched little man emerged from his gatehouse when a man on horseback galloped up outside. He saluted the rider and opened the gates to let the horseman through, then carefully closed them again.

The visitor came up the rocky road at a gallop. When he noticed us, he pulled his horse to a rearing halt and swept the white Stetson hat from his head in a courtly bow. "Good morning, ladies," he said gallantly.

I looked up at David Roberts, but this time I kept my composure. Despite Sarah's gasp, I answered calmly, "Good morning, Mr. Roberts." Before he could say more, I led Sarah away in further exploration of my new home. I was quite proud of my coolness, resolving never to lose it again, no matter the circumstances.

"Miss Shadow," Sarah almost wailed, "that man! He's always around, it would seem. Oh, dear, oh, dear." Then she tried to pull herself together. "I'll have to leave now if I'm to catch the train to New York, but I do hate to leave you here. Are you sure you want to stay?"

"Now, Sarah," I began, feeling our roles had been reversed. "I can handle anything that arises. After all, Miss Brigham said I was dependable, didn't she?" I smiled to reassure her. "I'm seventeen, remember, and quite capable, too."

We completed our circle of the mansion and reentered through the glass doors. The maids had readied Sarah's baggage, and Carlie stood in the hall with her traveling cloak.

"Are you sure you don't want me to accompany you as far as the wharf, Sarah? I can ride in the carriage with you, if you like. Oh, I will miss you!"

Her lips trembled when she looked at me. "No, Miss Shadow, I'll be fine. I remember you from the time you came to the school as a little girl. You were so shy . . . and your poor hands were burned in that terrible fire when you tried to save Diedre, and you were always so brave about everything. . . ." She swiped a tear from her cheek. "Now you're a young lady . . . still so brave. . . ." Her back straightened. "Well, there's nothing for it but to go, my dear. Now remember your training." She glanced at the hovering maid. "I've already said my say about other things. You'll remember my warning, won't you?"

"Yes, Sarah . . . I'll remember everything you told me, you and Miss Brigham, too." I wanted to put my arms around her, but knew it would only scandalize her, so I patted her gloved hand instead. "Thank you so much for coming with me. Talk to the other passengers on your way back, so you won't be so lonesome and the trip won't seem so long."

She nodded, saying, "Good-bye, dear," then walked to the waiting carriage. Tom Jordan helped her inside, then took his place on the box, clucking the horses into a walk. When the iron gates had closed behind them I was left with a feeling of loneliness and bereavement. Was the last friend I had leaving me in a hostile world?

But I was not alone. A low chuckle from behind brought me around to see David Roberts leaning carelessly against a doorway across the hall from the dining room.

"So the old dragon has flown away, has she?" he asked, then laughed again. "Didn't she get furious, though?"

"She should have, Mr. Roberts," I said coolly. "Your conduct was unforgivable."

"Oh-ho! So the flying fish I caught is now a princess of the realm, is she?" His blue eyes glinted wickedly. "Well, I'm your servant, ma'am."

He was bowing extravagantly when Julia sailed down the stairs. "What on earth are you doing, David?"

He ignored her question as he demanded, "Why are you dressed for town? I thought we had a date to go riding."

She drew on white gloves, waiting for Bertha to bring her cloak. "I'm going shopping, David. The Crocker ball is coming up and I simply must have a new gown. You may go with me if you like, if you've brought suitable clothing besides your riding habit."

"Your dressmaker comes here to work," he said indignantly. "And why should I lug town clothing with me when we planned to go riding?"

Julia's laugh tinkled in the morning air. "Oh, dear boy, don't be droll. Mother wants me to have a gown from Paris for the ball. Only provincials wear creations made by the local seamstresses."

"So we aren't going riding," David said. "Why didn't you send one of the grooms to tell me of your change in plans?"

"I forgot." She turned to Chung. "Have Tom bring the carriage round at once."

"I'm sorry, Miss Julia," Bertha said. "He's taking Miss Murphy to the wharf."

"Oh, bother!" Julia stamped her foot. "Have one of the other carriages brought round, Chung. Tell one of the grooms to drive . . . and hurry!"

The houseboy scampered away, followed by Bertha at a more sedate pace.

"What am I to do?" David asked.

"Oh, David, I don't feel like riding today. Perhaps tomorrow." Her glance fell on me. "Why don't you take my cousin for a ride? You do know how to ride, don't you, Shadow?"

"Of course, Julia, but . . ." My voice trailed off as I wondered if it were proper for me to go riding alone with her fiancé.

"But what?" Julia asked impatiently.

I glanced at David's serious face, noting his eyes were still wickedly amused.

"Will a groom accompany us?"

Julia's eyes opened wide. "Why should he?"

My voice was low as I answered, "It isn't proper for us to ride unattended."

"Little goose!" Her laugh was derisive. "David is engaged to me, which makes him almost your cousin. You really were raised in a nunnery, weren't you?"

The hated blush burned as I tried to will it away. "Of course not, Julia. However, we were taught to be ladies. My father's solicitor told me ways are different out here, and I fully intend to adapt. However, I do not intend to act like some street hoyden."

Inwardly, I felt satisfaction at the discomfited look on Julia's face. I had successfully pushed the painful blush out of sight and was sure I was in command of myself.

On closer inspection my cousin was not the really beautiful woman I thought I'd seen. She was attractively gowned and extravagantly bejeweled, but her nose was slightly overlarge and her mouth had a petulant twist that was quite unbecoming. She was a few inches taller than I, quite slender, and her eyes were beautiful. If she weren't so terribly spoiled, I decided, she would be much better looking.

Julia's head rose as she frowned at me. "You'll have to stop being such a little prude, Shadow. Do as you like about the ride."

A carriage rattled up outside and she turned back to David. "Shall we see you at dinner tonight?"

"Of course, my dear." He raised one of her gloved hands and pressed it to his mouth.

"Then I'm off."

David opened the door and Julia walked quickly to the waiting carriage.

I waited, uncertain what to do.

The carriage left, and David closed the door and turned to me. "I'm afraid I've been an awful cad, Miss St. George." His voice was regretful. "I've been teasing you before we were even properly introduced, and I don't blame you for not wanting to be alone with me."

"Really . . ." I began.

He held up a hand. "I haven't finished my apology yet, Miss St. George. I'm very sorry for my behavior and would like to begin our friendship anew, if you will allow me."

"Of course," I said uncertainly.

"I would like to show you the country and some of my ranch, if you care to see it. Ferd has some very good horses in his stable. I know you would enjoy the ride, and if you prefer a groom to accompany us, I'm sure it can be arranged."

The kindness in his voice unnerved me. I had

gotten off to a bad start, mostly because of his resemblance to my father, but also because of the free and easy ways of this alien western world. Was I being a silly goose?

David Roberts stood penitently before me, waiting for my decision, and suddenly I made up my mind.

"Your apology is accepted, Mr. Roberts. That is," I added, "if you'll call me Shadow. As Julia pointed out, we will be cousins before long."

He smiled, and I noticed how white his teeth were under the sandy mustache.

"I would like to go for a ride," I continued. "Some exercise would be most welcome." I paused, then added, "A groom will not be necessary, of course."

He bowed politely. "I'll make arrangements while you change, Shadow."

Turning, I ran lightly up the stairs to my room. Sarah would have been shocked at my words, but this was a new world.

While I changed into a riding habit, I silently thanked Mr. Arbuthnot for having had the dressmaker make such an extensive wardrobe for my new life. A feeling of happiness crept into my consciousness, and my heart beat faster than usual. Was I beginning a more exciting life than I had ever imagined?

Chapter Seven

It was only a few minutes later that I ran down the stairs. The admiration in David's eyes told me my new habit was a success. It was gray velveteen that contrasted nicely with starched white linen and an immaculate stock. A smoky veil over a tiny hat completed the outfit. As I pulled on white gloves, I slowed to a pace more befitting a young lady, then smiled at my escort.

David offered his arm. "You'll dazzle my poor cowboys and they won't be able to work," he said gallantly.

"I wish you'd stop teasing, David. I'm not a child any more." I gathered my train in one hand and put the other on his proffered arm.

My mount was more mettlesome than any I'd ridden, but I soon settled into the rhythm of her easy lope. I looked enviously at David sitting comfortably astride, and wondered why women were condemned to perch precariously with both feet on one side of a horse. Probably for the same reason they wore bulky long skirts while men traveled easily in trousers.

We rode along the dusty road for a while, then turned into a narrow lane that gradually changed to sand. Then there was a beach where breakers rolled in, and David guided our mounts into shallow water.

"Saltwater is good for their hooves," he explained. "I ride each of my horses through the sea at least once a month—it toughens their feet."

He led the way farther into the water, walking the horses slowly to allow the waves to splash around their ankles. When an unusually large wave rose to above their knees, the spray reached my veil and hung in the lacy webbing like sea dryads' tears.

"You aren't dressed for this," David said, "and I should have realized it. Your riding habit is getting sprinkled, and I'm sure saltwater can't be good for it. Come, let's get out of this and I'll show you my home."

We left the water and cantered the horses along the sand until it sloped upward onto a grassy hill. Above, I saw a long, low one-story building, weathered to a color that blended into the dunes. It was a picturesque addition to the tumbling hills of sand, and one that looked as though it had sprung up like the salt grass that surrounded it, a natural wonder of nature.

By the time we reached the hacienda a boy in high-heeled boots had come around the house to stand waiting.

"Hi, boss," he said with a grin.

"Chico," David acknowledged. "Put the horses in the shade and saddle up the little roan mare and my bay."

He held out his arms to help me dismount, shaking his head in dismay as he realized how damp my clothing had gotten in the flying spray. "I'm so sorry, Shadow . . . I'm a thoughtless clod. Come, let's go in and I'll introduce you to my housekeeper. Perhaps she can repair the damage I've caused."

Inside, a dark-skinned Indian woman in a neat gingham dress greeted us with a nod of her head.

"This is Shawohanee, Shadow. She takes such good care of me, I forget I'm an orphan," David said lightly. "This is Miss St. George, Shawohanee."

She motioned us to a table, then went to bring cups and a pot that steamed on the huge black range.

"I'm hungry," David complained.

Shawohanee went to get a towel-covered platter that turned out to contain a mound of prepared sandwiches and our lunch. She smiled as she placed it before us, but said never a word, then left.

"Are you an orphan, David?" I asked, adding, "I am."

He nodded. "But you know who your parents were, Shadow, and that's something I have never known."

"How can that be?"

A shrug lifted his shoulders. "As far back as I can remember, I was in a boys' boarding school back East. One of the best, which is strange. It surely cost a lot of money to keep me there, but nobody would tell me who was paying."

"You never saw either of your parents?"

"Not unless it was when I was too young to remember." He shrugged in resignation. "When I was fifteen, I ran away and came out here."

"Where'd you get the money?" I asked curiously, thinking of Juan.

"What money? I got a job as a hand with a wagon

93

train, and that was just for bed and board. After I arrived in San Francisco, I tried swamping out a saloon." He grinned. "That's one job I wouldn't wish on my worst enemy. Then I landed a job as a cowhand on a ranch."

"Then how could you inherit so much money?" I asked, and suddenly my hand flew to cover my mouth. Now David would know I had been gossiping about him!

He pretended not to notice my confusion. "An attorney from the city came looking for me when I was nineteen. He said I'd been left a bequest by someone who preferred to remain anonymous." He grinned ruefully. "By then I was tired of taking orders and even more tired of doing every ornery job that came along, so I didn't insist on answers. It bought me a ranch of my own where I can give the orders."

He offered me another sandwich. I chewed thoughtfully, digesting the information he'd given me. David was an orphan, another link we shared.

While we ate, David's eyes traveled over me, and he must have been taking measurements, for he reached a decision. "Why don't you go with Shawohanee and change into sensible clothing so we can really go for a ride?"

I had removed my drenched hat and veil, but now I stared at him, uncomprehending.

There was a glint of wickedness in his eyes when he laughed. "Shawohanee has clean clothing belonging to Chico that I'm sure would fit."

"I couldn't!" I gasped.

"Julia does," he said nonchalantly. "Why dress in that torturous way when there's nobody to see you

94

except me? I'll never tell."

My carefree days with Juan when I had donned a servant girl's coat to run through the streets with him returned to my mind. That had been daring, but nothing dreadful had happened because of it. Absently, I sipped at the hot coffee Shawohanee poured in my cup, and then I made a decision.

"Perhaps you're right, David. My gown is quite damp from the sea." I was aghast at my own words, but determined to go through with the bargain I had made for myself. I would adapt to this alien world as soon as I could, even if I had to wear a boy's clothing to do so.

Shawohanee led me into a cool bedroom and silently helped me remove the cumbersome riding habit. She brought a white shirt and clean trousers, then stood looking expectantly at my corset. I removed it slowly, feeling rather ridiculous standing there in my shift. Then she handed Chico's clothing to me and left, closing the door behind her.

The shirt fit well, I noted as I buttoned it. Then I slipped into the trousers. Chico must be my exact size. A mirror hung over a washstand, but it was too high for me to see how I looked. I pulled on my own boots and they felt strangely tight in contrast to the freedom my body was experiencing. When I looked down at my new self, I felt my cheeks burn. How could I possibly show myself in this garb?

A knock sounded on the door. "Hurry up, Miss Slowpoke. The day will be gone before we get our ride," David called.

My feet seemed reluctant to move, but I pulled them toward the door. A deep breath filled my freed lungs as I raised my head. I would go out even if I died of embarrassment.

David only glanced at me, then turned to the waiting housekeeper. "Where's a jacket and hat?" he asked impatiently.

He snatched the jacket she brought and helped me into it, started to button it, then relinquished the task to me when I pushed his hands away. "Now we can really ride," he said with satisfaction.

I donned the wide-brimmed hat Shawohanee offered, but David shook his head, so I removed it. "Braid your hair up under it so it won't be noticed," he said. "Shawohanee will do it."

The Indian woman quickly plaited my hair into two braids, then swirled them around my head like a halo. As she fastened them in place with hairpins, she nodded her approval.

"Thank you," I said, and pulled the hat over my hair. What would Miss Brigham think if she saw me now? I flinched, imagining her shocked displeasure. But I'm not at Miss Brigham's school anymore, I thought defiantly.

Chico had brought two horses from the stable. They were both saddled with men's saddles!

"Oh, I couldn't. . . ." I began, then stopped as David held out his hand.

"Try it," he urged. "It's really the only sensible way to ride—come on, I'll help you up."

He made a step of his hands so I could mount easily. The heat in my cheeks returned when I swung a leg to the other side and straddled the saddle. Lowering my head so the hat brim shielded my face, I fiercely willed the redness away. I would be neither a

96

silly goose nor a simpering idiot.

We returned to the beach where the spray from the ocean cooled my burning face. The strange feeling of freedom I felt soon changed to exhilaration as the horses went from a walk to a trot. How easy it was to balance myself when my legs could grip the sides of a horse! I kicked the little mare into a gallop, flying madly alongside the booming waves while foam churned beneath her feet. It no longer mattered that the salt spray spattered my clothing—these garments were made for anything a person wanted to do.

Never in my life had I felt so free! The light cotton clothing was wonderful, and a laugh came unbidden while the salty air rushed by. My feet were firmly in the stirrups, and there were no cramps in my back as I sat easily in the comfortable leather seat.

David was following, but now he brought his bay alongside. "What's funny?" he demanded.

I laughed again, slowing the mare to a walk. "I am, I suppose. I feel so . . . so free and so comfortable. I never dreamed riding a horse could be this wonderful."

"How you women stand the clothing you pile on yourselves is something I'll never understand. It would kill me!" His eyes went to my splashed clothing. "At least you won't ruin your new riding habit now. Come . . . I'll show you some of my ranch."

He led the way across grassy fields on the rolling coastal hills, pointing out an outstanding member of the herd of cattle we passed. Then he grew even more boastful, showing me a magnificent red stallion.

"I had him brought from England. All the way across the ocean by boat," he said proudly.

David was no longer the suave scoundrel of the ferry. He was but a small boy bragging about his possessions. My heart skipped a beat when he turned his smile on me. Why hadn't my father ever looked so approvingly at me?

We rode through wind-bent groves of gnarled oaks to other pastures. The day was like one out of a fairy tale. David waved at cowhands going about their work, or motioned them near to give an occasional order. After a casual glance the men ignored me, so my disguise was complete.

Soon the sun beat down fiercely, but in my light clothing I felt as cool as any colt. David was charming and kind—how could I ever have disliked him?

At the top of the highest hill he pulled to a halt and dismounted. "Let's rest a bit," he said, holding his arms to catch me as I came down. I slid against him, and the contact sent a shock through my body. I quickly pulled away to walk back and forth, ostensibly to ease my joints, but in reality to control my emotions. David was Julia's fiancé, and was only amusing a guest in her absence.

The view from our hill was a spectacular one. Breakers rolled in from the distant ocean swelled to bursting. They rid themselves of their burdens on the shore, then scurried back to the deeps. Soon more waves followed suit, and although the water looked flat beyond the turbulence, I could picture a sea of unrest, much like my inner feelings now.

David dropped the reins carelessly on the ground, leaving the horses to munch as they would. Removing his jacket, he spread it on the grass for me to sit on, then dropped beside me.

"Won't they run away?" My worried glance went from him to the horses and back. We were miles from civilization, and I didn't relish the thought of a long walk in my tight boots.

He shook his head. "They're ground-tied, Shadow. They'll eat the grass around them, but so long as those lines drag on the ground, they won't run away. They've been trained to stand that way. When you're working cattle and have to get to one in a hurry, you don't have time to tie your mount, even if a tree is handy."

We sat in comfortable silence admiring the view while the sun sparkled against the water and the breeze brought the smell of the sea.

"You have a beautiful ranch, David," I said dreamily. "Is all this land yours?"

His head rose defiantly. "It is as long as I can hang on to it." He rose and his gaze circled the country. "Too many people are coming West. Seems like the whole world thinks California is the promised land. Trainload after trainload of immigrants empty out every week, and every time a wagon pulls in with a plow in back I know another sodbuster is moving in to churn up the earth and fence it in."

"But there's so much room out here. . . ." I began, only to be interrupted by his impatient voice.

"Not enough! It takes acres of grass to make one steer fat, and thousands of acres to run enough cattle to make it profitable."

"Well, the settlers can't move onto *your* land, can they, David?"

He sank beside me again. "It isn't really mine, you see. It would take a great deal of money to buy as much land as I'd like to have, and I just don't have it. Enough money, I mean."

His words had taken me by surprise. Carlie had said David was rich, but perhaps his wealth was only great in contrast to her family's poverty. "Well, at least the Chinese don't take up much room," I said consolingly.

"Oh, no?" he asked with a scowl. "They're moving in everywhere. Since the railroads began bringing over coolies to work for them, they've come thicker than locusts from every ship that anchors in the harbor. In sixty-eight the fools in the city even signed a treaty guaranteeing China unlimited immigration of their population to the United States."

"If there are so many of them, now that the railroads are built, what do they all do?"

When David answered his voice was bitter. "First they moved into the mines. They almost took over before white men had enough and burned their camps. Then they moved to the cities like a yellow plague, working for wages no white man could live on, and even saving enough money to start their own businesses. They work day and night, cutting the ground away from white merchants by underselling them to a point where it would seem no one could make a living. Now they're starting to become farmers and are grabbing all the land they can get their filthy hands on."

David was growing angrier as he spoke, so I decided to change the subject. "David . . . what are vigilantes?"

A startled look crossed his handsome face, and then he frowned. "Why do you ask?" he said slowly.

"Before we could leave the city after we landed, a man was hanged from one of the lightposts." A shiver ran through me. "Tom Jordan said vigilantes had done it."

"Good grief!" he exploded. "And you *saw* it?"

"Our carriage was trapped by the throng of people and we had to wait until the horses could get through. Oh, David, it was awful!"

He stared, then muttered, "You really have had an introduction to our Wild West, Shadow, and I'm so sorry. . . ." His eyes remained on my face as he continued. "However, Tom Jordan must be mistaken. The vigilantes broke up years ago when law and order were established. They were good citizens who wanted a safer world for their families. Making examples of the worst criminals was their way of doing it."

My skepticism must have shown on my face, for David asked, "If there is a group calling themselves vigilantes now, I don't know who they are."

"But why would they do such a thing?" I persisted.

His shrug was eloquent. "Just stealing a horse can get you strung up out here, Shadow. Cheating at cards, rustling cattle, jumping a claim . . . they were all hanging offenses when the vigilantes rode, and even now, when crowds get excited over something they consider unfair, they can get very rough. But that you should have seen such a thing . . ." His jaw tightened. "Tom Jordan will certainly be taken to task for this."

"It wasn't his fault," I said quickly. "It happened so suddenly . . . all at once we were surrounded by a mob of maniacs. As soon as the sheriff's posse and the police arrived, he got us out of there in a hurry."

David continued to scowl, so I abandoned the subject for one less controversial. "It's certainly lovely out here," I said, rising to my feet.

David followed suit as his glance measured the sun. "We had better be getting back, or I'll be late for dinner and Julia will have my hide."

Once again he held his hands so I could reach the saddle, but my exhilaration was gone. He had reminded me he belonged to Julia—a fact that I had almost forgotten during our idyllic afternoon together.

We cut across the fields and reached the hacienda while the sun was still well in the sky. Shawohanee had cleaned my riding habit and it hung neatly in the bedroom where it had dried. She followed me in, indicating the full wash basin.

Regretfully, I removed Chico's clothing, wondering if I would ever return to gallop over the hills in such freedom. I washed, then donned the corset and let Shawohanee lace it up. She was as expert as Sarah, pulling it tight enough almost to stop my breathing. When I emerged in the velveteen gown with my hair brushed into ringlets around my shoulders, my eyes widened in surprise. David had changed from casual riding togs to a formal dinner jacket.

His smile was engaging. "Thought we'd return in the carriage, if you don't mind. I'll send Ferd's mounts back to him tomorrow. This time I'll surprise Julia by being early for a change."

"Of course, David."

The carriage waiting for us was as grand as the one Count Chauvanne sent to meet Sarah and me, and I wondered again about David's finances. Then my mind went to other things as David sat beside me on the soft leather cushion pointing out places we passed.

I studied his profile and the muscles in his jaw while he told me of this family and that. He was an unusually handsome man, as my father had been. His sandy hair was brushed to a shine against his well-shaped head. The silky mustache moved with the forming of his words. A lump came into my throat when I remembered the touch of it against my face on the ferry, and the disturbing lips that had brushed so briefly against mine. Then sudden dizziness made me weak, and it must have showed on my face.

"Did we ride too far today?" David asked gently.

His voice seemed to come from far away. Mentally I shook myself and straightened my back. "Of course not! Perhaps the sun was a little too much, glorious as it was. It's certainly brighter here than in New York."

The open iron gate passed by the window when the carriage turned from the road onto the mansion drive. The sun had slipped halfway into the ocean, bathing the world in golden iridescence. When the carriage rolled to a halt David got out, and the sun behind him formed a halo around his head, making him look like a picture of the angel Gabriel I'd seen in one of my school books. Then he helped me alight and I ran up the stairs.

Inside the house Julia was coming down the stairs, and I paused at the bottom.

"Well, you did make a day of it, didn't you?" she said, and her voice was sharp. "Perhaps I'd better not be so generous with my fiancé in the future."

Before I could reply, she sailed past, still talking, but now to David, not me.

"Darling, I'm so glad you're dressed. We must leave

103

right after dinner. Dorothy and Burt are having a party for Susan, and we simply can't miss it!"

My cheeks burned as I hurried up to my room. What an idiot I was! Just because David was kind enough to accept me as a substitute on the ride he'd planned with Julia, I had let my imagination run rampant. The angel Gabriel, indeed! He was only a man, and Julia's at that!

Chapter Eight

By the time Carlie helped me out of the riding habit and into a gown, it was time to go down for dinner. I would have much preferred a tray in my room, but pride forced me to walk back down the stairs. Voices came from the open door opposite the dining room, so I went in.

The initial impact of the magnificent salon made me gasp. Paintings hung in such profusion that the room resembled a museum. Gold-colored draperies were drawn over massive windows, and a golden carpet lay under matching upholstered furniture. Pure gold statues and bric-a-brac added dramatic accent to this most opulent of rooms.

"Come in, my dear," Count Chauvanne said when he saw me. "We've neglected you shamefully today, but Elizabeth had previous engagements we couldn't avoid."

A maid held a tray with filled glasses before me. I glanced uncertainly at my uncle, and as he nodded encouragingly, I accepted one of the goblets.

"Oh, Shadow wasn't neglected," Julia drawled.

"David showed her his ranch . . . probably the greater part of it, since it was an all-day expedition."

Her mouth had its usual petulant twist that made her nose seem even larger than usual. However, she was dressed in an elaborate party frock and wore diamonds around her throat and wrists, so the impression was one of beauty.

My aunt came forward to greet me. "We shall have to see that our niece is acquainted with other young people, Ferd. Tomorrow evening I shall have a small soirée in your honor, my dear."

David smiled, raising his glass in silent salute. "Which leaves this evening rather barren for you, doesn't it, Shadow?" He turned to Julia. "How about taking your cousin with us to the party, Julia?"

"We can't do that, David!" Julia exclaimed. "The table will be set for invited guests only, and an unexpected one will throw it off." She smiled placatingly. "I'm sure Shadow would much prefer to go to bed early, especially after her long and wearing horseback ride. Wouldn't you Shadow?"

"Of course, Julia."

I felt like an unwanted intruder. Their conversation continued, involving people I didn't know. My uncle returned to his position beside the blazing fireplace, while the talk swirled back and forth between the Chauvannes and David.

The liquid in my glass looked inviting. I had never tasted spirits of any kind, and now I remembered Miss Brigham's admonitions against the "devil's brew" she so hated. But here I was a Westerner, and I was determined to act as they did. Apparently Westerners drank wine, so I would also. The first sip was

106

quite delicious. I emptied the crystal goblet.

"Dinner is served, Madam Countess," Chung announced from the doorway.

A general movement toward the dining room started. My uncle offered me his arm as he and the countess passed by, and I accepted it with gratitude.

The wine settled smoothly into my stomach, but then strange waves of heat seemed to rise from it all the way to my head. The room shimmered in a golden haze as I sank into the chair positioned for me by Count Chauvanne. I reached for the glass of water before me and hastily gulped some of the contents. It provided a brief respite.

The meal passed in slow motion. I tasted the food put before me, and smiled the few times a remark was aimed at me, but I was glad when dinner was over. My eyelids were so heavy it was difficult to keep them from closing. Mostly I was ignored, so no one noticed. Julia and David held the center of attention until they decided to leave, then hurried out in a flurry of fond farewells. It was my chance to escape. I murmured my excuses and fled to my room.

The queasy feeling of unease grew to nausea as I threw myself on the bed. After one sharp look at my face, Carlie quickly brought a cold, damp cloth and laid it on my forehead.

"Are you going to . . . er . . . be ill, Miss Shadow?" Without waiting for my answer, she hurried to the washstand and brought the basin to me.

"No-o-o," I wailed, then promptly leaned over the bowl and began to retch. I felt Carlie's hands gather my heavy hair and draw it to the back of my head. Perspiration popped out on my face as my stomach emptied itself. When I had finished, Carlie carried the container to the stand and covered it with a cloth, then returned and began to undo the fasteners on my gown.

"Wouldn't you like to retire, Miss Shadow?"

"What's wrong with me, Carlie?" I asked, still gasping from my latest ordeal. My head was ready to split from the pounding inside, and never in my life had I felt so humiliated.

"Something disagreed with you," Carlie answered soothingly. "It happens to everyone at some time or other."

I moaned while tears came to my eyes. "I wish I were back home!" Sobs tore at my throat before I surrendered to a torrent of tears. Why had I come to this horrible place? Why had my father *condemned* me to it? Where was Carmelita? Where was Juan? Everybody had deserted me!

While I cried Carlie removed my clothing, lifting me around like an overgrown doll. She slipped the long nightgown over my head and positioned my arms in the sleeves, then pulled the covers over me, patting them consolingly.

"There . . . there . . ." she cooed. "I'll ask Bertha for something to settle your stomach. Please stop crying—you'll ruin your eyes with so many tears. Oh, dear!" She left me to my hiccupping sobs.

The major events in my life began passing through my mind. My day with Juan riding the horse cars in carefree abandon were the happiest days I had known. The saddest had been when Diedre died in the dreadful fire. I could still see the flames charring her beautiful hair, and a moan was wrenched from me when the agony of her dying tumbled through my thoughts. I sobbed piteously remembering the small coffin being carried down the stairs and the sad procession following it.

My father's disapproving eyes joined the parade. I could still see their cold look despite the dreary funeral that had buried his body in state and taken him from me forever. Would everybody I had loved die before I did? A moan came from my soul.

I relived the long trip with Sarah across the monotonous prairie before I saw Juan's laughing eyes above the tray of candies. Where was he now? Why hadn't he come to solace me? My sobs broke out anew at the thought of Juan shivering and hungry back in Ogden. Perhaps he was starving at this very moment. Perhaps he was dead!

"Drink this, Miss Shadow." Bertha had come in Carlie's stead with a steaming cup that smelled awful.

"I c-can't," I said tearfully. "I'm d-dying."

She put the cup on the bedside table before she propped me up with the pillows. "You aren't dying, Miss Shadow. Have you never tasted wine before?"

I shook my head.

"Next time, don't drink it so fast. Wine was meant to be sipped, and a long time taken between swallows." She held the cup to my lips. "Now, drink this."

Obediently, I opened my mouth for a tentative taste. A shudder ran through me when I swallowed. It was the vilest-tasting liquid I could imagine. Under Bertha's urging, I took another sip, and yet another. The taste was terrible, but soon welcome numbness came over me. Through a wavering haze I saw Bertha rise.

"You'll sleep now. . . ."

My sleep was not restful, for nightmares plagued me. Julia chased after me wielding a huge whip that cracked around my head like giant claps of thunder. Her face was horrendous, and from her mouth came a gibberish I could not understand. I ran until my lungs threatened to burst, then suddenly David was before me with open arms. Just when I reached their safety, his face changed to that of the hanging man—tongue protruding, eyes bulging, hands clawing at whatever they could reach. I screamed in terror as I eluded the clutching things I had thought were David's arms.

Perspiration bathed me when I woke shivering in fright. Dark shadows . . . darker even than the room around me . . . came threateningly toward me. My heart throbbed like a great drum and made it difficult for me to breathe. I cowered against the pillows, trying to squelch the imaginary figures coming from my mind.

A wrinkled face appeared just inches from mine, and I knew this was not a product of my imagination. When I tried to shriek, a tiny bony hand clamped over my mouth and stifled the cry in my throat.

"Sh-h-h," came a sibilant whisper. "You must leave here at once! Do you understand? Leave before you are killed!"

The face and hand withdrew, leaving me shaken and stunned. A slight rustling in the dark, the sound of a softly closed door, and all was silent.

With a gasp I came alive and bedlam shattered the night! I was screaming and couldn't seem to stop. I screamed until my throat ached with my screaming, then screamed some more.

Carlie came stumbling in, crying, "Miss Shadow? Oh, Miss Shadow?" before she fell atop me clutching my shaking body. "Are you all right? Oh, dear!" She scrambled from the bed and found the lamp and lit it, then came hurrying back to me. "What's the matter? Oh, Miss Shadow, are you hurt?"

I stopped shrieking and stared around the room. "She was here," I whispered. "A horrible old woman was here!"

"Who was here?" Carlie asked. "There's no one here now." She rose and quickly made a tour of the room, even opening the closet door and peering behind draperies. "No one is here, Miss Shadow." She returned to my bed and her arms went round me as she rubbed my back with soothing strokes. "There . . . there . . . you had a nightmare. It's the laudanum Bertha gave you. It always gives bad dreams."

Bertha burst in, long nightgown flapping behind her, frilly mobcap bobbing in agitation. "What is it? What happened in here? What's the commotion about? Miss Shadow, are you all right? Was it you who screamed?"

I nodded, saying, "An old woman put her hand over my mouth and sort of hissed at me. She said I would be killed if I didn't leave here." My voice quavered as tears again filled my eyes. "It wasn't a dream!"

Bertha looked startled, then glanced over her shoulder at the maids crowding into my room and motioned them away. "Go back to bed, girls. Everything is all right."

When they had gone, she closed the door and returned to my bed. "Are you sure an old woman was

111

here?"

"I'm sure," I quavered. She and Carlie exchanged a look that made me even more certain I hadn't been imagining the crone who menaced me.

"Well, I'll go check the latches," Bertha said briskly. "If anyone was here, they won't be back, I'm sure." She shot another meaningful look at Carlie and shook her head slightly before she left.

Carlie continued to hold me in her arms, clucking as though I were a frightened child. It reassured me, but I pushed away from her so I could sit up, breathing deeply to overcome my terror and shock.

"Who was it, Carlie?" I demanded.

She started to shake her head, but I cut into her denial.

"You know who it was! Tell me!"

"I'm not supposed to," she said nervously.

"Tell me anyway," I insisted. "Was it the 'old countess' Bertha said stayed on the third floor?"

Carlie's eyes opened wide. "You know?"

"Bertha mentioned her the day we arrived."

The maid shook her head. "It must have been a slip on her part. We have orders never to talk about her."

"Why not?"

Carlie rose, sighing. "Count Chauvanne brought his mother here from France a long time ago. I think the reason he left his home and came here was to keep her from being locked into a madhouse over there. At least, that's what Bertha says. The old madam has been secluded on the third floor all these years, poor soul. The only person who tends her is Bertha. Not even her son or the madam ever goes to see her, at least that I've ever seen."

"Is she insane?"

"I don't know for sure," Carlie admitted. "She's very old, and Bertha says her habits are terribly messy. I think that's why she's hidden away . . . you know, so the Chauvannes won't be shamed before other people if they happened to see her. The door to her room is always locked. I don't see how she could have gotten out during the night, but I guess she did."

"But that is awful," I said indignantly. "If she wasn't crazy to begin with, she would get that way from being locked in by herself all these years."

Carlie nodded. "That's what I think, too, but there's never a sound to be heard from her room even when I pass outside her door in the hall. I think she sleeps most of the time. Bertha gives her ten grains of opium twice a day so she won't get restless."

It was hard to believe she could calmly accept such a situation. In the course of our history lessons we had read about opium dens. They were shameful things, according to Miss Brigham, and she hurried us on when we asked too many questions about them, saying such topics as these were not meant for our tender ears. Opium eating seemed to be something that happened as far away as the River Styx and was certainly not to be accepted in any casual way. I had thought only foreigners did it.

"Oh, Carlie, she was as thin as a skeleton! And her skin was wrinkled and sort of yellow."

Carlie glanced around, then shushed me, shaking her head.

I dropped my voice to a whisper. "How can Count Chauvanne do something like that to his own mother? Does my aunt know this is happening? Does Bertha

113

forget to feed her when she's busy?"

"Of course not! Bertha is too kind ever to hurt anybody, and you know it. It's just . . . well, sometimes it's difficult to get her to eat," Carlie admitted. Bertha takes meals up, but lots of times they aren't even touched."

My fears were subsiding and pity for an old creature was taking their place, and then my curiosity came alive. "Why did she say I would be killed if I stayed here, Carlie? *Who* will kill me?"

Carlie shook her head impatiently. "That's just nonsense, Miss Shadow. Opium makes you hallucinate, just as laudanum gives you nightmares. That old woman could have been walking in her sleep, for all you know. Besides, how could anyone who has been inside one room for so long know what's going on out here? She probably didn't even know what she was saying, poor thing." She tucked the covers around me. "You go back to sleep now and don't think about it anymore. Bertha went up to make sure the old countess is locked in tight, so she won't bother you anymore." A worried look crossed her face. "You won't tell anybody I told you all this, will you?"

"Of course not, Carlie. It was silly of me to have hysterics, and nice of you to comfort me. I'll be fine now. What you've told me will be our secret."

"Do you want the light left on?"

"No, of course not, Carlie. Good night."

Alone in the dark, I discovered my bravery was not so firm as I had thought. Small creakings made me start even as my eyes tried to pierce the blackness. Wind rattled around the house, somewhere banging a shutter back and forth. What kind of world had I

114

entered? Hanged men dangling from lampposts, and mad old women locked into garrets . . . had my father known into what he was sending me?

As usual, the thought of my father brought another one of Carmelita that calmed me. With her image in my mind, I drifted into sleep.

The following morning no mention was made of the night's disturbance. I determined to forget it . . . or at least to ignore it.

Chapter Nine

That evening Countess Chauvanne gave the promised soirée to introduce me to San Francisco society, at least that part of the city's population she acknowledged. These were the elite of the city—rich, busy parents, and young people determined to make the hours pass swiftly in their pursuit of pleasure. There were more young men than women, so females were treated like princesses from whom a smile was worth more than gold.

As the winter rains began, I was swept into the activities of the wealthy. The weather curtailed our picnics and horseback rides, but elaborate indoor parties were substituted. At first I felt guilt at the uselessness of the life I led with my peers. Some of the young men were learning their fathers' businesses in the plush offices they occupied, but nothing was so pressing that it couldn't be postponed when a party beckoned. These offspring of the longtime rich had an indifference to money, or rather to the *making* of money, that was at times almost offensive when I contrasted their lives with those of the immigrants I had seen . . . and Juan's. But then, as the rains persisted, denying me outdoor exercise, I became as bored as they, and soon eagerly agreed to any amusement proposed.

Julia kept David at her beck and call, and I wondered when he took care of the business at his ranch. Then I decided he probably did like other wealthy men—gave orders to others as to what should be done. He and Julia were together both mornings and evenings and often in the afternoon, for she seemed unable to go anywhere without him.

A constant stream of callow youths accompanied me to parties and balls, but none of them fascinated me the way David did. I ached inside while smiling sweetly at my current escort, and did my best to banish David from my thoughts.

Julia went out of her way to make snide remarks whenever possible. Her witticisms about the oddity of my name offended me, but I refused to let her see I was hurt. The entire group was carelessly cruel to each other, mostly because they were constantly bored, and it was just something they did to pass the time.

Christmas loomed ahead to spark a surge of interest in the coming Crocker Ball. It was held annually, usually at the Pacific Club, but this year would be changed to the new Palace Hotel. The carriage had carried me past this imposing edifice a time or two, and I knew it was one of the most ornate hostelries in the world.

The Palace Hotel covered two and a half acres of land. It had a grand court in the center into which carriages could be driven so visitors needn't walk too far, especially in the damp on foggy nights. The hotel was like a city in itself—it boasted 437 bath tubs just for its guests to use, and over twice that many rooms.

The ballroom was a wide expanse of glittering elegance. Solid gold doorknobs graced the entrance, and solid gold table service was used at banquets in the spacious dining room. It was a man-made fairy-land only the fortunate could enter. High-nosed door-men guarded their entrances against the common folk.

Even before Thanksgiving, young men pressed their pleas to be accepted as escorts to this Christmas ball by the ladies of their choice. From the array of invitations I received, I accepted the one from Allen DeJung, a young attorney several years my senior who actually spent many of his days at work.

He was a serious person, which in itself made him stand out from the others. His father had died five years earlier leaving a prosperous practice to Allen. Since his mother was long gone, our mutual orphan status gave us much in common. My admiration for his diligence expanded into real affection as we became better acquainted. Beside his current clients, he told me there was an entire roomful of his father's records that he hadn't finished reading and sorting. So when he couldn't attend one of our gatherings, pleading the press of business as excuse, I felt no offense.

He was closing his office at noon for Christmas Eve celebrations, as did all the businesses in the city. Count Chauvanne gave his permission for Allen to take me to dinner at the Pacific Club where he was a member, and from there we would drive to the Palace Hotel for the Crocker Ball.

Julia had her Paris gown—an elegant confection that must have cost a fortune. My gown had been made in New York at the same time as the rest of my wardrobe. It didn't have the same dramatic flair as Julia's, but its warm, rosy color heightened the pink in my cheeks and made my eyes magically bluer, so I thought it would hold its own against any foreign creation.

The entire mansion was in an uproar of preparation by the time the evening of the ball arrived. While Carlie helped me with my toilette, I could hear the constant scurrying of maids running hither and yon as they assisted the other members of the family for their gala evening.

Allen brought a nosegay of miniature roses for me. It was an adorable tussie-mussie with a real lace holder instead of the usual one of paper. Long ribbon streamers flowed gracefully from bows beneath the tiny blossoms, and I wondered how Allen had matched my gown so perfectly.

He bowed elegantly as he presented the flowers. "You're the most beautiful lady in the entire city of San Francisco," he declared. "I shall be forever in your debt because you have favored me with your company this evening. My fellow attorneys will be green with jealousy!"

"Thank you, Allen. I'm sure you exaggerate, but thank you," I said with a smile. His earnest air secretly tickled me, since it was quite different from the flippancy of the other members of our group. "Shouldn't we be leaving? I declare, I'm quite ravenous."

He smiled, knowing I would only pick at the food,

no matter how delicious it was. No lady ever took more than two bites at any gala dinner, however much she protested a hearty appetite.

In his carriage, Allen leaned close. "Shadow, my dear, I'm quite in love with you, you know. Will you give me your permission to speak to your uncle about our marriage?"

I looked at him aghast. Marriage? To Allen? Oh, no! When I married . . . what about when I married? I hadn't really thought about it. I liked Allen, and he was quite eligible, but I could never marry him . . . of that I was sure.

"Oh, Allen, please don't spring at me this way," I said demurely. "Tonight I want to think about dancing and fun—not something serious."

His dejection lasted only a moment. When we pulled up before the Pacific Club he was again the genial young attorney. Inside, he proudly introduced me, and we settled to the meal with male voices and tinkling female laughter circling in the air. It was a happy gathering, and since we were all going to the ball, the meal was not drawn out with endless discussions. It ended in good time so we could make the short drive to the Palace Hotel and the gaiety awaiting us.

The orchestra was playing when we entered the great hall. Dancers already thronged the floor, black-clad men in dramatic contrast to their rainbow-hued partners. Julia and David waltzed by among the dancers—Julia talking, as usual, and David looking slightly bored. The Paris gown was almost invisible under the glittering array of jewels encircling Julia's neck and wrists, but a pout on her face signified an argument was most likely in progress.

Wistfully, I wondered how anyone in David's arms could be unhappy, then put it from my mind when Allen held out his arms to swirl me onto the floor. I remembered my dream wherein Carmelita and Edward St. George waltzed so magnificently and so beautifully. Could we possibly look as graceful?

Other young men cut in. I went through dance after dance, murmuring answers to their questions and thanks to their compliments. The transfer of partners became automatic until I found myself in David's arms, smiling happily into his incredibly blue eyes.

"You're much too popular tonight, little Shadow," he said, glancing at an approaching young man. Quickly, he swung me away and danced me over to the refreshment buffet. "Would you care for something to drink?"

At my nod, he accepted two glasses from the attendant and led me to one of the tables lining the wall. "If we sit this one out, perhaps your suitors will leave us alone," he said, smiling to remove any sting from his words.

Warily, I sipped the champagne cocktail, recalling the night I came a cropper on wine. Since then I had learned to drink carefully and sparingly, and only when it was expected of me.

"Julia looks lovely tonight," I observed. My cousin was passing from hand to hand on the dance floor, and although I was sure she was aware of us, never once did her glance come our way.

"You're always beautiful, little Shadow," David said huskily. "That's why I kissed you the first time I saw you on the ferry."

Hastily, I fanned myself with my kerchief as I felt a blush begin. "My! Isn't it warm in here!"

David rose, drawing me to my feet. "Come . . . let's get some fresh air."

He led me into the great courtyard where other couples strolled. I marveled at the difference between Christmas Eve in San Francisco and in New York. The soft fog had crept in, as usual, but the air was only pleasingly brisk. In New York there would be snow and icy slush. Blasts of arctic air would forbid any casual dalliance outside.

David slipped off his jacket and arranged it around my shoulders. Mischief gleamed in his eyes as he led me to a spot under a flickering light, and then he deliberately gathered me into his arms and kissed me.

My shocked gasp was smothered under his lips, but I managed to push him away. Laughter swelled from spectators around us as David pointed to a bouquet of gray-green foliage dotted with tiny berries pinned on the post holding the light.

"You are under the mistletoe, and I claim my forfeit," he said, bending his head so his mouth could again cover mine as his arms held me close.

This time I did not push him away. Perhaps it was the champagne, or more likely it was the spirit of Christmas accenting the loneliness always at the rim of my consciousness. As I felt the silkiness of his mustache and the warmth of his lips, I responded to his embrace. Time melted away as we clung together in a world all our own.

"So here you are!" a voice exclaimed, and I broke from David's arms. Julia's face was furious, contorted into ugliness from her anger. "You . . . philanderer!"

she sputtered, then tore his ring from her engagement finger and threw it at him! "I don't want it," she said, then whirled on her heel and returned to the ball-room.

Shocked faces watched the performance, then eyes were deliberately averted, as though to erase the happening. I saw Allen's disapproving gaze when he came to my side to claim me.

"I believe this is our dance, Shadow," he said gravely, handing David his coat.

I accepted his arm, wishing I could sink from sight to conceal my shame. We neared the doorway, and I glanced back to see David retrieve the ring from where it had landed.

"Please, Allen . . . will you take me home?" Tears pushed at my eyes. I would *really* die if I were to cry in public! Carmelita nodded approvingly when I raised my head to face the assemblage. No conquista-dore ever faced a fiercer enemy. Steely eyes and pursed lips of disapproving women marked our withdrawal, even as their partners tried to smooth the troubled waters by drawing them back into the dance.

We rode in silence until we neared the Chauvanne mansion. "He's a terrible cad, you know," Allen said quietly. "Have you a crush on him?"

I studied the miniature roses in my lap, examining each petal in the dim light. The horses' hooves made rhythmic sounds that were muffled by the drifting fog.

Allen sighed. "I suppose it isn't any of my busi-ness," he said sadly. "You didn't answer my proposal tonight because you don't love me . . . isn't that right?"

"I don't love anyone," I said miserably.

Juan's face came to mind. I remembered the look in his eyes when I had told him I was leaving New York. Was it love for me that made him look so unhappy?

Loving my father had made me unhappy, and he'd been unhappy after Carmelita died because he had loved her so much. Perhaps love was the basic cause of unhappiness. If so, I wanted no part of it.

"Thank you for rescuing me, Allen. That dreadful . . . *scene* beneath the lamppost—oh, Allen, wasn't it just perfectly dreadful?"

He pulled me to him so my head could rest on his chest. "It wouldn't have been if Julia hadn't made such a thing of it. Everyone kisses under the mistletoe on Christmas Eve. It's a respectable custom, you know."

I felt his lips touch the top of my head.

"I planned to take you there myself, Shadow, if ever I could separate you from your string of admirers," he said lightly. "I've been looking forward to it for ever so long."

The carriage stopped in front of the Chauvannes' wide front door and Allen got out, helping me descend before escorting me onto the veranda.

"May I come in, Shadow?" he asked, removing his hat.

"Please . . . not tonight, Allen. I'm quite tired . . . as well as extremely embarrassed." I stood on tiptoe and gently kissed his cheek. "Goodnight, dear Allen."

He stood motionless for a moment, then said, "Don't feel badly, Shadow. The things that happened tonight weren't your fault—remember that."

The door opened and Allen turned to see Bertha standing in the light. "Ah, good evening, Mrs.

Darwell." He raised my hand to his lips. "Get a good night's sleep, my dear. Tomorrow the world will look better, and I wish you a very merry Christmas," he said softly.

I watched him replace his hat and return to the carriage.

"You'd best come inside, Miss Shadow," Bertha said in her motherly manner. "My, but you're home early! The staff was making so much noise in the kitchen, I was lucky to hear you arrive."

A lump came into my throat that made speech impossible. Allen's sad eyes would haunt me, I knew. Had I lost a dear friend because of my desire for David? And what would Julia do to me? She had thrown her engagement ring away, but that was only a fit of temper. David had picked up the discarded ring and would probably bring it back to Julia tomorrow. Oh, *why* had he kissed me? Did he care for me? Or was he being the cad Allen said he was?

Oh, no, my heart protested. That was no casual buss under the mistletoe, no mere dalliance at a ball. My knees grew weak as I relived the embrace.

"Do you want Carlie to come help you, Miss Shadow?"

"No, of course not," I said. "Please go back to your party."

Wearily, I trudged up the stairs. It was a relief to shed my finery and slide under the covers onto cool sheets. I had thought to cry once I was alone, but weariness pulled me into healing sleep.

When Carlie pulled the draperies aside on Christmas Day, I woke to a feeling of dread. Gray drizzly fog blanked the wide window, echoing the dreariness in my heart. I was not looking forward to the day ahead.

"It's past ten o'clock, Miss Shadow," Carlie said cheerfully, "but I doubt anybody will bother with breakfast this morning. Oh, my! It was terribly late . . ." she giggled, "or rather *early* when everybody got in." She twirled across the sea-green carpet. "We had a *lovely* party!"

"Did you, Carlie? That's nice." Mine hadn't turned out that way, I remembered with dreadful clarity. "Will you bring me coffee, please?" Not being expected at the breakfast table gave me a reprieve of a few hours, at least.

"Right away, Miss Shadow."

By the time Carlie returned with a tray I had propped myself against the headboard, willing myself to face a world I knew would be hostile.

"Miss Julia got in later than anybody," Carlie announced, "and it wasn't Mr. David who brought her home. They sure have their differences, those two."

Hot coffee revived my spirits somewhat. I dawdled over drinking it, trying to postpone the meeting with my relatives as long as I possibly could. Then an idea came to me.

"Get my riding habit, Carlie, and then go tell one of the grooms to bring the gray mare around for me."

Carlie's look was doubtful when she glanced at the blankness outside the window. "Oh, Miss Shadow, look at the fog. . . ." She glanced at me and when I merely looked back, added, "It's terribly damp out this morning."

"I'd like some fresh air, Carlie. Go, go!"

126

She laid the soft gray habit at the foot of the bed, then scampered off to do my bidding. I had reached the corset stage of my toilette when she returned to lace me up and slip the velveteen gown over my head.

"You do look beautiful, Miss Shadow," she said.

"I wish I felt that way, Carlie." The dread feeling of being alone had returned to make me wish I were dead.

Once mounted on the spirited little mare, I nudged her to a trot on the road to the iron gate. The gatekeeper emerged, looking surprised to see me alone in the fog, but he opened the gate, bobbing his head as I urged the mare through. I was barely out of sight of the gate when hoofbeats sounded flatly in the thick air and a ghostly horseman came riding out of the fog.

"Shadow! What are you doing out here alone?" David exclaimed, pulling his horse to a halt as his shocked voice posed the question.

He was the last person I wanted to see this morning, but I forced my voice to remain even when I answered. "I doubt if Julia's up yet, David. I went to sleep early, but it was terribly late when everyone got in, I'm sure."

"I wasn't on my way to see Julia. I was coming to see you, Shadow." He paused, searching my face before continuing. "I'm terribly sorry about the row last night." His eyes closed as he groaned, then, "Seems like I'm forever apologizing to you for something, doesn't it?"

"It's quite all right, David. Allen said it's the custom to kiss under the mistletoe on Christmas Eve, so I'm sure Julia will understand when you return her ring."

Even through the mist I could see his blue eyes gleam. "I'm not going to return her ring," he said bluntly. "Damn! The mistletoe had nothing to do with the way I kissed you." Abruptly, he lifted me from my precarious perch to the saddle in front of him. "I love you, little Shadow. I've been falling in love with you ever since I caught you flying through the air on the ferry. Haven't you guessed?" Then his lips were on mine.

I responded to his kiss in a way I could scarcely believe. We drowned in a sea of emotion while he held me, and I would never be the same.

The fog was a caressing softness when we finally drew apart. David lifted me from his saddle and swung me over to my mare, his eyes tender. "Now I am going to see Count Chauvanne. I'll need his permission to ask you to marry me."

"David! You can't! Not this soon!" I said, shocked from my euphoria. "You must talk to Julia first to be sure she really meant to break your engagement."

His angry snort startled my mare. I grabbed for the horn to keep from being unseated and brought her under control.

"Whether she meant it or not, I did," he said grimly. His mood changed when he looked at me, and a grin replaced the frown. "If everyone is still in bed, let's go for a ride, Shadow, just as we did before."

I nodded, remembering the carefree romp we'd had on the day I donned Chico's clothing. It would be wonderful to be happy again instead of feeling dreary and unloved. David's, "I love you," still echoed in my ears. My heart throbbed in my throat like some small thing grown wild.

My mare pranced nervously, anxious to be on her way, so I gave her her head. She carried me through the fog ahead of David, and the dampness did much to cool my fevered face but nothing to slow my beating heart. At last I slowed her to a walk as we reached the sand.

David came up beside me, laughing in delight. "Your eyelashes are beaded with pearls," he said, handing me his handkerchief. "Whew! This is some fog!"

In truth, the fog had filled my lashes with drops of moisture that were beginning to roll into my eyes. I mopped away, laughing as I shook the water from the curls on my shoulders and settled my hat more firmly on my head.

"You're so beautiful, Shadow!" David exclaimed, reaching for me again.

This time I dodged away and kicked the mare into a trot that soon broke into a headlong gallop as we fled up the beach to the hacienda with David in hot pursuit. The wind of our passing pulled my hair behind me and my clothing was plastered against my body. I was filled with exhilaration and happiness that I wanted never to end when we arrived at David's house.

A tall man emerged from the bunkhouse and came toward the hitchrack. David jumped from his horse and came to catch me when I slid from the saddle. He held me in a tight embrace and once more I drowned in the ecstasy of another kiss.

When I pulled away from David, the ranch hand

still stood watching while the horses' reins lay neglected on the ground. Our eyes met, and I stiffened in surprise.

"Juan!" I left David to run to him. "Oh, Juan, you got here!" My arms went around his waist as I shamelessly hugged him like an exuberant child.

Chapter Ten

Suddenly remembering I was a grown woman, I stepped back from Juan's encircling arms. "Oh, my!" I gasped. "It's so *good* to see you, Juan! I was afraid you'd be stranded somewhere and we'd never see each other again."

"I told you I'd be along," he said gently.

David's icy voice broke into our reunion. "What are you doing here, Monterro? You're supposed to be helping move a herd this morning."

Before Juan could answer, David's sardonic voice was aimed at me. "I didn't know you went around hugging cowhands, Shadow. Do you know this man?"

"Of course I know him!" I said indignantly. "We've been friends since we were children."

"Oh?" His gaze flicked to Juan. "You didn't answer me, Monterro. What are you doing here?"

"My horse pulled up lame. I came back to get another." Juan paused, then continued. "I thought you were engaged to Miss Chauvanne, Mr. Roberts. Would you mind explaining your behavior just now?"

"Juan . . ." I began, then stifled a cry as David

lashed out with a double fist to knock Juan to the ground.

"I don't explain my actions to the help, Monterro," David said. "What I do is none of your business! And keep your greasy hands off Miss St. George."

Juan scrambled to his feet with murderous rage in every line of his face. Without a word, he launched into David, fists flying.

"Oh, stop . . . stop!" I pleaded, but my cry was lost in the thud of fists blending with grunts of pain as blows found their target.

"Juan . . . David, stop!"

But they didn't stop. They pummeled and lashed at each other, with first one down and then the other. Then Juan landed a blow that snapped David's head back and sent him flying to the ground with blood running from a gash in his lip.

"David . . ." I wailed, sinking to the ground beside him. I pulled out my kerchief and dabbed at the blood welling from the cut.

"Leave me alone, Shadow," he gasped. His enraged eyes focused on Juan. "You're fired, sun-grinner," he snarled. "Get your things and get out of my sight."

Between panting breaths Juan answered, "You're wrong, gringo. I quit!"

Then he looked at me, and his brown eyes were stern. "Get up, Shadow, this is no place for you to be. I'll take you back to your aunt's."

David lay with closed eyes as groans emerged from his bruised mouth. Fear filled me at the sight of the blood gushing down his chin. Was he dying? I cradled his head in my arms, crooning, "David, David, David."

Juan put a hand under my arm and tried to pull me to my feet. "Come on, Shadow, you don't belong out here. What can your aunt be thinking of to allow you to ride alone with this . . . *estiercal*!"

I thought David's breathing had stopped and my heart skipped a beat. He lay limp in my arms, eyes closed and a pale look to his face. "You've killed him, Juan," I whispered. Then I jerked away from his hand. "Get away from me! You've killed him. . . ."

"He isn't dead," Juan said scornfully. "He will be, though, if I see him touch you again."

I glared up at him, tears streaming from my eyes. "I hate you! I never want to see you again, do you hear me? Oh, you've killed David!"

He turned away, his shoulders sagging. I sobbed wildly, pressing David's poor bloody face into my riding habit. When the sound of hoofbeats faded away, a voice broke into my hiccupping sobs. "I love this, Shadow, really I do, but you're smothering me."

Incredulously, I loosened my hold and sat back. "You aren't dead?"

"Not quite," he said, gingerly massaging a jaw that was turning purple. "Your friend throws a mean punch, lady. I'd hate to be in the way when he really gets mad."

"You were shamming!" I said indignantly. "You let me think you were dying."

"Well, I didn't seem to be getting anywhere fighting," he said ruefully. "I didn't know that Mex was a friend of yours. How come you know him?"

"He isn't a 'Mex'! He's a Spaniard, just as my mother was. He was the only friend I had at the boarding school I attended."

I felt like a fool when David rose and extended a hand to help me to my feet, and then a pang of remorse shot through me. What had I said to Juan? I had been so angry and frightened I couldn't remember, but it must have been something awful.

"Oh, David, I have to find him before he gets away. I've made a terrible fool of myself again. Come and help me on my horse . . . please?"

His face hardened. "If you are going to be my wife, Shadow, you will have to choose your friends more carefully. I don't want you seen with trash like Monterro."

"Trash!" I gasped. "Why, you . . . *estiercal!*" I echoed, too embattled to feel shame at mentioning manure. "And who said I was going to be your wife? I didn't, that's for sure!" I forced my voice to iciness to overcome my anger. "If you'll help me onto my mare, *Mr.* Roberts, I'll trouble you no more."

Panic filled me as I stepped into David's hands to a seat on the saddle. What had I done? How could I have shouted the things I had to Juan? I had been waiting and waiting for him to find me and when he finally did, I had screamed at him like some fishwife. The best friend I ever had, and I had insulted him!

The thin crop carried only for looks came into use. I lashed the little mare, clinging tightly until her startled jump settled into a headlong gallop. I searched the horizon, but Juan was nowhere in sight.

He had gone in the direction of the Chauvanne manor, but his long-legged horse was too fast to overtake. At the mansion gates I halted the mare, craning my neck to see as far as I could. No living thing came to view save the gateman, who looked anxiously up at me. With a sad heart I walked the mare up the drive and turned her over to a groom.

Bertha met me at the door. "You missed dinner, Miss Shadow," she said softly. "I'm afraid there is an awful row going on." She rolled her eyes toward the open parlor door. The murmur of agitated voices reminded me of a swarm of angry bees.

"Send Carlie to help me change," I whispered, then ran up the stairs.

My heart sank as I realized the time had come for an angry scene with Julia. There was little doubt in my mind that my aunt and uncle would be lined up behind her. Carmelita, help me, I prayed. I would need a champion on my side.

Carlie brought a sandwich on a dainty tray when she appeared. "You'd best eat something, Miss Shadow, to keep up your strength." Her eyes rolled in mock terror. "Such a to-do there is!"

"Just help me change, Carlie. Bring something suitable for a carriage ride. I must go into the city." I tried to get out of the riding habit, but my fingers seemed all thumbs.

Carlie placed the tray on a table, then hurried to help me. "Do you want to slip out the back way?" she asked as though she were a conspirator.

"No, of course not! Why should I?" The trumpet of my ancestors had sounded in my blood. I would face my relatives, not sneak away.

I walked into the salon with head held high. "Good afternoon," I said calmly.

The Chauvannes ceased their bickering as they turned to stare at me.

"Well! There she is—Miss High-and-Mighty . . .

halfbreed!" Julia said spitefully.

I ignored her as I spoke to my uncle. "I must go into the city, Count Chauvanne. May I have the use of a carriage?"

"You will not go anywhere until we settle a few things," my aunt said. "I understand your conduct at the ball last night was unforgivable!"

"I doubt that, Countess," I said coolly. "Julia made a scene over a very trivial matter."

"Trivial?" Julia said angrily. "You call stealing my fiancé *trivial*?"

"Really, Julia, I didn't steal your fiancé. As I recall, you threw his ring in his face."

"You were kissing him."

I sighed as my desire to end this and go find Juan rose. "He kissed me under a sprig of mistletoe, which I understand is one of the customs of this country." I turned back to the count. "About the carriage, sir?"

"Why are you so anxious to be off to the city?" my aunt asked. "Perhaps I do allow you girls too much freedom."

"I insulted a friend, Countess. Now I wish to find him and make amends."

I heard a carriage rattle up outside and thought, with relief, that Bertha had most likely ordered it around.

"You aren't going to let her leave before this is settled, are you?" Julia wailed. "She's stolen David!"

"I have not stolen David, Julia." A stab of pain went through me when I remembered his proposal and, later, my icy negation of it. Oh, David, David . . . oh, why do I have such a terrible temper? To insult my friend, and then to rebuff the man I love

. . . I felt like crying, but that wouldn't help.

Count Chauvanne drew me to a seat beside him on the couch. He held up a hand in remonstrance as Julia and her mother started talking.

"Now hold off, my dears. I'll get to the bottom of all this. Shadow, just what is this all about?"

I told him of the morning's events, carefully omitting David's proposal of marriage, but stressing my long friendship with Juan. Julia's sputterings and her mother's face mirrored their displeasure as my tale progressed.

When I finished, my aunt rose. "Ferd, you will allow me to handle this," she said imperiously. "Shadow, I'm afraid our customs are quite too much for you to handle, although I hadn't realized it until now. This is Christmas Day, and nothing can be done until tomorrow, but then we will enroll you in an excellent boarding school I know."

Her eyes flicked to Bertha, waiting in the doorway. "You may dismiss the carriage, Bertha. Miss Shadow will remain in her room for the rest of the day."

"No!" I said rebelliously. "You can't do this to me." I had to find Juan! I *had* to!

"Go to your room at once, Shadow," my aunt said, and her voice cracked like the command of a cavalry officer.

"Oh, please . . ." Tears threatened to ruin my composure as I looked to the Chauvannes, but only stony faces and hostile eyes stared back.

My heart sank when I thought of being confined in a girls' school once again. Had I come all this way to return to the same life I had led at Miss Brigham's? Always watched, usually bored, and this time without

Juan?

I stiffened my spine. "I'm sorry if I've offended you, Julia, and you, Aunt Elizabeth. However, I've spent far too much time at school already, and I don't wish to attend another. If you don't want me in your home, I'm sure Mr. Arbuthnot can make arrangements for me to live elsewhere. It is my understanding my father left me a great deal of money, so it will in no way inconvenience you."

Count Chauvanne's startled gaze met mine as he said, "For one so young, you are quite headstrong, my dear. Mr. Arbuthnot is no longer involved in your affairs. Your inheritance has been turned over to me to tend."

"Mr. DeJung asked me to marry him last night," I countered. "Do you prefer that I do so?"

"No!" My uncle's answer came almost in a shout. He clasped his hands behind him and paced back and forth to compose himself. At last he paused in front of me. "You are much too young to marry anyone, Shadow, and will be for several years to come." He looked toward his wife and daughter. "This bickering among you ladies must cease," he said firmly. "I will not have my household put into such an uproar again. Julia, go fix your face. Shadow, go change into something more suitable. We are having guests this evening who will be entertained properly. Have you forgotten this is Christmas Day?"

I hadn't forgotten. I was hoping it would be different from the dreary Christmas days of my childhood, but it was worse instead of better. My relatives hated me, Allen was hurt by my refusal of his proposal of marriage last night, and I had sent Juan away. And

138

much the most dreadful of all, I had refused to marry the man I loved.

In the privacy of my room I threw myself on the sea-green coverlet to sob my grief into a pillow. My heart was broken and I would more than likely die from its pain. I cried for my lost love . . . and I cried because I didn't know where Juan had gone. Then I wept some more because I was an orphan and my father hadn't loved me. But why should he? I was detestable . . . spiteful . . . and with a dreadful temper! My fists pummeled the pillow in a wild orgy of self-hatred.

"You'll bruise the feathers, Miss Shadow."

When I looked up, Carlie wavered through my torrent of tears. "I wish I were dead," I wailed.

"Now, now," she soothed. "Count Chauvanne sent up a glass of champagne for you. He gave orders you should drink it to make you feel better."

She put the small tray down so she could help me sit up. After a look at my face, she fetched a damp cloth. "Hold this over your eyes, Miss Shadow." She tsked, surveying the damage. "We'll have to get rid of that redness before you go downstairs. There's company waiting."

"C-company?" I quavered. "What company?"

"Oh, friends of the Chauvannes." She took the cloth and resoaked it in cold water, then returned. "There's a particular friend of yours, too, I'm a-thinking."

"Who?" A ray of hope flared as I wondered if Juan had dared present himself.

"Mr. DeJung is here," Carlie said, smiling before she clapped the wet cloth over my eyes. "He's brought you a bouquet fair as big as his horse."

"Oh." I sighed in disappointment, but at least Allen was still my friend. Then a wild idea made my pulse race. Perhaps if I confided in him, he would help me. Perhaps he could find Juan and give him a message!

I rose and bade Carlie help me dress. We worked feverishly until I was arrayed in my most attractive gown, and when I looked at the results in the mirror, I noted the redness was almost gone from around my eyes.

Carlie glanced at the tray she had brought. "Wouldn't you like to drink the champagne Count Chauvanne sent for you?"

"You drink it, Carlie, I don't need it now. I really don't much like wine." I twirled across the carpet, my spirits high at thought of somehow reaching Juan. He would accept my apology, I was sure. He had always put up with my whims and caprices and wouldn't stop now.

Allen waited in the front hall, and I giggled at the enormous bouquet that filled his arms.

"This is my apology for being such a grump last night, Shadow." He drew a fresh bouquet of tiny rosebuds from its depths. "And this is for your lovely self."

"Thank you, Allen. I'm so glad to see you again, and I too wish to apologize for last night. You were wonderful, and these flowers are glorious. Whose garden was stripped for all these beautiful posies? Shall we have to sneak them back to keep you out of trouble?" My light banter was forced, but I knew it would be more politic to lead up to the request I had

140

in mind.

In the main salon a goodly crowd was assembled. My aunt's smile showed only friendliness when I greeted her. Even Julia covered her rage with graciousness now that we were surrounded with guests. It would take a while to disperse the scandal she had begun at the ball, but she was doing her part to assure our world we were friends. Would she be able to act her role if David were here?

My question was answered when David arrived. An ugly bruise discolored his jaw and a slight puffiness at the corner of his mouth marked the cut he'd received, but other than that he was dashing as ever and as sure of himself as any prince of the realm. Julia came forward to greet him with open arms, claiming him with fluttering lashes as though there had been no quarrel.

"Allen, I must talk to you," I murmured, drawing him aside.

He nodded. "I'll get your wrap. We'll have to go outside to have any privacy."

We walked out into soft night air laden with the scent of oleanders and the sea. Salty fog closed around us, erasing the features of the mansion and covering the pines with misty mantles. We were alone in a ghostly world.

Allen adjusted my cape so I would be warmer, then led me to one of the benches scattered over the lawn.

"Now, what are we to talk about? Have you reconsidered my proposal?" he asked.

"Allen . . . oh, you're such a dear! It wouldn't be fair if I married you when I'm not . . . not in love with you, now would it?" It came to me that I did love

141

Allen, but as though he were my brother and not a lover.

Mournful fog horns sounded at intervals from far away while Allen sat looking at me with sad eyes. Then he said, "I would marry you on any terms you choose, Shadow. I love you more than I ever loved anyone, and I think I could make your life a happy one." He straightened as he flashed a rueful grin. "I'm also prepared to wait until I can make you love me, if you prefer, my dear, for I would never rush you into anything." He brushed a kiss over the back of my hand. "Now, if that wasn't the subject you wished to discuss, what was it?"

"Well . . . I made a terrible fool of myself this morning . . . again!" I said despairingly. "Oh, Allen, I'm such a very terrible person!"

"Oh, no, Shadow. I shall fight even you if you say that again," he said solemnly. "You are sweet and wonderful and a young lady who can do no wrong in my opinion. I dare anyone to say differently!"

"Wait until you hear what I did," I warned him. Then I told him of the events of the morning and how I had mortally insulted my childhood friend by saying the things I did when I thought he had killed David. I ended my recital with the plea, "Will you find Juan for me, Allen? I must find him before he disappears again, and I dare not ask my guardians."

His eyes scanned my face while he sat in thought so long I feared he would refuse me. At last he said, "I don't know that I can, my dear. Do you know where he was going?"

"No . . ."

A sigh stirred the fog between us. "You have much

to learn, little Shadow. Our class—the rich and privileged—knows each of its members, but only because there are comparatively few of us. There are thousands of faceless people who mingle in the crowded sections of San Francisco such as Chinatown, blood alley, opium dens, and places too harsh to mention near your delicate ears." He rose, staring into the fog. "Men come here to lose themselves in the crowd, or fade into the wilderness around us, and many disappear without a trace." He extended his hand to help me rise. "However, I will try to find your Juan Monterro, my dear. I will comb the city and ask questions of people who might know of his whereabouts." He paused before asking gently, "Are you in love with him?"

"Juan?" I asked incredulously. "Of course not! He was my dearest friend when I was a child, that's all. I must find him only to apologize for my rudeness."

Allen's voice was barely audible when he said, "And David Roberts?"

A pang went through me, but my chin rose. "By now he and Julia are most likely engaged again. The liberties he took this morning were doubtless brought on by my indiscretion under that horrid mistletoe."

A smile twitched at Allen's lips, but he said nothing. He offered me his arm and gently patted my hand as we returned to the house and mingled with the guests.

David's eyes were stormy while he moodily listened to the stream of chatter Julia directed into his ear. I noted the ring was still missing from Julia's hand, but the fact gave me no solace. He had returned to her, and I felt drearily sure Julia could annex him if she

143

wished.

At a time when we were alone, Allen asked, "Do you want me to look for your friend tonight, Shadow? Or shall I stay at the party?"

"Would you mind leaving now, Allen? He was so angry when he left I fear he will leave the territory." I tried to smile. "I think I'll go upstairs to my room and rest. My head aches dreadfully."

We moved to the hall where he retrieved his hat and coat from the maid. "Goodnight, my dear," he said with a courtly bow. "May I call on you tomorrow about ten?"

"Please do, Allen." It was unnecessary to say more. I wanted to add no more fuel to the gossip that was rife in the kitchen. Allen knew I was anxious about Juan and would do his best to find him. We both knew it would be unwise for Juan to come here to see me in the event Allen found him, but Allen would arrange a place for us to meet. The thought of his capability comforted me.

Wearily, I trudged up the stairs. The events of the day had unnerved me to the point of exhaustion and I wanted only to be alone.

Carlie was usually waiting for me, but tonight another maid was in my room. "I'm Jane, Miss Shadow. Carlie took sick and I'm to take her place tonight."

I nodded, and was glad when I could dismiss her. A fleeting question crossed my mind about Carlie. How could a girl who was usually so robust and cheerful suddenly become ill? Then I recalled the night I had drunk the wine too quickly and the dire aftermath. Perhaps Carlie had partied too long and too well on

Christmas Eve.

She faded from my thoughts as I lay reviewing the day. David's laughing eyes came to haunt me. How they changed when he was with Julia! My lips tingled remembering his kisses, and tears came to my eyes when I knew I could never have him. I must keep in mind that he belonged to Julia.

Julia didn't love him, I thought rebelliously. If she did, they wouldn't quarrel so much. But she wanted him. Was it because he was considered such a good catch by the girls of our set? Perhaps pride was involved more than love.

Then I remembered my uncle's saying he would not allow me to marry anyone. Why? Most girls were married at a younger age than I had attained. Was it because Julia, who was older than I, was not yet married, and they didn't want her to appear to be an old maid?

Allen was an eminently desirable suitor for any girl. He came from one of the oldest families in California and, what was more, I was sure he was adding to its already considerable wealth. If the Chauvannes wanted to be rid of me, what better way than to give me away in marriage?

Chapter Eleven

Carlie's face was wan and pinched when she woke me the next morning. Her "Good morning, Miss Shadow," was nowhere so cheerful as her usual greeting.

"You look ill, Carlie. Are you sure you're well enough to be up and around?"

"Oh yes, Miss Shadow, I'm all right. It's just . . . well, I can't imagine what came over me last night. I've never felt that sick in my life until then."

"Did you party too much? Perhaps it's my turn to hold a basin for you," I said mischievously.

"Oh, no, ma'am, it wasn't that. Liquor never makes me sick, or at least I don't think that was it. My father always says I have a cast iron stomach."

She went about her usual chores helping me dress. I paid particular attention to my attire because of Allen's promise to call. Perhaps by now he had found Juan and would take me to where he was, I thought wistfully.

The dining room was deserted when I peeked inside, so I made my way to the morning room.

Bertha had unveiled the large windows to show a dreary scene of fog over a sullen sea, all in shades of damp gray. Still, it was not so dull as no ocean view at all.

She glanced up with a smile from where she was lighting the lamps. "We'll make our own sunshine this morning," she said cheerfully. "Count Chauvanne left early this morning, and the countess and Miss Julia prefer to sleep late, so I thought you might like your breakfast served in here."

"That will be fine, Bertha," I said. "I'll just have coffee and a croissant, please. I'm not very hungry this morning." I was taking on the ways of my aunt's household. A hearty breakfast no longer appealed to me, especially at a time when my world was in such turmoil.

I was dawdling over a second cup of coffee when Allen was announced, and managed a smile when he sat opposite me. We spoke the usual amenities until he was settled with a cup of his own and the maid gone.

"Did you find him, Allen?" I asked eagerly.

He shook his head. "I told you it would be difficult." He was neatly barbered, as usual, but his eyes had tired lines around them. "It seems we aren't the only ones trying to find your friend."

"What do you mean?"

He toyed with his spoon, eyes avoiding mine. "Did you ever hear of the vigilantes?" he finally asked.

A shudder ran through me. "Oh, yes. They hanged a man the day Sarah and I arrived," I whispered, then proceeded to tell him the entire story.

His frown deepened as he heard the events of that fateful day, and when I finished, he took a deep breath. "These aren't real vigilantes, Shadow," he said. "This is a small group of so-called citizens who mainly look out for their own interests. They hide their identity because they break quite a few laws, or at least they try to keep from being known. However, I know one of them quite well."

"Who is he? And why are they looking for Juan?" I asked, my heart plunging when a vision of Juan hanging from a lamppost came to mind.

Allen's eyes searched my face as his measured words emerged. "David Roberts is one of them."

Icy fingers touched my spine. "David?" I whispered. "How do you know he's a vigilante?"

"Never mind how I know," he said grimly. "Apparently, your Juan Monterro rode away on one of David's horses when he left. Now he's a horse thief."

"Oh, no . . ." I clasped my hands to control their shaking. "Juan is no thief!" And then anger overcame my fear. "We must stop them before they hurt Juan, Allen. I'm going out to see David."

"Do you think that's wise, my dear?" Allen asked, then after a look at my face, he rose. "I can see you're determined. I'll take you there in my carriage, Shadow, and see no harm befalls you. Today my office can go hang."

I winced at his choice of words and shook my head. "Thank you, Allen, but I'd rather go alone. This is something better left between David and me."

A maid entered and I bade her send word to the stables to have my mare brought round. Then I turned back to Allen. "You haven't slept at all, have you?"

"I had a commission from my lady, and I'm afraid

148

I failed to carry it out," he said sadly.

"This is all my fault," I said miserably. "Juan wouldn't have fought with David if I weren't such a fool. I'll explain to him . . . persuade him to stop the vigilantes . . . even pay for the horse, if that's what David wants. I'll insist that my uncle give me the money."

Allen shook his head and frowned. "I don't like your riding alone, my dear. Don't you know how dangerous it can be? Please let me go with you."

"Dear Allen," I said, touching his cheek with my fingertips. "It isn't far to David's ranch and there are few travelers out this way. This is something better done by myself. Besides, you need sleep." I urged him toward the door. "Will you dine with us tonight? I'm not sure just who will be here, but you're most welcome, I know."

"For one so young, you are quite headstrong, my dear," Allen said, echoing my uncle's sentiments, "but I shall do as you wish. David Roberts is a very dangerous man, so please be careful. Until tonight, then?"

When he had gone I sped to my room to change into riding clothes, then hurried outside to the waiting mare. A second horse was saddled, and I looked a question at the groom.

"I'm to go with you, Miss St. George."

"By whose orders?"

"Count Chauvanne's, miss. He said the young ladies will no longer be allowed to ride alone."

"You may stay here," I said firmly.

"I can't, Miss St. George. Count Chauvanne said he would have our hides if we let you or Miss Julia go out without an escort."

He helped me mount before leaping astride the other horse. I seethed inside, too angry even to ask his name. My mare was mettlesome and fell into an easy gallop at the touch of my heels, holding a lead well in front of my companion. Even when I slowed to give her a breather, the groom stayed the same distance away.

As we approached David's hacienda I saw him leading a horse from the barn behind. With a curt "Wait here," to the groom, I left to meet David alone.

"Good morning, Shadow," he said soberly. He held out his arms to catch me when I dismounted, but I stayed in the saddle and backed away from his reach.

His eyes were bleary, and I surmised he had stayed late at the party the night before. Had he made his peace with Julia? My pride would not let me ask. Besides, there were more important matters at hand.

"You must call off your vigilantes immediately, David," I said firmly.

He looked surprised, and then a wary look sealed his face. "What are you talking about?" he demanded.

"Juan Monterro. He isn't a thief, and you know it!"

David's lips thinned and his eyes grew cold. Once more I saw a younger version of Edward St. George, although a rather disheveled one.

"This is not female business, Shadow," he said bleakly. "Stay out of it!" Turning, he began tightening the cinch of his saddle.

"It is too my business! David . . . please, I'm sorry I quarreled with you, and sorrier still if Juan hurt you during the scuffle, but . . ."

"Your Mex didn't hurt me," he interrupted scornfully. "He's a thief!"

"No, he isn't! He was just angry when he left. He'll return your horse, David. Or I'll get enough money from my uncle to pay for it. Please . . ."

"How do you know so much about this?" he growled. Then a sneer twisted his mouth. "I forgot . . . your pasty-faced attorney probably snooped for you. Well, you can just forget it! No man knocks *me* down and walks away scot free." He snorted angrily, much like one of his horses. "He doesn't ride away on one of my horses, either."

"But they'll hang him, David," I pleaded. "Please . . . you must not do this!"

An angry flush covered his face. "I didn't know your taste was for sun-grinners, Miss St. George, or I wouldn't have bothered you." He swung up on his horse and touched the brim of his hat. "Good day," he said coldly.

The horse leaped under the touch of spurs, then settled into a headlong gallop until they were out of sight. I was left clutching the reins of my mare so we were not carried along.

I returned to the manor wondering how I could love David, but drearily acknowledging that I still did. Was I forever destined to love men who did not love me? What was wrong with me? Allen loved me. Why couldn't I love him?

The groom helped me dismount, then led the horses away. There was a hopeless feeling inside me. How could I save Juan when I didn't know where he was? Allen couldn't help me, and David wouldn't, so where was I to turn?

When Chung opened the door to greet me, an idea came to me. "Did Tom Jordan drive Count Chauvanne to the city today, Chung?"

"No, missy. Boss leave on horse this morning," Chung answered. "Ladies take carriage to do shopping, but groom drive. Tom is breaking in new team today."

"I need his help, Chung. Will you ask him to bring a carriage around? I'll be ready by the time he gets here."

Chung looked doubtful, but went to do as I asked. I hurried to my room to change. A listless Carlie helped, but it still seemed to take forever. It was such a bother to be forced to change to a different costume for each activity. Men didn't have to change their suits at the drop of a hat.

Tom was waiting by the carriage when I emerged with each button and bow in place. He removed his hat. "Will it be all right if a groom drives you, Miss Shadow? Count Chauvanne said I was to remain here."

"No, you must drive me, Tom, for I need your help." I looked around to see that no one was in earshot, then told him about Juan and Allen's failure to find him. "Now I want to go to Mr. DeJung's office. If he isn't there, I want to look for Juan myself, but I can't do it alone. You can help me better than anyone, Tom. We *have* to find him before the vigilantes hurt him."

Tom's face was grave. "Miss Shadow, this is something you'd best not interfere with. Why don't you wait until Count Chauvanne returns and ask him to do what he can. A young lady shouldn't be fooling with the vigilantes. They are a dangerous group of men."

"I'm not fooling!" I said angrily. "They aren't going to hang my friend. I won't allow it!" I climbed into the carriage without his assistance. "I'm ready to leave," I said defiantly.

He stood indecisive, then seemed to make up his mind. "I'll take you to Mr. DeJung's office, Miss Shadow, but if he isn't there, we'll return home. I can't be responsible for your safety without him."

The ride to the city seemed interminable. Allen's office was located at the corner of Montgomery and California Streets, and we reached it with agonizing slowness. Unlike the buildings on steep Telegraph Hill to the west, here a carriage could stop before a doorway with ease.

By the time Tom pulled the horses to a halt in front of the DeJung Building, I was in such a state of agitation I didn't wait for him to help me alight. One of Allen's clerks hurriedly opened the door when he saw me coming, and I fled past his greeting through to the inner office where Allen was usually found.

Today it was empty! I turned to the clerk in dismay. "Where is Mr. DeJung?"

"He's not here, Miss St. George."

"I can see that," I said impatiently. "When will he be back? Where did he go?"

"A messenger came with a note for him about an hour ago. He didn't show me the note and didn't tell me where he was going," the clerk said with an injured note in his voice.

"Well surely he told you when he'd be back, didn't

he?" I felt like shaking the eyeglasses from the timid little man, but he was not to be hurried.

"Well . . ." Deliberately, he removed his spectacles and tapped the side of his cheek with them. "Mr. DeJung said he might not be back today. He said I was to close the office at the usual time and go home." His narrow chest swelled with importance, much like a pouter pigeon.

"Are you sure he didn't say where he was going? Think, man! This is important."

"Ah . . . let me see now. Perhaps he did say something about that. . . ." He frowned in concentration. "Now I remember. Mr. DeJung said he would be in court today. Yes, that's what he said. He's in court."

I whirled around to discover Tom Jordan standing just inside the door. "We'll go to court," I announced.

"Miss Shadow, wait." He turned to the clerk. "There's no regular court this late in the day. Which court did Mr. DeJung say he was going to? Think careful now. Was it maybe the People's Court?"

The little man pondered the question. Then he said, "I do believe it was, now you mention it."

Tom held the door for me to leave. "We'd best go home, Miss Shadow. Count Chauvanne would not want you out after dark in this section of the city."

I swept past him to the carriage. "No, we won't go home," I said stubbornly. "We must find Mr. De-Jung, Tom."

He helped me inside, then stood without closing the carriage door. "Miss Shadow, you cannot go to this place they call the People's Court. It's just an old warehouse in the worst part of town. It's much too

154

dangerous for us to go there. It's where the vigilantes hold trials."

Fear turned my blood to ice. Vigilantes! Had they found Juan? Was that why Allen had gone there? Was he now trying to help my old friend?

"Hurry, Tom! We must get there before they murder another man! Do you want that on your conscience? Perhaps we can stop them from doing it. Don't stand there. Let's go!" My voice held a command I hadn't known I could muster, and it had its effect on the coachman.

He closed the carriage door and sprang to the box. His whip cracked, urging our carriage through the darkening streets at a faster pace than usual. Alone, I cowered in agony, wondering if we would arrive too late. If Juan were hanging from a post already dead, what would I do? How could I face the world if he were not in it?

True, after being swept into the endless gaiety of my life since the night of the soirée, I had seldom thought of him. But then I hadn't thought of him constantly when I was at Miss Brigham's school, either. I had just known he was there when I needed him, and that had been enough.

How could I have said the things I had shouted at him when I thought he had hurt David? Oh, Juan, forgive me . . . please. Oh, Juan, don't let them kill you!

Suddenly I realized tears were streaming down my cheeks. Impatiently, I brushed them away. This was no time for weak female sniveling. Carmelita wouldn't cry in a situation such as this. Trumpets sounded as I wiped my eyes and pulled myself erect.

We were nearing the waterfront. Crowds of people filled the narrow streets and rough men elbowed their way along. A drunken man rolled from the path of our horses to sit cursing as he brandished an angry fist. Tom's shouts mingled with the noise of his whip cracking menacingly in the air as he forced a passage for our carriage.

Soon he turned the horses into a narrow alley lined with darkened warehouses, slowing to avoid the piles of refuse here and there. The stench of rotting offal swirled around me. I pressed my kerchief to my nose, wondering how people managed to breath air this rank. Then an open yard lit by flaring torches appeared beside the carriage, and a heavily masked man with a gun in each hand glared angrily from the entrance.

"Get along there," he shouted, firing both weapons into the air.

The horses reared in panic, but our carriage remained where it was. "I'm here to pick up Mr. Allen DeJung," Tom called.

While the guard and Tom bickered, I slipped from the opposite side of the carriage into the dark alley. Terrible debris clutched at my skirts, but I gathered as much of the material as I could before I sped swiftly behind the guard and into the yard. Behind me, guns roared again. I heard Tom's angry voice as the panicked horses galloped wildly down the alley.

Before me huge piles of lumber lined a narrow walkway leading to the burning torches. When I reached the clearing, the scene that met my eyes made my knees go weak. A rough table was surrounded by a dozen masked men who were all talking at once. Allen stood before them with his back toward me, gesticulating with both arms as he tried to outshout them.

And then I saw Juan. He stood silently, his hands tied behind him, his face impassive. A burly masked man stood beside him with a rope in his hand that led to Juan's throat.

The night was filled with bedlam as shrieks rent the air, but this time I knew where they came from. They came from me! I gave angry notice that I would not let them hang Juan!

Allen's shocked face turned my way, and the masked faces of the men around the table followed his lead.

Chapter Twelve

"Shadow!"

The sound rang in my ears as Allen and Juan both shouted my name, but it didn't stop me. I ran toward Juan, butting my head into the stomach of his captor like an angry billy goat. The masked man staggered backward and sat heavily on the ground with a startled grunt.

Allen reached me, then, and I saw he'd drawn a knife from his pocket. While the men around the table scrambled to untangle themselves from their chairs, Allen slashed the ropes holding Juan's hands. The instant he was free, Juan swept me under his arm and ran for the alley with the rope still dangling from his neck.

My head spun from its contact with the guard, but still I sputtered in protest at being carried like a sack of potatoes from the arena with my skirts flapping damply around my ankles. I struggled to free myself, but Juan's arm just grew tighter.

The shouting behind us grew louder as we reached the end of the lumber-lined path. The guard who had shouted at Tom came toward us, but Juan used his free hand to shove him backward. The guard's feet tangled with several pieces of loose lumber lying on the ground, which undid him. He fell ignominiously backward into a thrashing heap.

Our carriage came tearing down the dark alley, Tom's frantic shouts urging the horses onward. I knew he must have discovered my absence and returned for me. Juan set me carefully on my feet and turned to meet the approaching mob. Allen was behind, brandishing the knife like a valiant hero in spite of the guns being drawn.

The carriage reached us and I yanked the door open. Juan's hands boosted me into the dark interior, then he and Allen scrambled inside. With a crack from Tom's long whip, the carriage lunged away.

I lay panting from my exertions while the shouts faded to faint roarings. Neither of the men said anything as they, too, tried to regain their breath. Then I ventured a question. "Where are we going?"

Allen groaned. "Do you realize what you've done, Shadow? Why didn't you let me take care of this? I could have gotten your friend off, I think. They were starting to come round when you arrived. Now we're all in for it!" He mopped his forehead. "Damn! If women would only stay out of men's business . . ."

"That's enough," Juan interrupted quietly. "I don't know who you are, and I thank you for your assistance, but you will please watch your language in front of Miss St. George."

I stared, trying to see his face in the gloom. Was this my old companion? This *man*? I recalled his fighting David because of me, and a strange sort of thrill rippled through me. "Juan . . ." I said uncertainly.

"Yes?" His voice was distant, and I knew he was remembering too.

"I'm sorry about . . . oh, dear." Tears suddenly gushed from my eyes while a lump formed in my throat. "I'm sorry I was so mean," I wailed, "and my head hurts, and I couldn't find you, and I was so scared."

"Quit bawling," he said gruffly, pulling a handkerchief from his pocket.

My bravery melted in a flood of weeping as I was overwhelmed by the evening's events.

"Sh-sh," Juan said gently while he mopped at my eyes. Then he started laughing.

I looked at him indignantly, my tears forgotten. Allen had subsided at Juan's interruption, but now I saw him watching us as the flickering lights from the street filtered into our carriage.

"What are you laughing at?" I demanded.

Juan doubled over in merriment, then straightened to look at me with streaming eyes. "You . . ." His glee almost strangled him before he resumed. "You looked so funny butting that man in the . . . er, middle!" His chuckles began again, and this time Allen joined him. They were whooping and hollering like demented men, much to my chagrin.

The carriage stopped while they still pounded their knees between fresh roars of mirth. Tom's puzzled face looked in at us. "Miss Shadow, are you all right?" He shook his head, puzzlement at the scene before him showing on his face. "Count Chauvanne will have my hide for this," he muttered.

Allen sobered as he opened the carriage door and asked, "Have we lost the vigilantes, Tom?"

Tom nodded. "For now, sir, but they know where they can find us."

"Yes, I know," Allen said, and there was no laughter in his voice now. He looked at Juan. "If you stay with us, Monterro, you'll endanger Miss St. George."

"I'm leaving," Juan said, "and I'd better do it now." His brown eyes were tender when he looked at me. "Thanks for coming to my rescue," he said softly. "I'm sorry I made such a mess of things." He held out his hand to Allen. "Thanks to you, too, Mr. . . . ?"

"DeJung," Allen said, grasping his hand. "Allen, to you. What did you do with the horse?"

"They have it," Juan said ruefully. "I wasn't thinking about horses when I left Robert's ranch. I was on my way to return it when that bunch picked me up." He shrugged. "I'd better disappear for a while."

"How did you ever come to be on David's ranch working for him?" I asked wonderingly. "It was such a surprise . . . Oh, Juan, I was so glad to see you! I'd been worrying about your being stranded in some dreary old town and never finding a way to get out here. Then you were so stern . . . and the fight . . ."

"Ah, the fight was the rub, wasn't it? Any man would hate being knocked down in front of a beautiful woman," Juan said. "As to my being there . . . well, I finally made it to San Francisco after I worked long enough to pay for a ticket. But then I was out of money again, so I went back to work." His voice was cheerfully resigned.

"But it's such a coincidence! I mean, your working

161

for David when he was engaged to my cousin. . . ." My voice trailed off when I remembered David's kiss, Juan's disapproval of it, and the fight that had ensued.

"It wasn't a coincidence, Shadow. The doings of rich people are common knowledge among us sungrinners." His ironic tone stressed the word. "I thought I'd get to see you sooner by working for your cousin's fiancé . . . and I did."

My face grew hot under his scrutiny. My cousin's fiancé, indeed! Oh, what must Juan be thinking of me? But there was no time for explanations now. We had to concentrate on Juan's escaping the vigilantes, so I pushed David out of my mind.

"Where will you go, Juan? What will you do?" I blinked away tears. "When will I see you again?"

"I'll be back, Shadow. No matter where you go, I'll find you again, just as I found you this time. I'll always be around, and you can count on it," he said gently.

He glanced at Allen. "Take care of her, Allen." Then he frowned. "What will they do? Is there any way they can harm Shadow? What sort of guardian would allow her to come out alone looking for me?"

Allen's smile was rueful. "I'm afraid Miss Shadow is very determined once she decides on a course of action, if you'll permit my saying so. I thought she was safely at home waiting for me to call on her this evening."

"Oh?" The word was noncommittal, but I saw the fleeting hurt that crossed his face as Juan realized I had still another suitor. I looked at him with newly learned understanding.

He left the carriage, murmuring his thanks to Tom while he shook his hand. Then he turned and walked away. I watched his broad back blend into the darkness of the night before he disappeared.

Tom Jordan was the first to stir. "We'd best be getting home, miss." He glanced at Allen. "Will you be going with us, Mr. DeJung?"

"Of course," Allen answered. He smiled, but his tone was purposeful when he added, "I think Miss St. George has traveled unescorted for the last time."

It suddenly dawned on me I would have to face my aunt and uncle and account for my performance. Tonight I had behaved as no girl ever should. I would have to pay the consequences, whatever they were. "Oh, dear! Allen . . . must we tell the Chauvannes about tonight?"

Tom and Allen exchanged glances. "I doubt we need to," Tom murmured.

"We won't tell them about tonight, Shadow. If Roberts keeps his mouth shut, perhaps they won't hear of the incident," Allen said. "After all, the vigilantes will never noise it around that they were bested by a slip of a girl." He grinned, obviously delighted by the havoc I had caused.

"Please don't start laughing at me again," I said primly. "I really don't know what I was thinking about to behave as I did." Then I remembered his angry words concerning women, and I added, "If men would conduct their affairs in a more seemly manner, women wouldn't have to interfere."

He bowed his head in acknowledgment . . . or was it merely to hide his laughter?

Then a discomforting thought pushed the others

away. "Oh, dear! Do you suppose Juan has any money? Oh, Allen, what will he do?"

I thought of Juan hungry and cold, without funds to remedy the situation. Why was I never given pocket money for an emergency? I had never asked for any, of course, but it suddenly seemed ridiculous that women were expected to rely on their escorts for everything. Especially rich women, and wasn't I wealthy? Mr. Arbuthnot had assured me I was.

"Don't worry about it, Shadow," Allen said absently. "Your friend seems quite capable of taking care of himself. We'd better go, Tom. We must take Miss Shadow home. I'll most likely get a dressing down for keeping her out so late. Just remember, we've been together the entire evening."

Our carriage moved at a more sedate pace this time. Allen was absorbed in his thoughts, and I was grateful not to have to make small talk. The enormity of what I had done lay heavy on my conscience, mostly because I dreaded the punishment that was sure to be meted out on me. What would Miss Brigham say if she knew of my behavior?

And my hat! It was a new one and had been beautiful. I had flattened it into something resembling a pie pan when I used my head as a battering ram. I must look a mess. My gown was wrinkled and the lower part was soiled from the refuse I had walked through to a point that would most likely make it uncleanable.

By the time our carriage rattled between the iron gates I was in a state of depression it would have been difficult to equal. Let everybody be gone or in bed, I prayed. I wanted only to go to my room and hide.

My prayers went unanswered. Chung opened the door, but Count Chauvanne stood behind him. He frowned, and his sharp eyes noted my dishevelment as they traveled from my battered hat to the mess of my skirt. However, all he said was, "Allen, Shadow, please come into the salon."

A chill ran down my back at his sternness. My feet seemed tied to the floor, but Allen's hand under my elbow propelled me forward. I tried to hold back, but his firm grip persisted, and I knew how Daniel felt when he was shoved into the lion's den.

My aunt waited, face stern as granite and eyes just as cold. "Where have you been, Shadow? What have you done to your gown? And your hat!" she exclaimed.

My uncle held up his hand. "Let us have no bickering tonight, my dear. It is clearly evident that our niece has lost control of herself. Mr. DeJung, I shall hold you partly responsible for her state, but I know how headstrong she is. We shall have to take steps to insure against this happening again."

"Well, I for one am going to retire," my aunt announced haughtily. "I can't imagine what my brother was thinking of to foist such a child upon us. I thought her training had been that of a lady!" She swept regally from the room.

Count Chauvanne turned to me. "As for you, Shadow, I can't imagine what you were thinking when you commandeered Tom and my carriage. Your conduct has become absolutely . . ." he struggled for a word and finally found one, "unsuitable! Definitely unsuitable, as well as being a disgrace to this house. You will go to your room at once, and you will stay there until we decide what is to be done about all this. Meanwhile, your meals will be sent to you."

I stared, unbelieving. I had known I would be punished, but not to this degree. Locked in my room? Confined—as his mother was confined on the third floor? My meals sent to my room where I would eat without companions or conversation? The thought was intolerable. And for how long would this go on?

"Go to your room," he repeated.

With a despairing glance at Allen, I went into the empty hall. Instead of going immediately to my room, however, I waited, straining to hear what was said.

"Allen, I'm most chagrined that you have seen fit to take such liberties with my ward," Count Chauvanne said.

"I took no liberties, sir," Allen assured him. "I have done my utmost to protect your niece in any situation in which we found ourselves."

"Let's not quibble, sir," my uncle said sternly, and then there was a pause. I surmised he was doing his usual pacing while he thought. Then he resumed. "As Countess Chauvanne said, our niece seems to have lost her head since she arrived. Our ways are quite different from eastern manners and no doubt added to her confusion. She seems unable to handle too much freedom, so we shall have to guard her more securely in future. Hereafter, sir, you will get my permission before you take her anywhere. Do you understand?"

"I would like to marry your niece, Count Chauvanne," Allen said. "May I have your permission to pursue my suit?"

"My niece is much too young to marry, sir."

I could hear the astonishment in Allen's voice when

he answered, "She's past seventeen, Count Chauvanne!"

"Nevertheless, you may not pursue your suit, sir! My niece will marry no one for some years to come."

"Why not?" Allen demanded.

Yes, why not, I silently echoed. Why was my uncle so determined to turn me into an old maid? He and my aunt would like to be rid of me, so why not marry me off? Other girls my age were betrothed. Some were even married. Others were already expecting a child. I had already heard catty remarks about Julia's age, and perhaps they were made about mine, too, without my hearing them. Why was I not being allowed to marry?

"I will overlook your impertinence, sir," Count Chauvanne said coldly. "Since my niece will be leaving here shortly, the question will settle itself. It will be best if you do not attempt to see her again." His voice grew louder as he neared my listening post.

I whirled and sped up the stairs before I was seen. Where was I being sent? No matter my destination, I knew I would rather not go. It was probably the school my aunt had mentioned, and I was much too old to return to that kind of life. Now what could I do?

Carlie was waiting in my room, as usual. "You'd best catch your breath, Miss Shadow," she said, leading me to a seat on the bed. "Land sakes! Whatever happened to your gown? It has garbage on it! And your hat! Oh, dear . . ." she said, drawing the pancake from my hand and looking at it in dismay. "Did you sit on it?"

"Carlie, they're going to send me away!"

167

"What, Miss Shadow? Oh, no, they wouldn't do that," she said, but her voice held a note of doubt as she added, "would they?"

I nodded.

"Where, Miss Shadow?"

Her question echoed mine, but I was still unsure. Count Chauvanne had mentioned no school while talking to Allen. I doubted any school would willingly accept a grown woman for a student, for it just wasn't done. But if not a school, where did he plan to send me?

"My, aren't you a pretty sight, though."

I looked up to see Julia standing inside the open door.

"You look as though you'd been strolling on a garbage barge," she said sarcastically. "Did David take you for a midnight walk?"

Anger bubbled inside me, but I held my tongue. I was a guest in her home, and my training was such that I could not quarrel with her.

"Well?" she asked sharply. "Were you with David tonight? Answer me!"

"No, I wasn't with David tonight," I replied evenly, wondering if I told the truth. "Allen brought me home just a short time ago. We had a lovely time." Then I couldn't resist adding, "Haven't you patched things up with David yet?"

Her trilling laughed was forced. "Of course not! It's better to keep men guessing, you silly goose. Let him sweat a while. I shall forgive him in my own good time, if I decide to forgive him at all," she said airily, and then her mouth twisted. "*You* won't be around for long!"

I caught my breath at her viciousness, but kept my voice cool. "Really? And just where will I be?"

Her head went up as a sly smile crossed her face. "You'll know when Elizabeth tells you, my dear cousin. You can be sure, however, that you'll no longer be around here, and good riddance," she said smugly, and with a shrug, left.

Carlie closed the door and returned to my side. "Don't let Miss Julia bother you, Miss Shadow. She acts strange at times, and Bertha says she can't help it." She looked at my dress again and her nose wrinkled when she touched the dampness of the skirt. "Wouldn't you like to get out of that wet gown?"

Weariness washed over me. What did anything matter? I let Carlie take off the soiled gown and the damp petticoats beneath.

"You're laced too tight," she muttered, loosening the strings of my corset. "It's a wonder you can breathe."

When I was clad in the comforting folds of a nightgown, she brought a damp cloth. "Let me clean your face, Miss Shadow." She clucked like a mother hen while dabbing gently at a spot beneath my chin. "My goodness, Miss Shadow, where have you been? How in the world did you get so dirty?" Her eyes twinkled. "Miss Julia wasn't right about the garbage barge, was she?"

Before I could answer, a light rap on the door preceded Bertha carrying a small tray. "Count Chauvanne sent you a glass of wine, Miss Shadow. He said it would remove any chill you might have gotten from the night air." Her eyes took in the soiled gown and Carlie's ministrations, but she said nothing.

"Thank you, Bertha. Put it on the table, please." I raised my chin higher so Carlie could see the rest of my neck. She dabbed vigorously at another spot of dirt.

Bertha shook her head as she left the tray, then went out, closing the door softly behind her.

"Now will you have your wine?" Carlie asked.

"No, thanks," I said, closing my eyes when my head touched the pillow. "Why don't you drink it, Carlie? And then, turn out the lights, please."

I was left in darkness with only my own thoughts for company, and they were not pleasant. My mind worried the questions circling in my head. If the Chauvannes wanted to be rid of me, why not marry me off to Allen? It would be a convenient method. He was no suitor of Julia's, and he was an excellent match by anyone's standards. Even though I didn't love him, he was infinitely preferable to another girls' school.

David had said he loved me, but that was before our quarrel over Juan. Despite what Julia said, I knew she would be wearing his ring if he'd offered it to her. Perhaps he had meant it when he said their engagement was over, but then why had he returned to her side? Did he still love me? Oh, David . . .

Every line of his face was printed indelibly in my mind. My heart beat faster remembering the feel of his lips on mine and the warmth from his body when he held me close. Had he been one of the masked men at the meeting tonight? About this, I hoped Allen was wrong. My cheeks grew warm as I remembered my rowdy behavior. If he had been there, could he ever again think of me as the girl he wanted to marry? I doubted it.

Then another thought came to me. If David were at the meeting of masked men, he'd been trying to hang Juan, for it seemed to me there was no dissension about the verdict except Allen's. Could he be that brutal and lawless? The hanged man's face I had seen the night Sarah and I entered San Francisco floated before me with horrible clarity. With a shudder, I banished it. Juan was safely away by now, out of reach of the vigilantes, whoever they were.

Or was he? If he had no money, how could he go anywhere? He was streetwise in New York where he could quite capably exist on his own merits, but California was entirely different, presenting problems he had not encountered before. Then I remembered his calm assurance in the carriage and felt reassured. My childhood companion had grown into a man, and a very wise one, too, in spite of the fact that he had allowed himself to be caught with a horse he'd forgotten could be classed as stolen.

He had a nice smile . . . and laugh. I'd never heard Juan laugh as heartily as he had this night in our carriage. The laughter was at my expense, but I supposed I did look pretty silly imitating a billy goat. With a sigh, I snuggled beneath the covers. My head was the only weapon I had, so what else could I have done?

When I awoke the next morning, another maid, Jane again, was drawing the draperies to let in the light. "Where's Carlie?" I asked, yawning.

"She's ill, Miss Shadow."

I sat up. "Again? Where is she?"

"The Jordans live in a cottage back near the stable, Miss Shadow. Carlie went home to her mother early this morning. She was taken bad sick during the night, and in spite of everything Bertha could do, she seemed only to get worse."

She bustled around assembling the clothing I would wear, then said, "As soon as you're dressed, I'll run down and get your breakfast. Bertha said you were to have your meals in your room today."

With a pang, I remembered Count Chauvanne's words. He would soon discover, however, that I was not a spineless old woman who could be locked away at will.

"That won't be necessary," I said. "I'm not hungry this morning. Change the gown you took from the wardrobe for my gray merino, and please bring my cloak."

Her eyes widened, but she obeyed.

"I'm going to see Carlie," I said. "Please say nothing about it to anyone."

I tiptoed down the back stairway, blessing the architect who had placed it there. A wrinkled old Chinese woman looked up from her post at the stove, then quickly turned back to the pots before her. She startled me, for I hadn't known the Chauvannes had another Asian servant.

Without pausing, I slipped through the back door into thick fog. It successfully concealed me from any curious eyes, but it also made it difficult to see where I was going. Walking through the dense mist gave me a curiously disembodied feeling when I looked down and couldn't see my feet. The world had a distinctly fishlike odor that rather delighted me. I could imagine the tumultuous heaving sea peopled with millions of denizens that ranged from tiny creatures to huge whales. Did they have as much difficulty seeing where they were going as I was having now? It was much as though I were swimming, only my feet touched bottom.

Several trees loomed ahead, and I walked slowly, with outstretched hands. Then I touched boards and knew I had found the stable. Soft snufflings and snorts came from inside where horses nuzzled their morning mash, and the odor of warm bodies and leather tack mingled with the smell of the sea. I felt my way along the side of the building until I came to a corner, then continued as before. Suddenly I stumbled and almost fell up two steps onto a porch. I was at the Jordans' cottage.

The door opened to my knock and I saw a straggle-haired woman holding a squalling baby against an old flannel robe. "Come in," she shouted over the cries of the child. "The fog is turrible this mornin'." She pulled a sugar tit from her pocket and stuffed it into the open mouth.

The wailing stopped as though turned off by a tap. "She's collicky," the woman announced. "Hasn't let me sleep a solid hour all night."

"I'm Shadow St. George," I said. "How is Carlie this morning?"

"Sick," she said promptly. "Came home several hours ago actin' drunk! I put her to bed." She tucked a stray strand of hair into her cap. "I know who you are, miss. If I'd knew you was comin', I'd 'a fixed up some."

"That isn't necessary, Mrs. Jordan," I said. "May I see Carlie?"

"Oh, sure." She walked into a back room, motioning me to follow.

Carlie lay in bed with her eyes closed. Her face had a bluish cast and her breathing was slow, laborious.

"Carlie?" I repeated her name without result, then felt her cheek. It was dry and much too warm. I shook her gently, but her eyes remained closed. "She's unconscious, Mrs. Jordan. Have you sent for a doctor?"

"We can't afford no doctor," Carlie's mother declared. " 'Sides, they wouldn't wanta come this fur out."

"Surely the Chauvannes have a doctor who comes to the manor," I protested. "Can't you ask Countess Chauvanne to send for him?"

Mrs. Jordan gave an audible sniff as she jounced the baby up and down. "She ain't never called him for one of us. For them, sure. She says Bertha is good as a doctor when one of us gets sick."

"Is Tom here, Mrs. Jordan?"

She nodded. "He's havin' breakfast now. Just came in from the stables, he did."

I walked quickly to the kitchen, fear making me almost run. "Tom, Carlie's sick. Go for the doctor as fast as you can. She looks dreadful."

He looked up, shaking his head. "Miss Shadow, I thank you for caring about my daughter, but I'm afraid the high living of the Chauvannes has been her downfall. She came in waking us all up, ranting and raving like a lunatic. She's sick, all right, but it's because she drank too much."

"You don't turn blue from being drunk, do you?"

"Blue?" He stared at me, then jumped up so fast his chair crashed to the floor.

174

I followed Tom to the small bedroom where Carlie lay as one dead. Her breath rattled slowly in her throat, and the blueness in her face was more pronounced. Tom shook her roughly until her eyelids opened. The pupils of her eyes were tiny dots gazing unseeing into nothingness.

"Opium," he said in a shocked voice, letting his daughter sink back onto the bed. "She's been eating opium!"

He hurried out, reaching for his coat from the tree beside the kitchen door. "I'd best ask Count Chauvanne for permission to go for the doctor."

"There isn't time," I said desperately. "Carlie's dying! Can't you see? Oh, Tom, go! Go quickly!"

A look of resignation crossed his face. "All right," he said slowly. "I'll probably get sacked anyway for letting you get mixed in that fracas last night."

He left while I stood wondering what to do. In a few minutes I heard hooves, muffled by the fog, fading away down the driveway. I hurried back to Carlie, praying she wouldn't die before the doctor arrived.

Chapter Thirteen

Carlie looked like one already dead. Mrs. Jordan wept and wailed beside her, her anger at Carlie's arrival now forgotten. The sugar tit had dropped to the floor, so the baby added shrieks of frustration to the bedlam.

"Mrs. Jordan!" I said loudly.

She turned, sniffling. "She's dead, ain't she, miss? My daughter's dead, and them at the mansion are responsible, ain't they?"

Then I saw the covers move ever so slightly. Carlie was still breathing!

"No, she isn't dead, Mrs. Jordan," I shouted over the baby's cries. "Why don't you take your child in the other room and tend to her? I'll sit with Carlie until the doctor gets here. Would it be too much trouble to fix some coffee?"

She nodded, hoisting the child to one hip as she left. The bedroom returned to comparative quiet, and I sat beside Carlie, calling her name with all the urgency I could muster, until she stirred again, fluttering her eyelids.

She looked at me in an unfocused sort of way and seemed to be trying to say something. Then her eyes closed and her breathing slowed until I thought it had stopped. I spoke her name again and again, but her eyes remained shut. In time her breathing seemed to improve, however, so I sat beside her, massaging her arms while I talked and talked and talked.

Mrs. Jordan brought a cup of steaming coffee. She looked fearfully at her daughter, then pleadingly at me. "Will she die, ma'am?"

"I don't know, Mrs. Jordan. Help me prop her up. Do you have more pillows?"

She hurriedly brought two pillows and we pulled Carlie to a position where I could spoon coffee into her mouth without drowning her. She choked at first, then swallowed. After a few sips the blue faded to a less lurid hue and her breathing became more normal.

Tom had said she'd had opium, but Carlie wouldn't take the drug willingly, I was sure. The old countess came to mind when I remembered Carlie's account of her incarceration on the third floor of the manor. Was it possible Carlie had accidently eaten some of the drug meant for the old woman? But she had also said only Bertha tended the old woman, so where could she have gotten it? Bertha was much too neat to carelessly leave anything where it shouldn't be left.

Then a thought raised goose bumps on my arms. The wine! The wine Count Chauvanne had sent to my room on two different occasions that I hadn't touched. Since the night I had become so sick from drinking champagne too quickly I hadn't really cared for wine of any kind. I sipped politely when everyone around me was drinking, but I didn't care for the taste. Carlie did, and I had told her to drink it. And each time she was taken ill shortly after. Carlie had drunk wine intended for me!

Shivers shook me as a lump of panic rose in my throat. Was my guardian trying to kill me. *Why?* Why would my uncle want me dead?

I heard voices outside the room, but it was too soon for Tom to have returned with a doctor in tow.

Mrs. Jordan stuck her head in the doorway. "You're wanted, Miss Shadow."

With a worried look at Carlie, I went into the other room, banishing the terror that had engulfed me. The trumpets had sounded and I was no longer panicked. If my aunt and uncle were trying to kill me, they would discover it was not an easy thing to do.

A maid from the mansion was waiting. "Bertha sent me, Miss Shadow. There's a terrible uproar, there is. Madam Countess discovered you'd gone out, and she's in a dreadful state. Will you come, please?"

"No, I won't," I said shortly. "Tell Madam Countess I will return when the doctor arrives. And tell her . . . no, I'll tell her myself later." When I could no longer be of help to Carlie would be soon enough to confront my guardians with my accusations.

I returned to Carlie's side to rub her arms and talk urgently into her ear. Somehow I felt I was her link with the world. At intervals I spooned more coffee into her mouth, but always I kept talking. So long as she heard my voice, perhaps she would not be drawn into death.

My back ached and my arms grew tired as the hours passed. Carlie's eyes fluttered occasionally, and once they opened wide for a second. The pupils grew larger and seemed to focus on my face. Her mouth opened as she made an effort to speak. "Miss Sha . . ." came weakly, then she lapsed into coma again. Try as I would, I could not rouse her.

By the time the doctor arrived my voice was hoarse. I looked blearily up at the gray-haired man.

"I'm Dr. Dijon," he said curtly. "You are Miss St. George? Tom Jordan said you told him to come for me."

I nodded, rising from my seat beside Carlie. "This is your patient, Dr. Dijon. I'm afraid she's extremely ill."

He bent over her, sniffing her breath and raising an eyelid to peer into her eye. Then he straightened. "Mph," he grunted, tugging at his neat goatee and looking beyond me to Carlie's mother. "I'll need your help, Mrs. Jordan."

Then he glanced at me. "You look exhausted, Miss St. George. Perhaps you'd better return to the manor and rest. I'll come over as soon as I'm finished here."

"What's wrong with her?" I asked, and my voice emerged in a croak.

"It looks like opium poisoning, Miss St. George. You look as though you're becoming ill yourself. Why don't you go home and get in bed? I'll give you a sedative as soon as I get there."

"I'm fine," I said wearily. "Will Carlie be all right? Can you help her?"

"Yes, I think so, if you'll get out of my way so I can work. I'll have to pump her stomach, and it isn't a pleasant sight." He noted the dregs in the cup. "She should have coffee. Lots of it."

Mrs. Jordan glanced fearfully at her daughter.

"Tell me what you need, doctor, and I'll get it."

"A basin, warm and cold cloths. Better make it two basins and put hot water in one and cold in the other. Hurry, Mrs. Jordan."

Impatiently, Dr. Dijon looked at me. "Please leave, Miss St. George. You are much too exhausted to be of help, you know. If you don't get some rest you'll just be another patient I have to tend."

I turned away. The doctor was probably right. I was so weary I could hardly move without groaning. I put on my cloak and left.

The world outside was gray and dreary, bereft of the sun that usually burned through the fog by midday. Light rain sprinkled down, changing to a downpour as I neared the manor. By the time I reached the kitchen, I was thoroughly soaked.

I hurried up the back stairway to the second floor, then paused. Tired as I was, there was something I must know before I could sleep, and perhaps the old countess could tell me. None of the maids were around, so I continued my climb to the third floor.

The hall was dimly lit, but it showed the threadbare carpet beneath my feet. Evidently the sumptuous furnishings stopped on the second floor. All the doors were closed, and I stood wondering which rooms held the old woman who had come in the night to warn me of danger. Then I saw the large iron lock and knew I had found her prison.

A key hung on a nail beside the door. When I tried it in the lock the door swung slowly inward. The room was dim, and not altogether from the dismal weather outside. There were no draperies at the only window, but heavy ivy covered the opening from the outside. It effectively screened from view the old woman who lived here.

My eyes soon grew accustomed to the lack of light. I glanced around until I saw the old countess sitting in a battered rocking chair. She moved slowly back and forth, taking no notice of me. She was humming a tuneless melody that was more like a mourning dirge.

I went to her and kneeled so my face was on a level with hers. "Countess Chauvanne," I said softly, "do you remember me?"

She continued her soft humming while my heart melted with pity at her plight. Blue veins stood out on the bony hands lying on the chair arms. A wasted face hung in wrinkles over bones trying to pierce the paperlike flesh. There seemed to be no substance under the old wrapper that hid her body. Did she weigh as much as the sawdust-filled doll I had had as a child? What were the faded eyes seeing?

"Oh, please," I pleaded. "You came to me once in the night to warn me I would be killed in this mansion. Can't you speak to me now? There are things I need to know."

The rheumy eyes shifted vaguely to my face. Mumbled words replaced the eerie hum. "Bad blood . . . bad blood . . . bad blood . . ." came through barely open lips. The ancient voice faded away and then returned. "Beware . . . must be stopped . . . no more . . ." Her eyes closed as her head dropped against the back of the chair. Her breathing became even and quite loud.

"Miss Shadow!"

Startled, I looked around to see Bertha coming toward me. "You shouldn't be here! You know you

181

shouldn't be here! Madam Countess has been waiting to see you." She glanced at the old woman snoring in her chair. "Have you been talking to her?"

"I've been trying to. Oh, Bertha, Carlie has been poisoned! The doctor said it was opium, and she might die! She looks dreadful and was barely breathing when I left."

Bertha's face blanched. "Carlie poisoned?" she whispered. "I thought she had just been tippling from one of the wine bottles, and drank too much."

"Oh, she drank wine all right . . . the wine my uncle sent for me," I said bitterly.

Her eyes widened with shock. "Oh, Miss Shadow, what are you saying? Do you think Count Chauvanne tried to poison you? He wouldn't do such a thing! If there was poison in the wine it must have been through an accident of some kind." She flapped her apron in agitation. "Oh, dear me!"

"I don't think it could have been an accident, Bertha, but I intend to find out. I thought perhaps the old countess could shed some light on why my uncle would try to poison me. After all, she did try to warn me, remember?"

Bertha gasped. "You must not let the count know you've been up here! We have all been given strict instructions not even to mention his mother. No one is allowed to enter this room, save me. No one! Oh, saints preserve us!" She urged me out the door and carefully locked it before she pocketed the key. "You won't tell anyone you were in her room, will you, Miss Shadow? It could mean my dismissal."

A look at her pleading eyes formed my decision. "No, Bertha, of course I won't tell . . . if *you* tell me all you know about this. You dose her with opium to keep her quiet, isn't that true? Is it done by lacing her wine with it?"

"Miss Shadow!" she exclaimed. "How do you know all this? Did Carlie tell you? I'll have to speak to her about her wagging tongue."

"Carlie told me nothing," I lied. "You know it was the old woman who frightened me so that night. Before she left she told me a few things." I would not tell her how few, I decided. "Did you know there was opium in the wine Count Chauvanne sent me?" I persisted.

"Of course not!" she said indignantly. "You must be as mad as the old woman if you think he would try to kill you. You're overwrought, Miss Shadow. Look at yourself. You've ruined another gown. You're soaked through and probably have a raging fever that is making you imagine all sorts of things. Come, let me help you to your room."

I let her shepherd me down the stairs into my boudoir. She bustled around helping me out of my wet clothing, then slipped a flannel gown over my head and tucked me into bed, and all the while her eyes had a haunted look.

When I was settled, she said, "Dr. Dijon is with Madam Countess, Miss Shadow. I'll ask him to come give you a sedative when she dismisses him."

"I don't need a sedative." The warmth of the bed coupled with my fatigue was making me drowsy. "Will you tell my aunt I would like to see her, please? It's very important."

She stood uncertainly, then frowned and shook her head. "The doctor will know best what you need,

Miss Shadow. I'll give Madam Countess your message, for she's been quite anxious to see you." Then, with another shake of her head, she left.

The ache in my shoulders subsided as blessed sleep claimed me. My last thought was that I could make more sense of everything if I could just rest for a time.

The prick of a needle woke me. Lamps were lit, making the man above me waver in shadows when he straightened with an empty syringe in his hand.

"Ah, you're awake, Miss St. George," he said smoothly. "I've given you something to help you rest easy."

It was Dr. Dijon, and there were matters I wished to discuss with him. "How is Carlie? What . . ." I began, but the room and the doctor began to circle around my head. No . . . no! I thought frantically. Darkness rolled over me like a giant wave while I struggled to maintain consciousness. Carmelita! Oh, Mother, help me!

She wasn't in the distorted world I entered. Grotesque shapes wavered in a menacing circle from which there was no escape. My feet . . . my feet were still there, but they would only move with difficulty. I ran in an exaggerated slow motion toward an opening in the circle, then the gap was filled with black creatures that oozed into place. I tried to scream, but had no voice. And I was tired . . . so very tired. . . .

How long I stayed in this other world I do not know. When it faded into solid blackness, again I felt the prick of a needle. Then the creatures returned to torment me and it seemed their torture would never end. How often this happened, I do not know, unless it was an eternity. How long is an eternity?

One morning I woke and saw Carlie drawing the draperies back to let sunshine flood the room. I stared unbelieving at the normalness of my surroundings, unable to grasp my return to sanity. "Carlie? Is that you?" I asked groggily.

She whirled and came to my side. "Oh, Miss Shadow! I've been so frightened! You've been so ill. . . ." She stopped to peer into my eyes. "Are you back to your full senses, Miss Shadow? I couldn't talk to you before. You've been raving like a maniac for weeks."

It was a struggle to push myself higher on the pillows, but I made it. "I've been ill? Oh, no, Carlie, *you* were ill. Don't you remember?"

Her capable hands propped pillows behind my head while she made soothing sounds. "Don't excite yourself, Miss Shadow. I was only sick for a few days, and not nearly so sick as you've been for such a long time. Dr. Dijon said you had pneumonia. You've been delirious, and I thought you were going to die. I'm so glad you're better."

"Pneumonia?" I asked stupidly.

"Dr. Dijon has been here every day, Miss Shadow. He said you took ill the day you came to attend me. It rained . . . don't you remember? Bertha said you came home soaked to the skin. Oh, I'll never forgive myself! It was all my fault for being so silly."

I stared up at her. "Silly?"

She nodded. "I'm not to touch wine anymore. Dr. Dijon said there is something in my blood that makes poison when it mixes with wine." She sighed. "I promised God I would never touch spirits again if you got well."

185

"What about the opium? When Dr. Dijon first saw you, he said you had opium poisoning."

"That's what he thought at first," she chattered on, "but then he found out different. It was just silly to think there was opium in the wine I drank. How could there be? The master had sent it up and he would never try to poison anyone." She patted my already smooth covers even smoother. "I'll go tell Bertha you've wakened. She'll make broth and tea for you to make you feel stronger. Will you be all right?"

"Yes, of course." So that was how it would be, I thought wearily. Poor silly Carlie, and poor me, too. Anything I said now would be construed as imaginings from the fever I had supposedly suffered from. Pneumonia, indeed! My hand went up to my cheek, and alarm shot through me. Was I as gaunt as the old woman on the floor above?

I reached for the hand mirror that lay on my bedside table and stared at myself aghast. My face was a pasty white, accenting deep blue circles under my eyes. My cheeks were sunken, and the bones protruded in a way I had never before seen. What had they done to me? Even my once glossy hair was now dull and stringy, like some old crone's. I dropped the mirror, sobbing in weak, impotent anger.

For days I lay in bed while Carlie and Bertha spoon-fed broth into my mouth. Then I graduated to custards and puddings. Soon I was able to rise and walk a few faltering steps around the room. When my shaky hands steadied enough to allow me to hold my own utensils, I felt as though I had accomplished a mighty feat, indeed.

One afternoon Dr. Dijon came to my room carrying

his black bag. Instinctively, I shrank into the pillows when he approached the bed.

"How are we today?" he asked, taking no notice of my obvious fear. He picked up my wrist and studied his watch for a few moments. "Your pulse is good," he announced with a genial smile. "I think we can safely say your bout with pneumonia is over, don't you?"

I pushed my fear away and braced myself. "I didn't have pneumonia, Dr. Dijon, and you know it. My illness was more like Carlie's, wouldn't you say?"

The smile left his face. "Well, now, perhaps I spoke too soon. If you are still hallucinating, a few more medicinal injections might be necessary."

Our glances met, and I was the one to look away first. What could I do to protect myself from his wicked needle? I decided this was not the time to be quite so brave.

"Perhaps it was pneumonia," I conceded. "I recall getting drenched in a sudden downpour after I left the Jordans' house." Our eyes met again. "However, Dr. Dijon," I continued, "I feel quite well now."

"That's fine," he said, once again the affable doctor. "Perhaps you can start taking your meals with the family in the morning."

After the doctor left, Carlie smiled at me. "Won't it be fine to be up and around again, Miss Shadow? You've become pale as a ghost, but the sun will fix that."

I said nothing, wondering how the Chauvannes would receive me at the breakfast table.

Next morning I found out. Carlie helped me to bathe and dress and I went carefully down the long stairway, determined to show a staunch front.

187

Count Chauvanne rose when I entered the dining room and smiled paternally. "Ah, Shadow, it's good to see you up and about again."

Julia watched me walk toward the table, an enigmatic smile twitching at her lips. "My, but you're thin," she observed. "Now you match your name."

"Good morning," I said.

My aunt's tart voice rose above her daughter's. "I hope you have learned not to walk in our winter rains, Shadow. They are quite deceptive, you know. Our climate is mild, but it can be deadly if you do not protect yourself."

"I'm sorry I was so much trouble, Aunt Elizabeth."

She frowned in annoyance. "I told you before, don't call me *aunt*! It's most annoying. Has your illness made you forget everything?"

"I don't think it's made me forget anything," I said mildly.

Count Chauvanne glanced at me, then returned to stirring his coffee. "Shall we all try to get along?" he asked. "After all, constant bickering will accomplish nothing."

"Ferd, we are *not* bickering, we are merely discussing," my aunt said sharply. "Isn't it time you left for the city?"

"Yes, my dear." He rose and held out his hand. "Will you see me off? It will make my entire day brighter."

Julia's eyes followed them out before she turned to me. "Your beau has been around to see how you were getting along. Dr. Dijon told him flowers were bad for sick people, so he brought no more after the first time."

"My beau?"

She laughed. "Your stuffy little attorney, goose." She waved her hand in the air to display the diamond she had regained. "I have accepted David's apology . . . the dear boy." Her smile vanished. "You are not to flirt with him anymore, do you hear me? You are to leave him alone!"

Her nose looked longer than I remembered, or perhaps the angry twist to her mouth only made it seem that way. My heart plunged to the depths when I saw David's ring on her finger. Was he that fickle? Could he say he loved me one day, then resume his engagement to Julia the next? Why was he marrying her? By now it seemed certain he wasn't in love with her, and what other reason could there be? My pride refused to allow tears, but my appetite for food vanished.

"Aren't you going to say anything, my dear cousin?" Julia demanded.

I rose, laying my napkin carefully beside my unused plate. "Of course, Julia. I hope you'll be very happy."

"Aren't you going to eat breakfast?"

Bertha came in, saving me an answer.

"May I have tea in my room, Bertha?" I said. "I'm not quite as strong as I imagined."

At once she was all motherly, urging me to lean on her arm for support. Carlie came to meet me in the hall just as the front knocker sounded. Bertha relinquished me to her care and went to open the door.

It was David. He was dressed in an immaculate morning suit. His eyes lit up when he saw me, then were quickly masked by cool politeness. "Good morning, Shadow," he said gravely. "It's good to see you are well again."

"David, you're early," Julia trilled, emerging from the dining room behind me. "You look very elegant, darling. As soon as Bertha gets my cloak, I'll be ready." She twined her arm through David's, tossing a triumphant glance at me. "We'll have a long, lovely day to shop, won't we?"

With Carlie's arm around my waist, I climbed the stairs. Halfway up I paused to catch my breath. A quick glance behind showed David staring after me while Bertha helped Julia into her cloak.

Our eyes locked for an instant, and it was long enough for me to see sadness and despair in the blue eyes I remembered as always full of laughter. His face looked somehow older than it had just a short time ago. Then Julia claimed him and they went out to the waiting carriage.

What had happened during the weeks I lay drugged? I could say that word to myself. If I dared mention it to anyone else Dr. Dijon would return with his needle and syringe and I would be returned to insanity, of that I was sure. I would have to be cautious.

"How long was I ill, Carlie?"

"Almost three weeks, Miss Shadow, although it seemed much longer than that," Carlie replied. She urged me upward to my room.

When we reached it, I left the support of her arm to walk to the window and look out. It was a lovely day and one full of promise, just as Julia said.

"Perhaps I had better have something to eat with my tea, Carlie. I think some toast and an egg would be nice, and bring some marmalade, too." Even though I wasn't hungry, I would eat. Food would give me strength.

She nodded, saying, "I'll get it now."

"Oh, and Carlie . . ."

"Yes, Miss Shadow?"

"The next time Mr. DeJung calls, please be sure to let me know. I want to see him."

"Of course, Miss Shadow." She hurried away and I was alone with my thoughts.

Allen . . . I must see Allen. He is wise and strong and will in no way be intimidated by my guardian.

And David . . . what had they done to him? His look of despair flashed before me. Had it been a plea for help?

Chapter Fourteen

In the days that followed nothing more was said about sending me away. Our lives returned to the normalcy they had had before Carlie's misadventure and my "illness."

Allen was somewhat skeptical when I told him my suspicions. "Dr. Dijon has been the Chauvannes' physician for as long as I can remember," he said slowly. "He is well thought of among his patients. It's hard to believe he would be party to such a thing. Do you have any proof that would stand up in court?" His eyes were troubled. "Why should your uncle wish to kill you, Shadow?"

How often had I asked myself the same question? It was constantly in my mind, despite the fact that he was now ever courteous to me. Would he do anything without my aunt's permission? The countess was so involved with her own affairs that she could scarcely be bothered with Julia's, much less mine. A more self-centered person I had not known, and Julia followed her pattern.

Julia kept David at her side, ordering him around

much as she would a servant. I knew he didn't love her, and by now Julia must have known it, too, unless she was deliberately dishonest with herself. But it made no difference. She was accustomed to getting whatever she wanted. At my first appearance she had been sure enough of her ownership of David to carelessly suggest he take me riding. It must have been a first for her when she discovered she might lose one of her possessions. The matter had been resolved somehow, and now David was at her beck and call. How had Count Chauvanne brought him to heel?

David was unfailingly polite to me, but that was all. His eyes always seemed to be avoiding mine. When our glances met accidentally, I glimpsed the yearning sadness again, but only for an instant. Then a mask fell over his face, and I was facing a man who appeared hardly to know me. Julia made sure we were never alone together, so there was no chance of my questioning him.

Allen was the rock I clung to, feeling cherished in his company. He neglected his work quite shamefully by calling often at the mansion to take me riding, either on horseback or in his carriage. He often brought a deliciously filled picnic basket for us to share. I regained the weight I'd lost during Dr. Dijon's ministrations and my hair grew lustrous and thick again, but my conscience nagged at me about Allen's neglect of his work.

One summery morning after we were settled in Allen's carriage, I broached a subject I had been toying with in my mind for some time. "Let's go to your office, Allen. I would like to help you work, instead of frittering away the days as we've been doing."

His eyebrows rose in surprise. "Are you getting bored with my company, my dear?"

"Oh, Allen, of course not! I know you've been neglecting your practice to amuse me and it makes me feel guilty. I want to be useful. I know how to pen beautiful letters and I can also add and subtract and even divide and multiply. I'm sure I could be as much help to you as any clerk you have, and I'll enjoy doing it."

"Ladies don't grub in offices, my dear," he said, shaking his head in disapproval. "Think of the scandalized gossip it would cause."

"I don't care," I said stubbornly. "You should be taking care of your clients instead of escorting me all over the country."

"Would you prefer that I not call on you so often, Shadow?" he asked gently.

"Oh, no! I couldn't bear to spend more time in the mansion—that's why I want to help you in your office. You can still take me riding, but your practice won't suffer."

He was silent, pondering my request, and then he nodded. "Well, why not? We could keep it secret for a while, at least. The old biddies won't peck at you until the news leaks out, and then we'll just face them down. We can say you are working for charitable causes, and it won't be a lie." He grinned. "You have no idea how much you contribute toward enlivening my life." His eyes rolled heavenward as he said, "What did you have in mind, Lord, when you created this lovely, headstrong angel?"

A boyish grin tugged at his mouth when he looked

at me. "My admiration for your Juan is growing by leaps and bounds, Shadow. He must have been strong indeed to shepherd you through a city like New York while you were growing up, and keep you safe while doing it."

By now I had told him all about our friendship. During our frequent outings we had exchanged confidences about our childhoods as well as our present circumstances. He knew about my parents—how my mother had died when I was born, and how my father blamed me for her death.

He had clucked in sympathy, saying, "I can't imagine anyone not loving you, my dear. You must have been an adorable child."

It was comforting to bask in his approval. My fondness for Allen grew, almost as though he were the older brother I'd never had. I could rely on him to supply fun and admiration and security.

Now we began going to his office together. He cleared a small space where I would be safe from the curious stares of his clients, and here I penned letters for him, blissfully sure Miss Brigham had taught me well.

When my curiosity got the better of me, Allen let me read the files his father had kept on clients in the past. My knowledge of the law of our land grew proportionately. The mysterious world of business that men so zealously kept from their women became one I knew well.

Many of Allen's clients were Chinese men of wealth. I had thought Asians were all laboring coolies or houseboys like Chung, but these were men of substance, just as David had said when he'd bitterly denounced these aliens. They owned cigar and garment factories, restaurants, grocery stores, and shops of various kinds. And laundries—almost every laundry in San Francisco was owned by the Chinese.

I discovered we were in the midst of a depression and had been for some time. White workers resented the Chinese to a degree that often resulted in violence. I had wondered at David's hatred of the yellow foreigners, but now I found the feeling was universal among white businessmen and laborers in the city. The ranchers whose lands were threatened by Chinese acquisition lobbied constantly to have them ousted from the country, but to no avail.

Allen liked the polite Asians who came to him for legal assistance. Mayor Bryant and his officials had passed a series of highly restrictive measures aimed at the Chinese, and when they violated any one of them, it was usually Allen who was called to their defense.

One ordinance sharply increased the license fees charged Chinese businessmen. Another prohibited Chinese laundries from operating in any except fireproof buildings, while still another barred them from appearing on the streets after two o'clock in the morning. There were others just as ridiculous.

When they came to Allen with their woes, he advised them to pay the fees, which they did, since most could well afford them. He suggested they honor the curfew because the early morning hours were the best for sleeping, anyway. But as to fireproof buildings—well, what building was?

San Francisco had always been subject to fires, both accidental and deliberate. During its turbulent life arson was a weapon that had been used on many occasions. Ten years earlier fire had destroyed the Chinese settlement at Hunters Point in a dispute over coolies' taking the place of white men at half the wages, and no one even considered that it might have been accidental.

Always when fire was discussed, or I heard the raucous clatter of a fire-fighting apparatus, the image of Diedre in the flames passed before me. My terror of such a holocaust was deeply embedded in my consciousness. While most citizens of the city rushed to follow the clanging processions to the scene of the catastrophe—Allen included—my fear made me want to flee in the opposite direction. Allen said I would have to overcome this feeling, but I doubted I ever would.

Whenever possible, I accompanied Allen on his trips to City Hall and court and on errands that took him to other parts of the city. San Francisco held an unending fascination for me. The motley crowds seemed more violent than those in New York. Chinese vegetable vendors in blue cotton garments, padded slippers, and broad woven hats carried poles across their shoulders with huge baskets of produce bobbing rhythmically with their swinging gaits. On Fridays the Chinese fishermen followed in their wake, weighing silver fish on their scales as servants of the wealthy made their purchases. There were ugly aspects to the city, too. Jobless workers often gathered in muttering groups. They were like powder kegs, ready at any moment to harass any coolie who came near, and even menacing more affluent Chinese who happened to pass by. Many of the white laborers were forced to take advantage of the free meals offered from wagons dispensing charity to the poor, and resentment simmered until it came to a boil.

Allen and I were riding across outer Market Street one afternoon when our carriage was stopped by other vehicles stalled amidst a throng of people. Unreasoning panic filled me as I remembered the hanging man in another angry mob. My face must have mirrored my fear, for Allen patted my hand.

"It's all right, Shadow," he said soothingly. "It's just one of the sand-lot orators."

A man with waving arms harangued the crowd of men surrounding him. "Crocker's pets are taking the food from your families," he shouted. "Chinks are tryin' to take San Francisco for themselves. Send 'em back where they belong! The yellow scourge must go!"

The men were already in an angry mood. Shouts of "Burn 'em out" and "Push 'em into the sea!" were heard. As the size of the crowd grew, voices merged into roars that rose and fell, much like the tides beating on a shore. The bedlam increased, until Allen's coachman was hard put to quiet his team, which had grown nervous and sweaty in the July sun. Carriages jammed together, and the passengers inside sweltered in the imprisonment of the street. Irate men yelled from swaying coach windows for the horde to make way.

The shouting grew even more hostile. Triggered by more words from their leader, the crowd headed for Chinatown, carrying us along as though on a giant wave. Allen's coachmen laid about him with his long whip, causing the trapped horses to rear and plunge, but the jam only intensified. He was pulled from his seat by a bearded ruffian who jumped to the box in his place and gathered the reins. He gave a shout to his companions, and at once our carriage was overrun by rough men clinging to the roof and hanging precariously on the two steps.

Two squeezed through the windows in spite of Allen's attempt to keep them out. "Keep quiet, guv-'nor," one said gruffly. "We just want a ride."

The other leered at me, touching his cap with the heavy cudgel he carried in a parody of manners. "Yer ladyship," he said, then guffawed, spraying the odor of stale beer and rotting teeth from his open mouth.

Outside, the mob rioted unchecked through the narrow streets and alleys. They smashed windows and kicked open doors. Our tormentors left to join them. Allen dragged me after him to the coachman's seat outside, then tried to extricate our carriage from the quagmire of people.

Fires blazed in laundries so close to us that our horses reared in panic to escape. Soon we heard the clang of the firebell, and companies of firemen arrived. They vigorously pumped water on the flames until the rioters cut the hoses.

Allen handed me his knife during an interval when the horses were quiet. "If anyone tries to touch you, use it," he ordered grimly. "Wish I'd brought a gun!"

With the rioters busy in the buildings, the street became passable. Allen gradually separated us from the morass of humanity until we could travel at a reasonable rate of speed, although the horses still shied nervously, keeping him hard put to hold them in control.

There was concern in his eyes when he had time to

look at me. "Are you all right, Shadow?"

I nodded, the lump of fear in my throat making speech impossible.

"Hang on to me," he said, whipping up the horses.

I clung to his arm with one hand and clutched the rail of the seat with the other while we jounced down the cobbled street. Allen's coachman stood in the sand where he'd been dragged off the carriage and we stopped beside him.

"Take over, John," Allen said, jumping down and holding his arms to catch me. He put me inside the carriage and closed the door. "I'm sending you home, Shadow. I'll be at the mansion to see you tomorrow, if I can."

I started to protest, but he held up his hand to stop me. "The city has been on the verge of an explosion for days. It's no place for any young lady to be. Just this once, my dear, don't argue . . . please?"

He slapped the nearest horse across the rump. The carriage lunged forward, throwing me back against the seat and jouncing me around as we bounced over the stones. Flames shot into the sky behind, covering the city with the burning smell I so hated. The way grew smoother when we left Market Street, and the coachman pulled the team to a slower pace. Sounds of rioting grew more distant, and the hated smell was diluted by the salty air of the sea. At last I could sit without clutching supports, but Allen's last words still circled in my mind.

Don't argue, indeed! I hadn't been to ask to stay in that . . . that melee! I had only wanted to tell Allen to be careful. I wished he had come with me, but men always did strange things that were hard to under-

200

stand. Where was he going? To help the firemen?

Allen's father had been a volunteer when the fire departments were manned by the socially elite. He told me they had had balls and soirées and had treated each fire like a contest. There was always the race to be the first to arrive, even endangering horses and firemen alike as the teams jostled their opponents, endeavoring to be first on the scene. I shivered, wondering how men could enjoy such a catastrophe as a fire.

I didn't see Allen the next day, or the next. Word was brought from the city to Count Chauvanne that he was needed, and he rode with Tom Jordan, leaving orders that no one leave the grounds for any reason. The gates were locked, and the gateman and two grooms given rifles to use in the event that looters came from the war in San Francisco. The maids were wide-eyed with excitement at the thought of our being in a state of siege. Being kept prisoner was not at all to my liking.

I was alone with the servants and two fretting women. My aunt bewailed the state of affairs that denied her the privilege of going to her usual teas and garden club meetings. Julia was testy because David was not at her beck and call, and, like her mother, she was unused to staying home. Evidently David had business with the upheaval in San Francisco, or I was sure he would have been summoned to attend her.

Then one evening my uncle and David rode in together. They were dirty and disheveled, but in high good humor, so the war must have gone as they wished.

Count Chauvanne gallantly kissed his wife's hand.

"The uprising has been quelled, my dear. Ah, it was a fine fight!"

With a grimace, she pulled her hand away and said, "Ferd, you are dirty!"

Glancing down at himself, he seemed surprised. "So I am! Forgive me, my dear. My attire certainly seems much the worse for wear, but you must remember I've been fighting in mortal combat." He looked proud of his condition as he critically compared it to David's, then said, "Perhaps we both better clean up for dinner, eh, David?"

"By all means," Julia said. "You smell of fire and . . ." she wrinkled her nose in distaste, ". . . other things."

By now I could scarcely control myself. "What happened? Is Allen all right? Did much of the city burn?"

"What happened?" Count Chauvanne echoed. "We reestablished law and order, that's what happened. The rascals will think twice before they dare to challenge us again. As for Allen, the good counselor is now a member of the Committee of Safety. Ho! We routed the enemy and put some in the Bastille!"

"Were many people hurt?" I asked.

"Any war has casualties, my dear," my uncle answered, "but details of such happenings aren't meant for the ears of young ladies." He dismissed me as he turned to David. "Julia's right, you know. Your wardrobe is in worse condition than mine. However, I'm sure my valet can remedy the situation. Come, my boy."

"Well, now perhaps we can get on about our business," my aunt said with a sigh. "Such a to-do!

Why don't the lower classes keep their affairs less turbulent!" She turned to the hovering housekeeper. "See to dinner, Bertha. Have it served in half an hour. Meanwhile, have Chung bring champagne to the salon. Come, Julia, let's make plans for tomorrow."

I was left alone in the hall wondering if I would ever become used to their rudeness. Then I heard a horse coming up the drive, and I opened the door to see Allen dismounting.

"Shadow, my dear!" he called, then bounded up the steps as agog with excitement as my uncle. "I'm really sorry I didn't get here sooner, but events made it impossible. You can't imagine all that has happened."

"I'm glad you are safe, Allen."

"Come in, Allen, and tell us what happened," my aunt called from the salon.

Allen raised his eyebrows at her cordial tone, but laid his hat on the hall table and offered me his arm. Together we joined the countess and Julia.

"David came in looking like a pig," Julia said, glancing at Allen's fresh barbering and clean clothing. "Whatever happened to keep you all so long?"

"We eventually dispersed the mob and put out the fires they had set," Allen answered. "But then Mr. d'Arcy got busy stirring them up again. This time the crowd spread over the entire city—not just in Chinatown—and we had the devil's own time getting after them."

"Was Mr. d'Arcy the man we saw?" I asked, then could have bitten off my tongue. My aunt knew Allen took me on frequent outings, but not that we went about his business in the city.

My slip was overlooked as Allen continued. "James d'Arcy is a scoundrel!" he declared. "Mayor Bryant warned him and his laborites the police were ordered to take any measures needed to suppress further violence, but he wouldn't listen. He kept goading the rioters on to more destruction. The police couldn't handle the situation, however, so we formed the Committee of Safety to quell the revolution, and we took care of them!"

"Well, don't stop now," Julia said when he failed to continue. "What did they *do*?"

"They set fire to a waterfront warehouse containing goods imported from China and then tried to stop the firemen from dousing the flames," Allen said indignantly. "About a hundred of us went to help the police. We treed the rebels on a bluff near the warehouse." He grinned at the memory. "They threw rocks at us, if you can believe it." His grin faded. "We charged up after them, and Jack Ellery was shot in the chest. He died yesterday."

"Oh, Allen," I murmured. Jack Ellery was one of our group—an only child of doting parents, and I could imagine the mourning his passing would cause.

"Well, we have the leaders behind bars," Allen said, "and they will be prosecuted to the full extent of the law. And I'll see they are, you can be sure."

The men relived the skirmishes throughout dinner while my aunt and Julia and I smiled admiringly at their deeds. My smile was false, for I could feel only dread at the tales of burning and looting that unfolded.

In the days that followed I no longer went into the city with Allen. He said it was unsafe, and instead regaled me with the current news on his frequent visits. William Coleman, the old head of the second Vigilance Committee, was now leader of the Committee of Safety that had been formed. It was known as "Coleman's pick-axe brigade," and Allen was part of it, as were David and Count Chauvanne. It seemed to liven their routines, as they were always being called to meetings or assemblies for discussions that lasted far into the night.

The passing of summer also marked the end of the riots. Our lives settled back to normal when the committee was disbanded and our men were once more available as companions and escorts.

Suddenly it was October and my eighteenth birthday. I felt infinitely older, searching my mirror for wrinkles, although Allen constantly assured me I was still young and beautiful. He also made another proposal of marriage.

"Yes, Allen, I'll marry you," I said, and watched his face light up with pleased surprise.

I still loved David, but I knew I could never have him. Allen was dear, and I knew he loved me. Life would be infinitely more pleasant with him than it was with the Chauvannes. And safer. I couldn't forget, although I couldn't prove, Count Chauvanne's attempt at murder. It seemingly made no sense, but I wanted to be out of his reach in the event he decided to try again.

Allen was closeted with my uncle for an hour or more, then emerged with a stormy face and drew me into the garden.

"Your guardian still insists you are too young to marry. He practically accused me of being after your money!" He paced up and down, then stopped before me. "I don't give a hang for your money! You know that, don't you Shadow?"

"Yes, Allen, I know that," I answered. "There's something strange going on, I know. You wouldn't believe me when I told you my uncle tried to get rid of me, but he did. Why doesn't he want me to marry?"

"I wish I knew! Perhaps *he* wants your money." Allen's eyes met mine. "Did your father's will specify that you would receive all your money in the event you married?"

"I think that's what Mr. Arbuthnot said, but what difference would that make? Doesn't Count Chauvanne have a great deal of money of his own?" I was bewildered. My father had been wealthy, but his style of living was in no way as lavish as his sister's.

A speculative look crossed Allen's face. "Fortunes are often made and lost within a short time, Shadow. Here a man can be a pauper one day and a king the next. Or the reverse can happen," he said. "I think it might be well if I contact your Mr. Arbuthnot for a little more information. Some discreet probing into your uncle's finances might shed light on the situation also."

He offered me his arm. "Shall we go in, my dear? Perhaps I had best return to the city to start the wheels rolling. I don't give up easily, Shadow, and I intend to make you my wife before too long." He escorted me inside, making a date for the next Saturday to take me to a fall picnic that was planned. Then I watched him leave in his carriage, thinking how sedate he was in contrast with David.

The bay David rode was as wild and free as its

owner. Or rather, I amended, as David had been before he resumed his engagement to Julia. What had happened to make him so . . . so what? Listless? Unhappy? He stayed at his ranch more than he ever had, and while he had once galloped up the drive like a centaur, now he usually came in a carriage, his coachman driving the team at a discreet pace.

My heart ached for my lost love, but the hopelessness of our situation changed it from a pain I could scarcely bear to a dull throb I had learned to live with. It was much the same despair I had felt when my father would not show his love for me, no matter how often I prayed to an uncaring God.

Chapter Fifteen

My unhappiness slowed the passage of time, in spite of the constant activity of our group. Days dragged along instead of passing quickly as they had when I had first arrived in this turbulent world. We sailed on the bay in fine weather, or played at archery contests and croquet on the lawn. Horseback riding was an every-morning affair, until the rains began. When the skies poured seemingly endless torrents of water, we moved inside before crackling fireplaces for giggling sessions of gossip.

There was always one miscreant in our circle who scandalized the world by being seen in a carriage with a member of the opposite sex who shouldn't have been there. Or a new fashion in skirts or bathing dress was introduced by someone daring enough boldly to appear in it in public. At times a fresh engagement was discussed, or a broken one commiserated. Other hearts were broken besides mine, but it was small comfort.

The Committee of Safety was dispersed, but an outlaw band of vigilantes still occasionally hanged some poor wretch. To my peers these doings were as remote and unreal as the doings of witches and goblins. But to me, they were terribly real. My disgraceful conduct the evening the vigilantes had tried to hang Juan had never been mentioned, but at times I had nightmares wherein masked men dragged Juan at the end of a rope. Always just before they hanged him, I would wake in a sweat, trembling and terrified. I wondered where Juan had gone, and if he would ever return as he had promised.

On the day our picnic was planned, Allen called for me, and this time Julia and David rode in the carriage with us. Amidst inconsequential chatter we rode in the parade of carriages until we reached the beach where the event was to be held. Julia was in an unusually good mood and had refrained from any disagreeable remarks, a fact that raised my spirits considerably.

Servants had gone ahead to set up tables and benches, build a fire, and place baskets of food on top of the tables so sand wouldn't filter into the sandwiches. Then they discreetly departed, leaving us to our gala.

The ocean was much too cold for swimming, but a ball game was started and an impromptu game of tag. Allen surprised me by taking off his jacket and joining in the childish pastimes with much enjoyment. I decided to forget my unhappiness when Allen tagged me, drawing me into the game. We raced shrieking around the beach like carefree children, until I paused, laughing, to watch while I caught my breath.

Suddenly a hand pulled me behind a large dune and I fell into David's waiting arms. Before I had time to protest, his mouth covered mine in an urgent kiss.

I knew I should make him stop, but I didn't. The touch of his lips made me weak enough to melt into his embrace, while my heart beat madly with joy.

"I love you, Shadow," he whispered. "And I have to talk to you."

"We'll be missed," I said, pulling away.

"Come to the ranch when you can, Shadow . . . please?" He released my hand so I could return to the others.

"There you are!" Allen said, panting as he trotted up. "Where'd you go?"

I laughed, from sheer happiness as well as at the sight of his dishevelment. "I went to catch my breath, Allen. You had better do the same before you melt."

Perspiration streamed down his face. Sand clung to one knee of his trousers. He regarded himself ruefully. "My clients would never trust me if they saw me acting like a child, would they?" He bent to brush the sand from his clothing. "Shall we get something to drink? This is thirsty work." His grin was admiring. "You are beautifully rosy, but I'm most likely just red."

My pulse pounded from David's kiss, and I went with Allen to the refreshment table feeling like a cheat. Why was life so complicated? I wanted to love Allen . . . I did love him . . . but I wasn't *in* love with him.

But David . . . ah, a shiver ran through me when I thought of him. A certain wildness inside him called to a like feeling I hadn't known I possessed until he kissed me. To gallop beside him while the salty spray rose from our horses' hooves! That was sheer delight. We had had such fun together, and when we were together he had looked so happy.

I sighed in frustration. Why wouldn't he break with Julia and claim me openly? What had Julia done to him? More likely, what had her father done to him? It was all such a mixed-up puzzle!

"Why so quiet, Shadow?" Allen asked, handing me a glass of punch.

"Oh . . . I was just thinking."

"What about?"

"Oh, us . . . and what a lovely day this is . . . you know." I tasted the punch and found it refreshing. "Did you write Mr. Arbuthnot yet?"

He nodded, glancing at our noisy playmates. "We had better not talk here. I found out something interesting on the other subject we discussed, too."

"Oh?" That would be my uncle's finances, I decided, dropping the matter. A plate of sandwiches was offered. Allen and I each took one, then joined in the general chatter going round the table.

We had no chance to break away from our companions before the evening ended, and I didn't see Allen for several days after. David's words stayed in my mind, pushing thoughts of my uncle's finances into obscurity.

At the first opportunity, I slipped out one morning and rode my mare toward David's ranch. My uncle had not relented on our riding alone, so a groom accompanied me.

When we arrived at the hacienda, I said, "Please wait here."

Before I could knock at the door, David opened it

and smiled a welcome. "Shadow! Come in, come in. . . ."

Shawohanee placed cups on the table, then discreetly disappeared.

"I can only stay a minute, David," I said breathlessly. "You said you had something to tell me?"

He reached to take me into his arms, but I eluded him. "You mustn't, David."

"Why not? I love you, Shadow . . . only you."

"But you are going to marry Julia, aren't you?" I held my breath, waiting for his answer.

"I have to," he said savagely. "Ferd is going to announce our wedding date at Thanksgiving dinner. We're to be married Christmas day."

"What do you mean . . . you *have* to? What has my uncle done to force you into such a marriage?" My mind seethed with speculations, for I thought only women were forced into marriages of convenience. What would force a man into such a predicament? And then I began to learn the truth.

"If I don't go through with it, I'll lose my ranch," David said, and there was desperation in his tone. A sudden burst of anger showed when he smashed a cup against the brick fireplace. "Damn!" he muttered.

Then he came and held both my hands in his as he said, "I don't love Julia, Shadow. I haven't loved anyone but you since the first time I saw you. You know that, don't you? You do believe me . . . you must!"

"How will you lose your ranch, David?"

"Ferd lent me a great deal of money in return for a mortgage he can recall any time he wants. If I don't marry Julia . . . well, he'll take everything I own."

There was a pleading look in his eyes that made me want to melt into his arms, but this time I restrained myself. My uncertainty as to how things stood between us must be dissolved once and for all.

"Does your ranch mean more to you than me, David?" I asked slowly.

A groan emerged from his lips. "No, of course not! But we couldn't be happy if we were poor. You are used to fine clothing and servants and a mansion to live in. I couldn't bear seeing you do without everything you've had all your life. Oh, Shadow . . . I want to marry you more than anything in the world, but I can't if I'm poor!"

"Have you told my uncle this?"

"Yes, I have! He said that Julia wants me, and that seems to settle it as far as he is concerned. He has always gotten her everything she ever wanted! Even if I broke with Julia, though, he wouldn't allow you to marry me. He made that very clear. Why is he so set against your marrying?"

"I don't know, David. Count Chauvanne has made it most clear to me, too, and that is surprising, since he's also made it known that he prefers me not to be a member of his household. Allen said it might be that he needs my inheritance. I'm under his guidance until I reach the age of twenty-one or marry, and he can refuse to let me marry anyone, if he wishes."

David drew me into his arms. "It's all so hopeless," he said drearily. "I need you, little Shadow. I need you so much. Let me love you now, my darling. Once we are one, even if I'm forced to marry Julia, it won't make any difference with us. We'll have each other."

My blood turned to ice when I realized what David

was saying. I wrenched myself from his arms. "You
. . . you . . . you cad!" I sputtered. "Allen was right
about you!" I struck him across the face with the crop
that dangled from my wrist. "I never want to see you
again, Mr. Roberts!"

He stared at me in hurt shock as his hand rose to
feel the welt my crop had left on his face.

The sight of his damaged face made tears come to
my eyes, and I whirled and ran from the hacienda. I
was almost blinded by the time I reached the horses
and the groom helped me into my saddle. Without
waiting for him, I kicked the mare into a run and fled
sightlessly in the direction of the mansion. What
matter if she plunge us off a cliff or into a tree? I
wanted to die!

From that day on I avoided David as much as
possible. His offer of illicit love had so shocked my
Puritan senses that I was unable to feel anything save
shame. He must think me a common woman indeed
to have made it.

Thanksgiving Day was the occasion for an unusually large gathering at the Chauvanne house. David
had told me the reason, of course, but it was only
revealed to the other guests when Count Chauvanne
rose to propose a toast before the general dispersal at
the end of the meal.

"Ladies and gentlemen, it is my pleasure to announce that my daughter, Julia, will marry David
Roberts on Christmas Day!" He raised his glass of
champagne. "Shall we drink to the happy couple?"

Amidst excited chatter and congratulations,
David's gaze met mine for an instant before I looked
away. The red welt had faded from his face and he

214

looked his usual suave self, but in the seconds our eyes had met I had noted the pleading of his cause, and this even as he accepted congratulations and responded to the laughing banter surrounding him and his bride-to-be.

Desolation filled me. Despite my outrage at his proposal, a faint hope still remained that he would decide to defy my uncle. So long as he was unmarried, there was still a chance for him to claim me.

"I wish we could make it a double ceremony," Allen said in my ear. "You would make a beautiful bride."

The salon had been turned into a ballroom merely by removing most of the furniture. A small orchestra played in the alcove at one end.

Allen led me through the first dance, then whirled me into the hall. "Let's go for a walk before I lose you to your hovering admirers," he suggested.

I nodded, accepted my cloak from a maid. Any excuse to get away from the sight of Julia in her triumph was welcome. The garden looked beautiful, and the velvety lawn was soft underfoot. I glanced at the ivy climbing to the roof of the manor and wondered if the old countess watched from behind her heavy green screen. Perhaps she was missing the gorgeous day in its entirety, if she were lying drugged in that dismal room.

"I have a present for you," Allen said, drawing a small box from his pocket, "that I hope you will accept. Your engagement ring, Shadow." He slipped a huge diamond on my finger, then pressed a kiss on my hand.

It was a beautiful ring, sparkling with a mysterious life of its own, and it made me miserable. "Allen . . .

oh, Allen . . . I can't marry you!" Sobs I couldn't suppress shook me as I removed the ring and handed it to him, saying, "I d-don't l-love you, Allen." And then my voice became a wail. "I w-want to, but I c-can't!"

He gathered me into his arms, patting my back and letting my tears seep into his jacket. "Now, now . . . please don't cry, my darling . . . sh, sh." He drew me closer, murmuring soft endearments into my hair until my crying stopped. Then he pulled a handkerchief from his pocket and dabbed at my eyes. "There . . . now blow your nose," he ordered.

While I was blowing and mopping he put the ring back into its box. He waited until I returned his handkerchief, then placed the box in my hand, folding my fingers around it. "I want you to keep it anyway," he said. "You'll get over him, you know. Once he's married to Julia, you'll forget all about him. You'll have to, Shadow. I'll wait . . . I told you I would wait forever, didn't I?"

A flush burned my cheeks. "How did you know?" I whispered. Had I been that obvious in my infatuation? Was everyone laughing at my mooning over David?

"I know because I love you, my dear, and not from anything you've done," Allen said, brushing a stray curl from my forehead. "Don't look so stricken—you haven't given yourself away."

"I'm such a fool," I said angrily. "Oh, why do you put up with me?"

"I love you."

Allen's simple answer supported me through the wedding preparations in which we were engulfed. The entire household had the event as its target, with plans to decorate the mansion to resemble a bower of flowers. Julia's gown must be the most expensive and elaborate ever contrived. She and my aunt made countless trips to the city, amassing enough jewelry and garments for two lifetimes.

Through it all I forced myself to smile when it was necessary. Allen came to the mansion as often as he could to stand staunchly beside me or escort me to any of the countless parties planned for the happy couple. He became my buffer against David.

When David sought me out, Allen steered me expertly away, doing it in such a manner as not to embarrass anyone. He grew more dear, but my treacherous heart still yearned for David, much as I had yearned for my father during the years at Miss Brigham's school.

By Christmas Eve everyone was exhausted from the round of parties, but we attended the Crocker Ball, as usual. It was too much a coveted privilege to be passed over lightly, so our entire group rallied to attend.

Everyone expected me to choose Allen as my escort, for by now we were considered a pair. Allen allowed other men to dance with me, but when David came to claim a dance, Allen appeared at my side to whisk me away.

Julia glittered under an array of jewels. She seemed blissfully sure that David was as happy as she, and even smiled at me. "Dear Shadow . . . I hope you'll be as happy as I someday," she said warmly. "Just imagine! We're going to Paris on our honeymoon! The shops there must be wonderful, and there are so many of them!"

Allen suggested we leave early. "Since you are one of the bridesmaids, my dear, you should get some rest. I do believe you're about partied out."

"Do I look dreadful?" I asked in alarm. "Oh, dear, I just knew I was getting old!"

He laughed . . . the nice chuckly sound I knew so well. "Shadow, you look gorgeous, and as young as a child of eighteen should look, and I love you." Nevertheless, he returned me to the Chauvannes' home and didn't ask to come in.

"My, you're home early," Carlie remarked. "But then, it's just as well. Tomorrow will be a busy day. If you have your proper rest, you'll be prettier than the bride, Miss Shadow."

I dismissed her as soon as I could. The dismal feeling of wanting to cry filled me, and I wanted to weep alone. Tomorrow was David's wedding day! My hope was a faint one now, but after he and Julia were married, I would have no hope at all. Oh, David, David . . . how can you do this?

The night seemed endless. Sleep would not come. I tossed and turned, pummeling the pillow, but to no avail. Every creak and rattle was unusually loud. I heard the Chauvannes return and their chatter as my aunt and uncle bid Julia goodnight. When everything was quiet, I imagined stealthy footsteps and chided myself for my childishness. At long last I fell asleep, welcoming the oblivion that erased all thought.

Carlie woke me next morning with a cheerie, "Merry Christmas, Miss Shadow."

My heart was heavy and a headache throbbed against my temples, but I determined to ignore my discomfort. "Merry Chri . . ."

A shriek rent the air! With a startled glance at me, Carlie ran out toward the sound. Another scream followed, and another and another. I grabbed my wrapper, tying the sash as I ran. The din came from Julia's room, and when I arrived at the open door, I froze in horror.

The scene before me was like one from Dante's Inferno. Shrieking women supplied background to carnage and death.

Julia lay face up on a blood-soaked bed. The handle of a knife pointed ceilingward from a place on her skin that could only cover her heart. Her eyes stared blankly at a horror only she had witnessed. Julia was dead!

Chapter Sixteen

"Mon Dieu!" Count Chauvanne exclaimed as he brushed by me. He pushed the cluster of servants aside so he could stare down at his daughter. *"Mon Dieu . . ."* His voice trailed into an unintelligible monotone as he stood helplessly gazing down at the bloody havoc.

"Come away, Miss Shadow," Carlie whispered, drawing me into the hall.

I followed her numbly, unable to believe what I had seen. Julia dead? Why? Why would anyone kill her? Behind me an anguished shriek announced my aunt's arrival. Then Carlie closed the door of my room and the pandemonium outside was muffled.

"Sit down, Miss Shadow, before you fall."

I sank to the bed, shaking knees about to betray me. I clasped my hands together to stop their trembling, and all the while I saw the same dreadful sight.

"You are white as a sheet," Carlie exclaimed. "You aren't going to faint, are you?"

Slowly, I shook my head. "No . . ." The word came in a whisper through a throat too dry to function properly. I would not faint if I could help it.

Carlie poured a glass of water from the carafe and held it for me to drink. Then shock made my shudder and a sudden chill made my teeth chatter. "Wh-what sh-should I d-do, Carlie?" I asked.

"You'd best get under the covers," she answered.

Her practical voice and brisk manner made me ashamed of my weakness. I straightened, and long-gone trumpets sounded in my mind as I took a deep, steadying breath. "I'd better get dressed, Carlie. Perhaps I can be of some help."

My bridesmaid's gown hung limply beside the dressing table, and the sight of it renewed the shock of seeing Julia bathed in blood. I closed my eyes so I would not see it, and when I opened them again, Carlie had whisked the dress away.

I was soon presentable in a sensible gray merino, but as I started to leave, Carlie stopped me. "Miss Shadow . . . hadn't we best stay close together? I mean, may I go with you?" She opened the door and glanced nervously into the hall. "I'm afraid," she whispered.

Julia's death had shocked me almost to insensibility. I hadn't even thought about the murderer who had done the deed. Could he still be lurking in the mansion? Had Julia been slain because she was Julia, or was a madman loose for whom any victim would serve?

Carlie's frightened eyes made my decision. "Perhaps you're right. Until the mystery is cleared, it would be better not to be alone. Shall we go down?"

We descended to a house hushed by tragedy too immense for even whispered discussion. Carlie peered into each corner and doorway, and I confess my own eyes kept busy assuring me no one was following us.

Bertha was in the morning room. After a glance that sent Carlie to the kitchen, she asked, "Will you have something to eat, Miss Shadow?"

"Just coffee, please."

Her face was ravaged from grief and her eyes were red from weeping. Julia had treated her as callously as she had the rest of the world, but the tragic death had evidently affected her deeply.

When the housekeeper returned with a steaming silver pot in one hand and a cup and saucer in the other, I noted her trembling hands. "Sit down, Bertha. Have some coffee with me," I suggested.

Tears filled her eyes as she sank into a chair. "Oh, Miss Shadow, who could have done such a thing? She was my child more than she was theirs!" Her reddened eyes looked accusingly from her careworn face. "They were always too busy! I took care of Miss Julia. I saw she was washed and fed. You and Miss Murphy thought she was so awful the evening you arrived, but she wasn't. Not really. When your parents don't care about you . . . well, Miss Julia just pretended she didn't care either." Wild weeping shook her shoulders as she buried her face in her hands.

"Oh, Bertha . . . we really didn't think she was awful," I said, rather untruthfully, but in a spirit of kindness. "You mustn't give way like this."

The idea of Julia's parents not caring for her was one I hadn't taken into consideration. They lavished her with expensive trappings, but perhaps they had been niggardly with their affections. If your mother was alive . . . and she didn't have time for you . . .

well, that would be worse than not having a mother at all. Perhaps Carmelita was closer to me than Julia's mother had been to her, even though Elizabeth was alive and Carmelita dead. It was a dreadful thought, but one that I realized could be the reason for Julia's behavior.

I glanced up from the sobbing woman when a maid peered into the room. "Bring another cup, please." I filled my own cup and placed it before the housekeeper. "Come now, Bertha," I said firmly. "Stop crying . . . please? There is no way we can help Julia now, but perhaps we can assist in finding her killer."

My own words made a finger of fear trace a cold line down my spine. Whoever had murdered Julia . . . could he still be here in the mansion? Had it been some prowler looking for jewelry? Then a thought gave me pause. Had anyone checked to see if things were missing?

Bertha's tears stopped as her pale eyes stared at me. "The killer . . ." she said uncertainly. "Who killed Miss Julia? And . . . and why? Why in the world would anyone kill Miss Julia?" Bewilderment replaced her grief.

The maid brought another cup and poured it full. Her eyes were curious, but I dismissed her with a thank you. I urged Bertha to drink some coffee, then took several sips to set an example.

"Has Mr. David been notified, Bertha?"

She sniffled and blew her nose before answering. "Tom went right away, but Mr. David wasn't at his hacienda. His stable boy said they didn't know where he had gone."

Once again the finger of fear did its work. Where

was David on the morning of what should have been his wedding? Why wasn't he home getting dressed for the occasion? Did he already know Julia was dead? Had *he* killed her?

I remembered stealthy footsteps in the night that I had dismissed as a trick of my imagination. Had they been real? Did the footsteps belong to David as he crept into the mansion to murder the bride he didn't want?

Then I tried to dismiss the thought. David wasn't a murderer! Please, God, let it not be David who did such a dreadful thing. He was being forced to marry Julia, but he wouldn't kill her to stop the marriage, would he?

The image of Juan with a rope around his neck came unbidden into my mind. If David had been one of the masked men deciding Juan's fate, he would have voted to hang him. Juan had knocked him down. And it was David's horse Juan had taken. However, it was probably easy to go along with a mob of blood-thirsty men after they'd been brought to fever pitch. That was a much different thing from a cold-blooded stabbing.

David was weak. He had allowed Count Chauvanne to blackmail him into a marriage he didn't want. His illicit proposal to me showed a shameful lack of character, but could a man such as this have the necessary courage to plan and commit the murder of a girl he once had loved? It seemed doubtful. Prayers again circled in my mind that David not be involved. In spite of his faults, I still loved him. A tiny voice seemed to whisper, "Now he's free," but I refused to listen, cringing inside at the unworthiness of the thought.

The sheriff and his deputy arrived, coming with hats held carefully in hand. Chung brought them into the morning room, looking a question at Bertha. Like the good housekeeper she was, Bertha pulled herself together and rose to greet the men.

"Would you be wanting to see Count Chauvanne?" she asked.

The sheriff harrumphed as he cleared his throat. "Well, er . . . where's the . . . er . . . ah, victim?"

A moan escaped Bertha, then was quickly stifled. "I'll show you," she said. "This way, please."

"Mrs. Darwell . . ."

She stopped at the sheriff's words. "What is it, Sheriff Thompson?"

"We can find our way," he said gently. "Perhaps you would rather wait here?"

"No!" she said sharply. "Come this way."

They left me alone with my thoughts. *Where* was David? If he didn't know Julia was dead, wouldn't he be arriving soon? Oh, David, please, please come. I didn't want him to be the killer—I wouldn't be able to bear it.

Chung ushered Allen in, and he came quickly to my side. "Are you all right, Shadow? Good God! What a terrible thing for you to see!" He pulled me to my feet and held me close. "My dear, my very dear, what other ghastly sights will you behold before I can take you away from here?"

I sighed as I extricated myself from his arms. "I'm all right, Allen. Only . . ."

"Only what?" he demanded. "What can I do to help?"

"David is missing," I said miserably.

"What?"

"David is missing," I repeated. When Tom went to get him, he wasn't at his ranch. Chico said he didn't know where he was."

"Perhaps he is on his way here," Allen said slowly. "He might have gone for an early morning ride, or perhaps he was too excited to sleep."

"No . . ." Turning, I walked to the window and stared out. The morning was foggy and grey, more suitable for a funeral than a wedding, I thought dismally. "Will you find him, Allen?" I swung around to face him. "Will you go find David for me . . . please?"

His eyes searched my face with unspoken questions I knew couldn't be answered. Then, with a nod, he was gone. I heard his voice in the hall and realized the sheriff and my uncle were there, but I couldn't hear what they were saying, and somehow, I was too weary to care.

Bertha came in, her face still a tragic mask. "Will there be anything else, Miss Shadow?"

"No, thank you." Then, as she started to leave, I asked, "Do they know who did it yet?"

She stopped, and I saw tears fill her eyes. "No . . . only, it had to be some sneak thief, I know. Nobody who knew Miss Julia would stab her to death. Nobody!" Her mouth closed stubbornly, defying the world to say her child was unloved.

"How is my aunt taking it, Bertha? Would it help if I went to her?"

"She's taken to her bed, Miss Shadow. Dr. Dijon will be here soon to take care of her." Bitter lines formed when she added, "Now that Miss Julia is dead, she's a terribly bereaved mother!"

"Oh, Bertha . . ." I said lamely, "you must not say things like that."

"Yes, ma'am," she answered, and left.

With a sigh of worry I forced myself to return to my room, weariness making me forget the fear of being alone in the shadowy hall. Perhaps I would be the most help by keeping out of the way.

Carlie was absent, so I lay atop the sea-green coverlet trying to sort the events of the morning from the happenings that were purely of my imagination. Julia's death was real, that was sure. That I had heard ghostly footsteps in the night was not so sure. Exhaustion drew merciful blinds over the horrible scene and closed my eyes in blessed sleep.

"Miss Shadow! Miss Shadow!" Carlie's voice brought me from the dreamless sleep that nurtured me. It took several moments to realize where I was, and then I saw it was dark outside. How long had I slept?

"You haven't eaten a thing this whole terrible day, Miss Shadow. Aren't you getting hungry? It's almost time for dinner. Wouldn't you like to go down and eat?"

Dinnertime already? I thought drowsily, then came fully awake. Had Allen returned? Was David here?

"Has Mr. DeJung returned, Carlie? I wanted to be waked when he arrived, but you weren't here to tell when I lay down." My voice was peevish, and Carlie looked alarmed.

"He brought Mr. David in a little while ago. He said not to wake you, that he had to get back to the city right away." She wrung her hands. "I thought you needed sleep."

"Is Mr. David still here?" My heart had quickened at her words, and I was strangely breathless.

She nodded. "I think so . . . unless Count Chauvanne *killed* him."

"What? What are you saying, Carlie?"

"Oh, I didn't mean killed, exactly. It's just that the count got so mad when he saw Mr. David. He was . . . well, er, well, Mr. David was drunk. Mr. Allen helped him into the parlor before he left, and Mr. David couldn't even walk by himself, he was that tipsy."

"Get me another gown, Carlie."

Carlie went to do my bidding, still chattering. "The count made such a racket in the parlor, it was dreadful. He yelled so loud, I was sure it would wake you." She poked her head out of the closet. "Which gown do you want, Miss Shadow? There are no gray ones."

"Is the black presentable?" Sarah had packed my funeral clothing, although I had decided not to prolong my period of mourning for my father. Now I had need of it again.

She shook out the folds as she brought my black gown from the rear of the wardrobe. "With Miss Julia just carried dead from the house, I thought it was awful to make so much noise," she said virtuously. She shook the gown again and eyed it critically. "Shall I get the iron to press this?"

"There isn't time, Carlie. It will have to do as is. Now help me into it." I wished Allen had waited, but at least I could find out what had happened from

David.

"I'll go with you," Carlie said quickly.

"The house has been searched," I said impatiently. "No prowler was found, but if there was one, he's gone now. Wait for me here, Carlie." I saw her glance nervously at the shadowed corners and added, "Wedge a chair under the knob, if you are frightened."

The hall was deserted when I emerged and went down the long stairway. Evidently the servants had decided to wait out the storm in the kitchen. Light beamed from the parlor door and angry voices rose and fell inside. I peeked inside.

David stood facing my uncle with clenched fists. "I didn't kill Julia! How can you even think such a thing? I have told you and told you—I didn't do it!"

"Even if you did, it won't do you any good," my uncle said with a sneer. "You will never marry my niece, sir, never! Tomorrow I will begin foreclosure proceedings on your property, and you can go back to being the unknown ragpicker you were before you so mysteriously came into a fortune. I hope you starve! Why my daughter would pick a . . . a *bastard* like you, I'll never know."

David's hand lashed out across my uncle's face. The noise as flesh met flesh echoed like a shot against the high ceiling. Then David's voice came as cold as ice as he said, "You will apologize for that, sir!"

Count Chauvanne staggered, then drew himself erect. "I will apologize with a sword, you drunkard! That is, if you are man enough to meet me on a field of honor."

"I'll meet you," David said between clenched teeth.

He strode toward the door, then paused. "My second will call on you in the morning. Any time and place you name will suit me just fine."

I had stayed in the shadows during the exchange, but now I slid past the lighted doorway and let myself out into the night. I had to see David. I had to!

He emerged like an angry bull and was down the steps and part way up the drive before I caught up with him. "David, wait for me," I gasped.

He whirled around. "Shadow? Where did you come from?" He noticed my cloakless condition and slipped off his jacket. "Here, let me put this around you before you get a chill. We can't have you getting sick again."

I wrapped my arms around him while he was arranging the coat and held him close. "David . . . oh, David, where have you been?"

"I'm not fit to be near you," he growled. "I need a bath and a shave and clothing that doesn't stink of whiskey." A stubble of beard covered his chin and cheeks. The silky mustache looked stringy and he did smell quite rank.

"Where have you been, David? Oh, David, where were you last night?"

He stared at me. "You, too?" he asked bitterly. "Do you think I killed Julia? Oh, Shadow, why would I? I had already decided not to marry her."

"You had?" I felt foolishly happy. "Oh, David, when did you decide?"

"While I was getting into the shape I'm in," he said. "I started drinking to get enough courage to get married, and instead, I found guts enough not to get married, so I just stayed away." He struggled helplessly. "I wish I had come back and faced Julia with my decision, but then I try to avoid the difficult things in life." He turned and walked faster toward the iron gates.

"Wait, David! Oh, slow down for a minute. Are you going to your ranch? Where's your horse?" I had to run to catch up with him.

He slowed his pace, but kept walking. "Your beau brought me out here. I don't suppose it occurred to him I would have to walk home."

"You don't have to, David. I'll order a horse brought for you." I clutched his arm. "Come back with me."

"You'll get your hands dirty on my sleeve," he said, stopping as a smile twitched at his mouth. "I'm surprised you even speak to me after all I've done."

"If you didn't kill Julia, everything will be all right, David. You didn't kill her, did you?"

His smile vanished. "No, I did not murder Julia," he said, stressing each word. "Ferd thinks I did because I told him I didn't want to marry her, but he's wrong."

"Well then, why not prove your innocence? You were surely drinking with somebody, weren't you? All you need do is have them say so."

A sigh came from deep within him. "I was drinking with strangers, Shadow. From one bar to another down on the wharves. Even if they could see me through the smoke, nobody remembers strangers they drink with."

"If you can find them, perhaps you can jog their memories. Why not go find some of the men you saw in the bars?" I asked, grasping at straws in my desire

231

to help.

"Oh, Shadow, I was so drunk I couldn't tell you whether or not Gabriel was standing next to me. I don't even remember the places I visited."

I was quiet as doubts returned. Was it possible? Had he come to the manor and stabbed Julia without recalling he had murdered her? I strained to remember the stealthy footsteps, then silently chided myself for being so foolish. Didn't I know that David was no killer? Was my faith so shallow that I wavered at each hint of trouble?

"Let's go to the stables, David. It would be better not to bother Count Chauvanne again," I said, knowing it would be *much* better. "Are you really going to duel with him?"

"I am if I can remember how to wave a sword," he said grimly. "I haven't had one in hand since my fencing lessons at school. Ferd has killed two men in duels, so after tomorrow my troubles will most likely be over."

My heart plunged at his words. It was to be expected that Count Chauvanne was an accomplished duelist. He would use all the skill he could muster to kill the man he thought had slain his daughter, if not because of love for her, for reasons of honor. Another reason could be to keep David from marrying me. *Why?* Was he in need of money and using my inheritance for himself?

We reached the stables, but none of the grooms were in sight. "Why don't you just saddle one of the horses yourself, David? It will be faster than hunting up a hand."

"I don't want to be a horse thief as well as a

suspected murderer," he said glumly. "I'll go check the tack room to see if there's a groom there."

He returned with a stable boy behind him. "Tell him I'm borrowing a horse, Shadow. That way we'll have a witness to the fact I didn't steal one."

"Oh, David! Saddle a horse for Mr. Roberts, please."

David leaned against a stall. "For one so young, princess, you give orders as to the manner born. But then you know who your parents were, which is something I suppose I will never know." One eyebrow raised quizzically. "Your uncle was right, you know. I probably am a bastard."

"Don't say that, David," I said in protest. "You surely know something about your parents, even if they died when you were very young."

"But I don't princess. The first thing I remember is the school I grew up in. Good old Hopkins Grammar School in New Haven, Connecticut." A wry smile crossed his face. "Whoever left me there must have been very wealthy. The headmaster and his wife kept me under their wings, mostly to keep the flow of monthly payments coming. I tried every way I knew to find out who was making them, but they paid for a screen of anonymity that was impenetrable."

"No wonder it bothers you so much," I said sympathetically. "You don't even know if they're alive, do you?"

He shook his head. "I don't know if my birth embarrassed a wealthy woman or a rich man, but you can bet it was one or the other. I've always felt I must have been illegitimate or I wouldn't have been dumped while I was just a baby. Until I was three or four years old I thought the headmaster and his wife were my parents. Then they told me they weren't, but that is all they would tell me. I ran away when I was fifteen and came out here."

"But surely you know who left you a great deal of money when you were nineteen," I said, then felt a blush rising as I remembered I had been gossiping with Carlie when I learned this bit of information.

David laughed, tracing the warm red in my cheeks with a gentle finger. "So you've been talking about me!"

He stirred restlessly, peering into the gloom to see what was keeping the stable boy, then he resumed.

"Well, I don't know who my benefactor was. I was working on a ranch when a little old man came out in a carriage one day and said he was an attorney. He handed me a bank draft for ten thousand dollars. All he would say about it was that it had been left to me by a person who wished to remain anonymous."

"That's a lot of money, David! It's a fortune! How ever did you get so deeply in debt to Count Chauvanne? Why in the world would you borrow so much money?" I paused as a thought struck me, then said, "Why don't you force the attorney who gave you to money to tell you who it came from?"

He held up both hands. "Slow down, princess. One question at a time. I did my best to get information from the attorney but he absolutely refused to divulge his client's name. He wouldn't even tell me his own name. Anyhow, what's the difference? Maybe I'm better off not knowing."

"Oh, no, David, everybody should know their forebears. It's . . . well, it's strengthening." I thought of Carmelita and how many times just knowing she was my mother had given me courage.

"Well, maybe," he conceded. "As to how Ferd has me in his clutches, well, I just wanted too big a piece of the world too fast. If I had used the money to buy a small ranch, then earned the price before I tried to expand, I wouldn't be in such a mess as I am in now."

A stable boy led a saddled horse to where we stood and David straightened. He raised my hand to brush a kiss across it. "It's nothing for you to worry about, Shadow. As I said, after tomorrow, or whatever day Ferd chooses to duel, my troubles will most likely be over."

"Oh, don't say that, David . . . *please*. Dueling is against the law. When Count Chauvanne cools down, he'll surely call it off."

I started to remove his jacket, but stopped when David shook his head. "Leave it on until we get to the house. It's too chilly for you to be out dressed so lightly."

"You'd better not go to the manor, David. If my uncle sees you he'll just get angry again."

He led the horse outside, offering me his arm. "I can't let you run around by yourself when there's a killer on the loose. I know this isn't the time to say this, with Julia just dead, but I'll always love you, no matter what happens. I want you to make sure one of the servants is always with you, wherever you go. Will you promise you will?"

I nodded.

When we reached the veranda David took both my hands in his. "Your uncle has a streak of killer in him, Shadow. Oh, I don't mean he killed Julia. It's just that I've seen a sort of madness gleam in his eyes at times, and I know he can be more ruthless than most men. I can't believe your father would have put you in his care if he had known him. He dominates your aunt, you know, even though it might seem the opposite. You must guard yourself while you are in his house. There's a kind of . . . oh, evilness around him."

Light from the door shone around us as Chung opened it. I ran quickly up the steps, then turned and watched David gallop down the drive. His words brought a chill that had nothing to do with the cool night air.

The dining room was darkened, as was the parlor. It was too late for supper, but I was hungry. I ordered Chung to have a tray sent to my room before I went up the long staircase.

The warning from the old countess returned to haunt me. Her sibilant whisper echoed in my mind. "Leave here before you are killed!" I imagined the tiny, bony hand clamped over my mouth.

But Julia had died—not I. A shudder rippled through me as I recalled the look of horror on her face. Had she seen the evil I had been warned against? Would I be the next victim?

I looked fearfully at the dim shadows wavering in the hall, then ran panic-stricken into my room.

Chapter Seventeen

Sheriff Thompson returned the next morning. His questioning determined that nothing was missing; therefore, it was not robbery that had motivated Julia's murder. It was unthinkable that any member of the family should be suspect, so the sheriff was forced to leave with the crime still unsolved.

Allen came to see Count Chauvanne and they were closeted in the study for quite some time. Since my uncle had given orders they were not to be disturbed, not even a maid could enter, and I was left wondering what was happening.

When at last Allen emerged, he asked if he could talk to me. I wrapped a shawl around my shoulders so we could walk in the garden for privacy.

"You're looking rested, Shadow," he observed. "I was afraid you would go into shock over the gruesome events, but your uncle tells me you slept most of yesterday."

"I'm fine," I said impatiently. "What were you two talking about for so long a time? What have you found out that I should know?"

He pulled my hand through his arm while we walked, and seemed to be considering his words before he said, "Well, my dear, it seems as though there is to be a duel between your uncle and David. I was asked to be David's second, so I came to talk to Count Chauvanne. I did my best to persuade him to stop this madness, but I'm afraid I didn't succeed."

"Allen, you must stop it! David said my uncle has killed two men dueling. Oh, Allen, he won't have a chance against someone so skilled. Can't you do something?"

He stopped walking and faced me. "You are really in love with him, aren't you, my dear?"

"I can't help it, Allen . . . I really can't."

"Don't cry, Shadow. I suppose I knew all along you would never marry me. Damn!" He startled himself with his own swearing and hastily begged my pardon before he said ruefully, "I should let Count Chauvanne kill the rascal." Then he scowled and said angrily. "The death of David Roberts would benefit the race of man!"

The savageness of his voice surprised me. This was a side of Allen I hadn't known existed. When he was at my side he had always been polite and gentle, but then all men had a streak of brute in their makeup, didn't they?

"How can you say that?" I asked, then decided to try a different tack. "Dueling is against the law, Allen, isn't it? Please . . . won't you stop them?" I pleaded. "If Count Chauvanne kills David in a silly duel, it will be like murdering him."

He sighed, and his anger had dissolved. "Men settle arguments with their guns every day, my dear.

That, too, is illegal, but it doesn't stop their doing it. Out here there are too many people and too little law, so people are more inclined to take the law into their own hands. It is a situation that can only be remedied by strengthening the forces of law and order, and in time this will be done."

He resumed walking, although this time he did not pull my hand through his arm. "What I really wanted to talk to you about was something else, Shadow. There was no robbery connected with your cousin's death, and this means there's a killer still around. Apparently there was no motive for her murder, so some sort of madman could be lurking on the premises."

Again Allen paused to face me. "I feel you're in danger, although why, I do not know. As long as you remain in this house I am uneasy about your safety. I spoke to your uncle about your visiting my aunt for a time until this mystery is cleared up. He agreed, although I must say it was quite reluctantly. There's something strange going on, I'm sure." He looked at me expectantly. "Well, my dear Miss St. George, will you pay my aunt an extended visit?"

"You've very kind, Allen, and I'm sure I would love your aunt, but I can't leave until this matter is cleared up. If someone wants to kill me, he could do it just as well when I'm at your aunt's home, or in the carriage, or almost anywhere as easily as here. Besides, I intend to do what I can to stop my uncle from dueling with David."

He shook his head in despair. "You are the most stubborn . . . well, that's beside the point. Perhaps I can persuade you another way. Your Juan has returned to San Francisco. Do you wish to see him?"

"Oh, yes!" I exclaimed. "Why didn't you bring him with you?"

Allen studied my face. "A lot of changes can happen in a year, Shadow. Your friend is quite different from the boy who walked off into the night after we removed the rope from his neck."

"Different? How?" Juan was Juan and always had been, since our childhood. How could he be different?

"Well . . . perhaps I had better start at the beginning. Johnny Monterro came to see me yesterday. He asked about you, of course, but he also wanted to engage me as his attorney to manage his affairs."

I stared at him in surprise. *"Johnny?"*

A chuckle shook him. "Your friend is thoroughly Americanized now, I can assure you. Apparently, he's been back for several weeks living in San Francisco. I doubt very much you would recognize him."

"What do you mean?"

"Mr. Monterro is now a very wealthy man, my dear. He is one of the few successful gamblers I know."

"Juan?" I realized my mouth was gaping in disbelief and hastily closed it. "But . . . but . . ." I sputtered.

Allen led me to a bench. "Perhaps we had better sit down, Shadow." He sighed, but there was laughter lurking in his eyes. "I most likely have another of your suitors to contend with, although he's apparently almost afraid of you."

"Juan is afraid of me?" I asked incredulously.

"All men are afraid of good women," Allen said. "Didn't you know? And Monterro has you firmly planted on one of the highest pedestals I have ever seen a man imagine."

"You're making fun of me," I said crossly. "Now stop it and tell me about Juan."

"You will have to start calling him Johnny or he won't know you're talking to him." Laughter was still in Allen's eyes, and I remembered the night he and Juan had guffawed so boisterously at the spectacle I'd made of myself. Then he continued, "He has grown larger, or perhaps it just seems that way. Wealthy men have a way of appearing bigger than they really are."

"How did he get rich?"

"In the silver fields in Nevada, and don't ask me *how* rich. He's my client, and I can't divulge anything he's told me."

"Did he *mine*?"

Allen cocked his head to one side and considered the matter. "You might say that, I suppose," he said slowly. "He let the others do the digging, of course, then separated them from their silver over a gaming table."

"Juan is a *gambler*?"

"Johnny," he corrected mildly. "Yes, I would say that. At least he plays the part. He wears an expensive black suit, complete with silver watch chain across his middle and silver spurs on his heels."

Then his voice grew more animated. "He rides the most beautiful black stallion I have ever laid eyes on! You can't believe how magnificent an animal it is!"

I tried to digest all this information, but without much success. It was difficult to imagine Juan any way different than he had always been. He was familiar and comfortable to be with, wasn't he?

Then a thought occurred to me. "Why does he need an attorney, Allen? Is David still giving him trouble about that horse?"

"No, no, Shadow. I doubt David knows Juan is in these parts . . . or cares. Your friend engaged me to be his investment counselor, so you'll be pleased to know he doesn't intend to fritter away his fortune."

"When can I see him?"

"Anytime you wish, my dear. He said he is at your disposal."

This needed thought. Tomorrow Julia would be buried, and it would be unseemly if I didn't allow Allen to take me to the funeral. Our friends had taken our engagement for granted, so it would seem strange if I suddenly stopped seeing him now. Perhaps he would take me to meet Juan afterward.

I presented my most appealing look as I asked, "Will you be taking me to the funeral tomorrow, Allen?"

"Of course. And after the funeral, would you like to see your friend?"

"Do you always read my mind?" I asked tartly.

"Only when its workings show so clearly on your face, my dear. Forgive me if I've offended you."

"You haven't offended me, and you know it, Allen DeJung. It's just as well we won't marry, for it would be simply dreadful to live with a man who knows my every thought." I smiled to remove any sting from the words. "But it's very comforting to have you around to arrange things."

"Ah, yes," he agreed. "I am pleased you find me useful. Now, just what else am I to arrange?"

I rose and looked toward the sea. "When will the

duel be held?"

There was no answer, so I glanced around. Allen had risen, too, and his face was stern.

"When?" I insisted.

"The duel between Count Chauvanne and David Roberts is no business of yours, Shadow. There will be no butting of heads in stomachs at this meeting."

"I don't intend to repeat my outrageous behavior, Allen. However, you can't let Count Chauvanne kill David. I won't permit it, you know. You must think of a way to stop him," I said. Then I laid my hands inside his. "Please, dear Allen? Please?"

He sighed. "Because of Julia's funeral arrangements, Count Chauvanne will not meet David until next Monday morning. In the meantime, perhaps he will reconsider. I'll try to talk to him again about not proceeding with this madness after he has time to cool down. Right now he is very distraught over his daughter's tragic death."

"Poor Julia," I said, then told him of Bertha's outburst about the Chauvannes' neglect. "Perhaps she had reason to act as she did."

He nodded in agreement.

Then a different thought came to mind. "You never have told me what you found out about my uncle's finances, Allen. Is he using my inheritance for himself?"

A frown crossed his forehead. "I don't know for sure, Shadow. However, he lost a great deal of money the year before you arrived. He gambled on a gold mine and lost. The only reason I can think of for his not wanting you to get married is your money. I heard from Mr. Arbuthnot, by the way, and he asked me to send you his regards. When you wed, your fortune goes immediately to your husband."

"And I can't marry without my guardian's permission until I'm twenty-one?"

He nodded. "I could hate that man for not giving his permission when I had you agreeable to marrying me."

"It isn't fair," I said rebelliously. "Women are much more capable of handling money than men. At least we wouldn't gamble it away!"

"I agree with you, my dear, but the laws are very explicit."

"Well, they should be changed!"

The sun was throwing warmth from high in the sky as I flounced away. Then I remembered my manners. "Will you stay for lunch, Allen?"

"I'm afraid I can't," he said with a smile. "I must get back to my office today. What time shall I pick you up for the funeral?"

"At eleven," I said absently. "Oh, dear, there are so many things to think about. Can you arrange a meeting with Juan . . . Johnny, I mean, afterward? I do want to see him again."

Then I stamped my foot. "You *must* find a way to stop the duel, Allen. You must!"

He stood looking at me, mirth still in his eyes. "Yes, ma'am." His face remained solemn. "And may I say it's just as well we won't marry, for it would be simply dreadful to live with a woman who gives so many orders?"

"I'm sorry . . ." I began, then realized he was making fun of me again. "Oh, Allen, you are positively silly at times," I said chidingly.

"Yes, ma'am, I am," he said, trying to act contrite.

We walked to the veranda where his horse was tethered. His gaze went over my face, studying each detail, it seemed.

"You are the most beautiful woman I know," he said softly. "I don't think I will withdraw from the race quite yet. With the balance of your suitors mostly idiots, you just might end up marrying me as the best of the lot."

He mounted before I could answer, waving as he urged his horse down the drive.

Dear Allen . . . what would I do without him? Idiots, indeed! David was no idiot, and neither was Juan. Juan? Allen must surely have been jesting to say Juan was my suitor. He was dear . . . almost a brother, like Allen.

Halfway up the steps I paused when Tom Jordan brought Count Chauvanne's carriage around. My uncle emerged from the manor at the same time. I started to greet him, but he frowned at me and continued to the carriage, giving Tom orders as he got inside.

His rudeness startled me, for he was usually most polite. Thoughtfully, I watched the rig going down the driveway. With my uncle safely out of the way, perhaps it was my opportunity to talk to my aunt alone.

I went to her room and rapped lightly on her door. It was opened by a maid, and with a smile, I went past her to see the countess. "Aunt Elizabeth . . ."

Her appearance dismayed me, for I had never before seen her disheveled. She was propped on pillows, her hair in disarray, and she stared listlessly out the window. Her eyes were unseeing as she turned restlessly in my direction. When at last she focused on me, no smile greeted me.

"Oh, Aunt Elizabeth, I'm so sorry about Julia!" I said, and found to my surprise that I really meant it.

Tears filled her eyes. "My little girl . . ." she murmured. "My dear little girl."

A maid hurried to her side in alarm, but my aunt dismissed her with a wave of her hand and we were left alone.

"Why don't you get married? Or just go away?" she asked plaintively. "There's been nothing but trouble in this house since you arrived . . . you and your prying companion." She dabbed at her eyes with a kerchief, then broke into a wail. "Oh, how could my dear brother have sent me so much grief?"

Bewilderment filled me at her words and I said, "But, Aunt Elizabeth, how have I caused you trouble? What have I done? As for getting married, Count Chauvanne will not give his permission. Allen has asked and asked, but your husband will not allow it."

She sniffled as she looked at me accusingly. "That is ridiculous!" she said indignantly. "Why would he do such a thing?"

"I don't know," I said gently. "I thought perhaps you could tell me why . . . and a great many other things I am curious about . . . if we just had the opportunity to talk for a while."

"I don't feel like talking," she said pettishly. "I have lost my daughter . . . my only little girl." She broke into wild weeping.

Perhaps Bertha was mistaken and the countess really had loved Julia. The tears running down her cheeks were proof enough of a bereaved mother.

I sat on the bed next to her and gently kissed her forehead. "There, there, Aunt Elizabeth," I said soothingly. "Please don't cry anymore."

She looked up through tear-filled lashes. "Do not call me *aunt*!"

"Why not? You are my aunt, aren't you?" Then I thought to distract her and asked, "Did you know my mother?"

"Your mother!" Anger replaced grief as she spat out the word. "Your mother took my brother from me. She was a horrible child . . . and you're just like her."

For a moment I felt hurt. Then I sighed. "Aunt Elizabeth, I wasn't yet born when all this happened, so I can't see where any of it can be blamed on me. I have long been curious as to just exactly what occurred, but my father refused to discuss it with me. Why don't you tell me what happened?"

There was a silver coffee server on the tray by her bed. I filled the cup beside it and handed it to her. "Try some of this," I urged.

She took a sip and then several more before she replaced the cup on the table.

"I can't imagine why Edward would refrain from telling you your history. Perhaps it was bitterness at losing your mother because of your birth," Elizabeth said. "Your mother was only nineteen when he married her—less than half his age. She was such a child I could hardly believe he would marry her." Her gaze traveled over my face, as though to memorize my features. "You look so very like her, Shadow . . . almost her twin."

Her eyes returned to the window while she collected her thoughts. When she spoke, it was almost as though she talked to herself. "Edward was such a handsome man. How he adored the ladies! I think that is why he didn't marry for so long—he wanted to be free to court them all." She sighed, remembering. "We had grand parties when we were young. I met Count Chauvanne at one of them. He had come East on business. When he returned to California, I came with him as his bride."

She looked down at her hands. "I never saw Edward again," she said sadly. "I had almost convinced him to follow us out here when he met your mother."

She was quiet for so long I feared she wouldn't continue, so I prodded, "Where did Carmelita de la Cruz y Cuadro come from?"

Before answering, Aunt Elizabeth picked up her cup and sipped reflectively. "Carmelita de la Cruz y Cuadro—daughter of an ambassador from Spain, and the scandal of society! She was wild and free, doing things that would not have been condoned in any other woman. But she was so beautiful . . . at least that's what Edward said . . . no one refused to receive her, no matter her actions."

My thoughts turned inward. Carmelita . . . wild and free. No wonder I had imagined her dancing the flamenco so often as I daydreamed. And Edward St. George—it was hard to imagine him laughing and flirtatious when he had been so bitterly hard during the time I knew him.

"Aunt Elizabeth," I said timidly. "Why did their marriage divide the family?"

"I'm afraid that was my fault. I wanted Edward out here with me, and I knew if he married he would stay in New York. I gave him an ultimatum and I lost," she said regretfully. "Many a time I repented of my hardness, but my foolish pride refused to let me apologize."

Tears welled in her eyes. "I always meant to spend more time with Julia. I knew she needed a mother, but somehow my committees and clubs seemed important, and I just never got around to doing the things with her that I should have. Now I wish I had. Oh, God, how I wish I had! My little girl—stabbed! In the heart . . ." Her voice trailed off into a muffled moan as she buried her head in her kerchief.

"Please, Aunt Elizabeth, don't cry anymore." I rubbed her shaking shoulders until her sobs turned to sniffles.

"Go away," she moaned. "Please go away."

With a sigh, I left her. I had learned things about my parents I hadn't known, but not much about the mystery surrounding Julia's death.

And I had discovered that my aunt, at least, was not party to my not being allowed to marry. Perhaps in time she would become my ally.

Chapter Eighteen

The skies joined in to mourn Julia's passing. Her funeral was held at St. Anthony's Cathedral to the accompaniment of a steady downpour of rain rustling in the trees outside.

Allen had brought his black suit out of storage to wear, and I knew he was remembering the death of his father whom he had dearly loved. We stood together in our mourning attire to pay our last respects to Julia.

Real tears flowed from my eyes, for I regretted not making more of an effort to be her friend. Now that I knew why she had had such a brittle exterior, I could understand and forgive her sharpness.

Because of the weather the service was held inside the church. There were even more flowers surrounding the coffin than there had been at my father's funeral, and the air was heavy with their cloying scents.

Julia was so young to have died so tragically, I thought dismally, then sobbed into my kerchief mumbling, "Her nose wasn't really too long."

Allen raised an eyebrow and formed a "what" with

his lips, but I shook my head. All around us women were sobbing and men blowing their noses, so no one else noticed my foolishness. I straightened and stifled my sobs. What difference did looks make once you were dead?

The service seemed interminable, and my sympathy went out to my aunt. Her sorrow at her treatment of Julia must have been ten times more excruciating than mine. She slumped against her husband, crying almost hysterically. Count Chauvanne sat stoically erect, his face like an image graven in stone. Did he really care about anyone?

What sort of man was my uncle? One moment he was charming and debonair, the next . . . almost anything. David's words returned to me as I watched Count Chauvanne in the pew with the rest of the family. True, my uncle was ruthless, but did he have the same streak of madness as the old countess, his mother? Then another thought pushed itself forward. Was the old countess really as insane as everyone took for granted? Or had her son subdued her with daily doses of opium for other reasons? Why had he made her a prisoner and placed her in solitary confinement in his home?

Allen's hand at my elbow urging me to stand made me realize the eulogy for Julia Chauvanne was over. We made our slow way through the rain to Allen's carriage. Inside, the racket was tremendous as drops pelted the wood. I felt sorry for the coachman on his open box, but he was dressed in a slicker and brimmed hat, much like a ship captain, and surely was used to such weather.

Carriages milled around, the downpour causing

more commotion than usual as drivers tried to position their vehicles close to the cathedral exit.

I breathed a sigh of relief, glad the ordeal was ended, but still sorry about Julia's demise.

"Funerals are ghastly affairs, aren't they?" Allen said.

"They're barbaric!" I shuddered, pulling my cloak more tightly around me. "Why are they allowed? I would much rather remember people as they were alive instead of as they look in their coffins."

"Then let's do," Allen said decisively. "We'll remember Julia when she was laughing and happy." He frowned. "I can scarcely recall the times when she was anything but discontented, come to think of it. What do you suppose made such a lovely girl so chronically unhappy?"

"Perhaps she had less than we all supposed," I said.

"Ah, yes," he agreed. "Such as a fiance who was in love with her cousin?"

Guilt swept over me, but I pushed it aside. "I don't think Julia really loved David. She was looking forward to shopping in Paris on their honeymoon more than just being with her husband," I said, then paused, hoping I hadn't sounded catty while stating a simple fact. "Julia had to collect possessions . . . accumulate people and things . . . perhaps to fill some emptiness inside her."

"Well, at last we seem to be moving," Allen exclaimed. "Now we can go meet your friend."

I had almost forgotten Juan in my preoccupation with Julia and why she hadn't been happy. Then I realized with a start I hadn't been thinking about

David, either. Since there was nothing more to be done for my poor cousin, perhaps I had best concentrate on the affairs of this world.

"Where are we to meet him, Allen?" I asked, looking doubtfully at the pouring sheets of water splashing against the carriage windows.

"We will drive out Point Lobos Road to the park and meet him at the main arbor."

"But it's raining!"

"I know it is raining, Shadow. However, I didn't know it would be raining when I made the appointment."

The park beside the Golden Gate was an accomplishment of which San Franciscans were justly proud. Brush-covered sand hills had been converted into tree-sheltered areas of beauty. Flowering eucalypti rubbed elbows with Monterrey cyprus and wind-bent pine trees. Many a time we had picnicked beside one of the seven lakelets and rested beneath the arbors. But that had been when the sun was shining, not when the world was sodden and the air almost solid water!

Mud sloshed up from the carriage wheels splattering the windows. Rain poured from the heavens to dissolve the mud and wash it away. Was this how it felt to be immersed in the ocean?

Then I heard a shout as the blurred image of a rider showed through the downpour. The carriage stopped.

Allen opened the door, shouting, "Get in!"

The rider dismounted and poked his dripping hat inside the carriage. Juan's dark brown eyes were beneath it. He removed the hat and slicker that protected him, then entered, making the carriage rock dangerously as he scrambled inside.

"Beautiful day," he said cheerfully. "Hi, Shadow . . . Allen."

"Juan . . . ?" His name came in a whisper as amazement made me gape. Allen was right—Juan had grown *much* bigger. His shoulders were broader, dwarfing the seat on which he sat. His legs seemed cramped in the small space our feet were allowed. The rain had framed his tan face in dark curls. Gleaming white teeth made his skin even darker. His brown eyes mirrored the laughter I remembered so well, only they were somehow . . . surer?

He grinned at me, much as he had the first time we met in the stables when I was twelve years old. "My name is Johnny," he said. "What's yours?"

"Johnny!" I echoed indignantly. "Why have you changed your name?" If he were no longer Juan, then he was no longer as much a Spaniard as Carmelita, and somehow that made me feel deprived.

"Well now," he drawled, "Johnny just seemed to fit in with my surroundings better than Juan. It seemed not to lead to epithets like sun-grinner and greaser so often, and when those were aimed at me I felt called upon to do something about it. Less trouble, you see?"

I nodded, still staring.

He continued, "Besides, Americans have most of the money, so in order to play cards with them, I decided to become a full-blooded American."

"Gambling is a sin, Juan, and you know it!"

"Johnny," he corrected with another grin. "Then we're all most likely sinners, for living is the biggest gamble of all, Shadow. But are you just going to scold

254

me, or are you going to say hello?"

Confusion brought the hated blush when I realized I had been sounding like a shrew. Before I could answer his question, however, Juan turned to Allen and they held an animated conversation concerning some sort of investments in which they were involved. How dare he ignore me? Indignation dissolved my confusion.

Their voices eddied around my ears while I took a good look at Juan . . . Johnny. He was clad as Allen had said—an expensive black suit fit his wide shoulders perfectly, then tapered to hug slender hips. My eyes widened at the black gunbelt slung around his waist. A wicked-looking silver grip protruded from the top of the holster.

His long legs were covered with the same expensive black fabric that disappeared into his black leather boots. Despite the mud covering them, I could see they were fancily carved. Jingling silver spurs clung to Juan's heels, dripping water into miniature puddles around his feet.

"Well?" he demanded.

With a start I realized their conversation had come to an end and he had been watching me take inventory. Telltale warmth warned me of another blush, but I drew myself up and said coolly, "Well, what?"

"Are you going to say hello to me, Miss Shadow St. George?"

"Of course. Hello, Johnny Monterro."

"Now you're mad, aren't you?"

Allen interrupted. "Look . . . I didn't mean to intrude on your reunion. If you'll loan me your slicker, Johnny, I'll get up front with the coachman."

"You'll do no such thing, Allen," I said, still smarting from my gaucherie. "We have nothing to say that can't be said with you here."

Johnny removed the glove from my hand and pressed a kiss into my palm. Even his eyes had grown solemn when he looked at me. "I've been teasing you, and I shouldn't. You aren't the little girl who ran through the streets of New York with me. You have grown into the loveliest young lady I know." He paused, looking at my face as though he were committing it to memory. "I would be most proud if you would allow me to call on you properly, Miss Shadow St. George."

I looked at him doubtfully. My old friend was dressed like a nabob, and he could display very acceptable manners, but to call on me at the Chauvanne house? The day David had insulted him, Juan had knocked him down. If my uncle insulted him . . . well, Johnny had a sureness about him . . . and a gun at his hip. If Count Chauvanne snubbed him, as he most assuredly would, and Johnny killed him, there would be a rope around his neck no one could remove.

"You mustn't, Johnny. The Chauvannes have just lost their daughter, and I doubt they'll be receiving visitors for some time."

He nodded. "I'm sorry about your cousin. Has a motive for her death been uncovered?"

I shook my head.

Allen said, "I tried to get Shadow to visit my aunt for a while, but she refuses. Your former employer is going to duel Count Chauvanne over some fancied insult and Shadow thinks she can stop it if she stays at the mansion. I told her there would be no stomach butting allowed."

Johnny regarded me thoughtfully. "I would kill for you, Shadow. Did Roberts remove the obstacle between you?"

"No, he didn't!" I said angrily. "David didn't kill Julia. How dare you even think such a thing?" Then the full import of his words sank in. "What do you mean—you would kill for me?"

He shrugged, then changed to the Juan I had known when he said boyishly, "Oh, you know— dragons that menace the fair princess, cruel stepfathers, ill-natured stepmothers, and things such as that." Then he lost his boyishness. "I would kill anyone who tried to hurt you," he said. His voice was carefully casual, but somehow it made a shiver run up my spine.

He glanced out the window. "Ah, the rain seems to have stopped." Then his brown eyes returned to me. "Are you glad that I'm back and still unchanged, Shadow?"

"Yes, of course, . . . Johnny. Drat! I'll never get used to that name," I said, frowning at him. "I do wish your occupation was something other than gambling. You know what Miss Brigham said about gamblers, don't you?"

His head tilted backward in a hearty laugh, and even Allen chuckled. "I don't know and I don't care," Johnny gasped, then collapsed into mirth again.

When he stopped chortling, little devils of mischief peered from his eyes. "Shadow . . . oh, Shadow, perhaps you *are* still the little girl who likes to ride the horse cars and eat hot pretzels from street

257

vendors."

"Every time you two are with me you make fun of me," I said indignantly. "I don't think I said anything at all ridiculous. Not even the richest gamblers are received by anyone in our set, so the occupation must be one that is considered disreputable."

I raised my nose so I could look down it. "If you remain a gambler, *Johnny*, I doubt very much my uncle will allow you to call on me. This is a very different society than you knew in New York, but some things just aren't done." I had emphasized his name, making it sound more rakish than it was.

Juan's brown eyes had a hurt look that made me wish I had swallowed my words before I let them out, but his face was impassive as he scooped the still-wet slicker from the carriage floor and held the damp hat carefully in his hand.

"I have no doubt you are right, Miss Shadow." He picked up my ungloved hand, again pressing a kiss into my palm, then folded my fingers over as though to preserve it. "This meeting will be a pleasure I shall long remember. Especially if I'm to be barred from calling on you," he added.

With a nod to Allen, he leaped from the carriage to the back of his waiting horse. The big black quivered beneath his weight, but stood firm while Johnny tied the slicker behind the saddle. At a touch of the silver spurs, the stallion pawed the air and then took off in a flowing gallop.

"Beautiful!" Allen said.

I tried to cover my confusion by replacing my glove, but couldn't find it.

"What are you looking for, Shadow?"

258

"My glove," I said crossly. "I can't find it."

"I think it's in Johnny's pocket," he said quietly. "It will give me great pleasure to replace it with a new pair, if you'll allow me the liberty."

"Oh, just get it from him when you see him again." I flounced back against the seat feeling strangely upset, but by what I didn't know.

Through most of my childhood, and especially when I was so unhappy about my father's neglect, Juan had been the rock I clung to and the friend I needed so badly. Just knowing he was near had been enough to comfort me, but being with him had brought the most happiness I had known. Now his presence made me uncomfortable . . . uncertain about how to act. Had he changed so much?

Allen called to his coachman to return to the Chauvanne estate, then rubbed my chilly hand. "I can ask Monterro for your glove, but I doubt he'll give it up, my dear."

"Whatever would he want with an old glove?"

There was no answer to my question. Allen just smiled while he held my hand.

"Well?" I prodded.

"Your Johnny is a romantic, Shadow."

"He isn't *my* Johnny," I said, feeling unreasonably cross.

"Whether you want him or not, I'm afraid he is. Ah, Shadow, Shadow . . . have you any idea at all just how desirable you are?" He smiled a sad sort of smile. "He's been in love with you ever since you were children, I would imagine."

"Oh, that's silly! We were children, and children don't fall in love. And what has my glove to do with

259

this?"

"He is your knight in shining armor and your glove is the banner he will fight under." He paused before adding, "To the death, my dear."

Chapter Nineteen

The Chauvanne mansion was gloomily quiet in the days that followed. Even the servants spoke in whispers or in unusually low tones. My aunt took to her bed and gave orders to admit no one. My uncle left early each day and did not return until late at night.

Rain fell with such monotonous regularity I thought I would go mad. When I tried to order a carriage, I discovered Count Chauvanne had left instructions that no horse or vehicle be allowed to leave the premises without his express permission. As the day of the impending duel approached, I was trapped in my guardian's house.

Then it was Sunday night and I lay sleepless in bed thinking of the coming day and what it might bring. David had stayed away since the funeral—was he preparing for death? Or perhaps he had left the country, preferring dishonorable flight, and that was fine with me. David, stay alive, I prayed. Be a coward, if you must, but don't die!

Approaching dawn lightened the sky while I wondered bitterly where the rain was now. If it had poured sufficiently hard, perhaps the duel would have been called off. But the downpour had ceased during the night and I had no doubt the sky would be clear. I rose and looked out the window—had I wearied God with my endless prayers, to the point where my pleas were being ignored?

A horseman cantered down the drive and I saw it was Count Chauvanne. A second rider followed. I recognized him as an acquaintance of my uncle's, but his name eluded me. They must be going to the dueling ground, wherever that might be located.

I dressed without waiting for Carlie and fled down the back stairs and out to the stables, nearly colliding with Tom Jordan when I ran inside.

"Slow down, Miss Shadow," he said. "You're out mighty early in the day."

"Saddle my mare, Tom. Hurry!"

"I can't do that," he said slowly. "Count Chauvanne left orders."

"I don't care what he left, Tom. He is going to murder David Roberts if someone doesn't stop him, and apparently I am the only person who cares." I brushed around him. "If you won't saddle my mare, I'll do it myself."

"Now, Miss Shadow . . ." He caught up with me before I reached the tack room and caught my arm. "Please, miss, you can't do that."

Angrily, I yanked free of his restraining hand. "I couldn't let your daughter die either, could I?" I was momentarily ashamed for demanding payment for a favor, but then the thought of David lying crumpled on the ground stiffened my resolve.

Tom looked over my shoulder at an approaching

stable boy and told him to saddle a horse for him. Then he reached for my side-saddle and led the way to where my little mare crunched her morning oats.

"You'll get us both killed on one of these expeditions, Miss Shadow," he said gruffly, "but I'm going with you again on this one. Let's hope the good Lord is on your side this morning."

I started to kick my mare into a gallop when I was safely perched on her back, but Tom grabbed the bridle.

"We had best not let Count Chauvanne see us following him," he said.

"Do you know where they are going?"

He nodded. "Yes, I know . . . but what do you intend doing when we get there?"

A feeling of helplessness washed over me. "I don't know. . . ." What would I do when we arrived at the dueling area? A sick sensation in the pit of my stomach was my only answer.

Tom led the way up the drive while my mind went in circles searching for a plan of action. What *would* I do? What could I do? Would my presence be enough to stop the duel? I doubted it.

Then my guide raised his hand in a signal to halt after we had ridden through a wooded area for some distance. We paused at the edge of an open glade. Through fluttering leaves I saw a scene I would not soon forget.

David and my uncle stood facing each other a short distance apart. Each held a naked sword in his hand pointed down toward the earth. Allen stood behind David even as Count Chauvanne's second backed him. Dr. Dijon was at the side, the black bag in his hand. A sixth man stood with his back toward me, handkerchief held high.

I gasped when the handkerchief fell and the clash of swords rang out, and urged my mare closer despite Tom's restraining hand on the bridle. The sound of steel against steel grew more frantic as the men lunged and parried, but David gave as good as he took for several minutes. Then his inexperience began to show. My uncle pushed relentlessly forward, sword tip flashing first one spot, then another, as he forced David to retreat.

Then catastrophe struck before my horrified eyes. Count Chauvanne's blade touched David's arm and cut a wide slash just below his shoulder. I screamed in terror at the sight of the gushing blood as my mare leaped forward into the clearing.

Startled faces turned my way all save Count Chauvanne's. His blade hit David's, sending it sailing into the air. David stepped back to escape the punishing edge and fell onto the soft turf. The Count raised his sword to plunge into his helpless adversary, ignoring my shrieks while the mare covered the distance between us.

His hand stopped in midair when mounted men broke from the opposite woods and a pistol fired like the crack of doom. Rage suffused my uncle's face at the interruption. He glared at Sheriff Thompson dismounting beside him, but surrendered his sword at the sheriff's demand.

"Are you all right, Roberts?" Sheriff Thompson asked roughly, extending a hand to help David rise.

David grasped it, pulling himself erect, then tried to stop the flow of blood from his left arm. Dr. Dijon led him to a fallen tree where he could sit while the gaping wound was sewed shut.

Count Chauvanne glanced at Tom, then pointedly ignored us, addressing himself to the sheriff. "This is an affair of honor, Thompson. I'll thank you to stay out of it."

"Dueling is against the law, sir, as you well know," the sheriff said, holstering his gun. "You are both liable to prosecution, and the lot of you would have to answer if there had been a killing today."

"Who told you about this?" my uncle demanded. "I'll have your badge for this day's work!"

"You'll have my badge when the people of this territory un-elect me," the sheriff answered.

He looked down to where Tom and I sat our horses. "Why don't you take Miss St. George on home, Tom? This is no place for a young lady to be."

I looked toward David, but he ignored my presence. My eyes met Allen's. He stared coldly at me, not a trace of a smile now. Would no one help?

Tom resolved the issue by crowding my mare around with his horse and slapping her on the rump with his reins. Her lunge snapped my neck, but I stayed with her as she settled into a lope toward home.

Rebellion surged within me as I thought of the past few minutes. Fool men! Wanting to kill each other with slashing cuts, or a rope around the neck, or a bullet. Fool me! Screeching like a fishwife to stop them. My face burned at the thought of how I must have sounded. And after all that, nobody even thanked me for stopping a murder! Not even David! I had practically risked my life for him, and for what? Nothing!

We stopped to give the horses a breather in a patch of shade. Over the sound of their restless pawing I heard pounding hooves in the distance. I tried to see who it was but trees blocked the line of vision.

"We'd best get on, Miss Shadow," Tom said. "I don't know who is coming, but if it's Count Chauvanne I'd as soon get to the mansion before he does." He sighed. "Maybe he'll have cooled down by then."

"No . . . please wait." It might be David coming to give me belated thanks for coming to his rescue.

But it wasn't David. It was Allen, and his face was set in unforgiving sternness. "Get on home, Tom. I will escort Miss St. George."

He waited until Tom was gone before he spoke again. "Do you realize what you have done?" he asked in tones colder than ice. "Is there no end to your meddling? You asked me to take care of this matter. Couldn't you allow me to handle the situation in my way for a change?"

"I didn't know you intended doing anything," I said weakly. This was another side of Allen I had never seen, and I didn't like it.

"Women should not meddle in men's affairs! You told me the problem and that was all you needed to do," he said. "Your uncle will be rightly furious with you, and there's no telling what he will do."

"Oh, Allen . . ."

"If you were *my* ward, I should be most tempted to give you a hiding!" He jerked his horse for emphasis, making the poor beast toss his head in panic.

A gasp of outrage shook me. How dare he talk to me in this manner? If I were a man he would not be so daring.

"Women should not meddle in men's affairs," I mimicked. "If I hadn't, David would be dead and my uncle would be a murderer! Deny that, if you can, Mr. DeJung!"

"Who do you think had Sheriff Thompson come break it up?" he demanded. "You don't suppose he got the information from the seagulls, do you? All you did was make a blasted fool of yourself again."

"Oh, dear . . ." I blinked rapidly, but the tears wouldn't be held back. My anger dissolved into a feeling of despair. I kicked my mare into a gallop and fled down the trail wishing I were dead.

Pounding hoofbeats made me kick harder, but my mare was no match for the long-legged horse Allen rode. He pulled alongside and grabbed the cheek strap, almost pitching me over the mare's head when she suddenly stopped.

"I'm not through talking to you yet," he said grimly. "You are a headstrong, self-willed . . . brat!" He jumped down from his horse. "Now get down!"

I dismounted while tears streamed down my cheeks.

"All you think about is David, David, David," he said angrily, "but you've shamed him this day to where he won't be able to hold up his head."

A sick feeling filled me as I realized he spoke the truth. I'd been thinking of David's life. Like all men, he would be more concerned with his honor. Would he hate me because of what I had done?

"Oh-h-h." Pain brought the wail from my lips before I could stop it.

"You had better cry," Allen said roughly, "and pray

to the Lord to be forgiven for your stubbornness. Johnny paid your uncle the money David owed him so he wouldn't lose his blasted ranch. He did it because he's so crazy in love with you he'll even give you to another man if that's what you want. After what you've done, now your David will most likely leave the country from pure shame!"

I cowered against my mare, watching Allen swell with anger.

"Why, in the name of God, do men love you to distraction? You make fools of us all and still we come back for more. You are a silly, childish . . ." He stopped, taking a deep breath that emerged in a groan. "And God help me, I love you more than any of them!"

He pulled me to him and his mouth covered mine in a kiss that left me breathless. When he straightened, we stared at each other until his eyes shifted away.

"Now it's I who have made a fool of myself," he muttered wearily.

We rode home in silence while I thought about the events of the morning, or tried to. My emotions were in a turmoil of uncertainty, shifting from one thought to another without rhyme or reason. And through it all there was the feel of Allen's lips on mine. I glanced at him from time to time, but he kept his eyes focused ahead and would not look at me.

Instead of stopping at the veranda, I urged my mare to the stables, knowing Allen would have to follow. There were still things unsaid between us, and we needed no chaperone to say them.

The stable boy relieved us of our mounts and led the horses away.

Allen turned to me, bowing rather formally. "I'm afraid I made a dreadful ass of myself, Miss St. George," he said. "I hope you can find it in your heart to forgive me in time."

I let him get no farther. "Oh, no, Allen, it's I who should ask forgiveness." I swallowed, trying not to cry. "I have embarrassed everybody, including myself. It's just as you said. I start on a course of action and not even the Lord can stop me."

"Oh, no, my dear, I was wrong!" His arms went around me and his voice was again the soft caress I had gotten used to. "You are sweet and beautiful, my dearest darling, and in no way a brat. Oh, Shadow, can you ever forgive me for that terrible word?"

My suppressed tears changed to a sort of hysteria, and I giggled against his chest.

"Don't cry, my dear . . . please don't cry. I have never in my life been such a cad before, and I never will again. Please don't cry, my darling."

"I'm not c-crying, Allen."

He held me at arm's length so he could look at my face. "You are laughing! Oh, Shadow, you're laughing at me. And why not? We should both be laughing. We're about the two silliest people I know!"

We stood grinning at each other like idiots, then broke into laughter that was born of hysteria. We clutched each other for support as we laughed until we were both crying from too much mirth.

When I could speak again, I said, "Oh, Allen, do you suppose we can just forget this morning?"

"*We* can, Shadow, but I wonder if Count Chauvanne and your precious David and all those other men can. I had better escort you to the house, my dear."

I stood on tiptoe to kiss him. "Thank you for everything, Allen. Oh, dear . . . what if my uncle really gave me a hiding?"

"Why don't you visit my aunt for a few days? The permission your uncle granted before this morning is still valid." His face grew grim. "It seems I am as wild as your Johnny. I, too, would kill anyone who harmed you. My dear, please come away from here now."

"You're such a dear, and this time I'll do as you wish. I would love to visit your aunt. Will you wait for me while I change?"

"Of course."

He spied Tom Jordan coming from the tack room and motioned him over. "May I borrow a carriage, Tom? Miss St. George is to visit my aunt, and it would hardly be appropriate for her to arrive on the back of a horse. I will send the carriage back immediately we arrive."

"Yes, sir," Tom answered. "It might be just the thing if Miss Shadow were to go visiting."

The apprehension in his eyes made me ashamed that I had forced him to take me to the duel. "Oh, Tom, I'm so sorry I've gotten you into trouble again. I'll tell my uncle I forced you to take me, and then he won't blame you."

Tom shrugged. "I've been serving Count Chauvanne for a long time, Miss Shadow. He's changed from the man I first knew and seems to be changing even more lately. I have a feeling I won't be around here much longer."

Allen clapped him on the back. "Well, don't fret about it, Tom. A good coachman like you is a rarity these days. I'll see you get another position. It's the least I can do to reward you for your heroic efforts on behalf of Miss St. George. You have served her well on several occasions."

I hurried to the house to prepare myself for a visit with Allen's aunt, but my thoughts were desolate, perhaps as an aftermath to my wild hysteria with Allen. It was not only Tom I had harmed by my headstrong behavior. Would David ever forgive me? Had I ruined our chance for happiness by disgracing him in the eyes of his peers? Perhaps now his love for me had turned to hate. Oh, why was I so impulsive?

"Because you are my daughter!"

Startled, I looked around, but no one was in sight. Then realization made me smile. The words were only in my mind but they had come from Carmelita. Beautiful, impetuous, brave and proud, she would never grovel in self-pity as I had been doing. It was time I stopped.

Chapter Twenty

Allen's aunt was a delightful hostess. Miss Wilhelmina DeJung greeted me with open arms, beaming with pleasure when Allen escorted me in with Carlie just behind.

"Welcome, Miss St. George," she said cordially. "I feel as though I know you quite well, and for a long time now. Allen does nothing but sing your praises. I do wish you would marry the dear boy. You make such a beautiful couple, and I don't wish him to end up in the same state of solitude as I."

"That is quite a speech, my dear aunt," Allen said fondly, "but please don't frighten the lady of my choice with too much pressure. I'm stalking her, but circumspectly."

"Oh, Allen, stop," I said, smiling at their banter. "I'm very happy to meet you, Miss DeJung, and most grateful that you offer your home as my temporary shelter. And please call me Shadow." I motioned my maid forward. "This is Carlie Jordan, my maid, companion, and friend."

Miss DeJung acknowledged the introduction before

turning to her woman to suggest she take Carlie to our rooms while the rest of us had tea. Carlie took my cloak and bonnet and followed the other woman from the room.

"Come, dear," Allen's aunt said, taking me by the hand. "Why don't you call me Aunt Mina, as Allen does, and perhaps some day I will be your aunt. I'm an incurable matchmaker, as you can see."

Allen and I exchanged glances as she led us into her parlor. He looked quite pleased about something.

A houseboy who could have been Chung's twin served our repast. While Allen and his aunt engaged in animated conversation, I sat quietly observing the scene.

Aunt Mina was a birdlike little woman with snow-white hair piled in drifts atop her head. Her hands were never still, fluttering in the air like tiny hummingbirds. Her clothing was a bit old-fashioned, but shiningly immaculate.

After a brief exchange with her nephew, she brought me into the conversation by chatting of events and people we all knew. She made sure my teacup was full and urged me to have another scone, flattering me with her attention. I thought how different this meeting was from my first encounter with Julia and then my aunt and uncle.

The house of Mina DeJung was unpretentiously beautiful, with deep bay windows fronting on Nob Hill. I relaxed into the comfort of her protection with a feeling of relief, somehow believing my shaken life would be smoothed to acceptability in time.

In the days that followed, Allen called at Aunt Mina's home frequently to escort me to the gatherings of our set, and it seemed that our lives were returning to normal.

My heart cried for David, especially since he attended none of the events. We mourned the passing of Julia, and it was not thought strange that David stayed away. After all, it had been his bride who had been murdered on her wedding day, and society decreed that he observe a proper period of grief. But I wanted to see him again.

Julia's death was still discussed in almost every conversation, but by now hope that the perpetrator would be found was fading. Count Chauvanne's accusation of David was regarded as patently foolish, and since there was no solid evidence of David's guilt the matter was dropped. Discreet speculation and suspicion still wafted around him at times, but it was mostly idle gossip.

Everyone knew Count Chauvanne had wounded David in a duel, but apparently none of the participants had mentioned my part in the affair, for there were no twits given me about it. Most assumed the duel was a result of the madness of grief that possessed Count Chauvanne because of the violent death of his only daughter.

I knew better. My uncle wanted to kill David because he was in love with me instead of Julia. I was safe in a haven of Allen's making at present, but my visit would soon come to an end. It would be unthinkable to impose myself on his aunt for an interminable length of time. What would happen to me when I returned to the mansion?

It was a week from the day of my arrival when Allen came one afternoon to call, and this time he brought a visitor. Aunt Mina and I were chatting in the parlor when Allen and Juan were ushered in.

Allen kissed his aunt's cheek. "I've brought a friend to see you, Aunt Mina. May I present Johnny Monterro? Johnny, this is Miss Wilhelmina DeJung."

To my surprise, Johnny raised the small hand to his mouth and kissed it as he expressed his pleasure at meeting so lovely a lady. It was such a skilled gesture, he must have practiced it often.

Then Allen said, "Of course, you have already met Miss Shadow St. George."

Juan's eyes found mine as he said, "You are looking more beautiful than ever, Miss Shadow." He bowed, then an outrageous wink closed one eyelid when no one but I could see.

Flustered, I managed to murmur a greeting.

"I love when you bring handsome men to call, Allen," his aunt said coyly. "Mr. Monterro, you are an outrageously attractive young scamp!"

"Ah . . . yes, Aunt Mina," Allen interjected. "Will you show me the latest flowers in your conservatory? I have been meaning to ask you for some time."

When they had gone I said, "You must stop teasing me, Johnny Monterro. We aren't children, anymore."

He sank to the sofa beside me and began memorizing the features of my face again. "You are right, of course, Shadow. In the future I shall behave with the utmost decorum. Is everything all right with you?"

"I suppose. . . ." I said vaguely. "Have you seen David Roberts since the duel?" Then I remembered his magnanimous gesture. "It was very good of you to help him out of his financial difficulties."

He shrugged. "He has simply traded one master for

another. He insisted I take a mortgage on his ranch, which I'm sure he'll pay off in time. And no, I haven't seen him since the duel." An ironic smile preceded his saying, "I hear you've been a rescuing angel again."

Warmth suffused my cheeks. "Who told you?" I asked indignantly. "Was it Allen?"

This time Johnny laughed out loud. "It was in confidence, so you needn't worry I'll mention it elsewhere. After all, I was once the recipient of your—shall we say—violent mercies."

I sat silent, wondering if I were to spend my life being laughed at, when he changed the subject.

"I thought I'd drive out to see Roberts in the morning. It will be somewhat different to return as a toff to the place where I was once a lowly cowhand and almost came a cropper as a horse thief. Will you do me the honor of accompanying me?"

"Oh, yes," I said eagerly. "Juan, it's so wonderful that you're rich and all—much better than before. Remember when we were afraid to talk to each other on the train? I thought it was such a bunch of silliness!"

"I remember," he said, looking down at his boots. "I remember a lot of things about us. Do you?"

"What do you mean?"

"Oh, the good times we had together in New York. The horse cars, and eating hot bread—racing to get back to the school so you'd be on time for supper."

"Oh, those! Of course I remember, but we were children then. Now we're grown."

"Yes," he said soberly. "Now we're grown." He rose. "Will one o'clock tomorrow be agreeable with you?"

"Earlier, if you like. The country is lovely in the morning."

He frowned down at me. "I'm sorry, Shadow, but I can't manage it in the morning. I have an appointment that must be kept."

I rose to keep from getting a crick in my neck looking up at him. "Then, of course, it will be in the afternoon."

Allen escorted his aunt into the room and she was still chattering. I wondered if he had gotten a word in edgewise while they were gone. He nodded politely at intervals, but his gaze went from Johnny to me.

When at last she paused for breath, he said, "I'm afraid we must be going, Aunt Mina."

She looked astonished. "But you have just arrived! Don't you want tea, Mr. Monterro?"

"Just meeting you and seeing Miss Shadow is all the refreshment I need, Miss DeJung," he said, bowing over her hand. He turned to me and said, "Your servant, ma'am." His eyes were full of mischief, but he observed the proper decorum.

They left, and Aunt Mina chattered on about how nice they both were. I agreed, although I was somewhat miffed. Why did I always feel as though this new Juan were making fun of me?

Allen's insistence that Johnny was in love with me was ridiculous! *Johnny!* A stupid name had changed the Juan I'd know and trusted for most of my life into a *roué*, a gambler, and almost a stranger.

A thought brought me up short. I'm going riding with him tomorrow . . . I'll be alone with him in a carriage! I felt strangely uncomfortable at the prospect. But would we be alone? Perhaps Allen would go with us. After all, he was Johnny's attorney.

"Is something wrong, dear?" Aunt Mina's gentle question brought me from my reverie.

"No, of course not," I said with a sigh. "I'm afraid my mind was straying. What were you saying?"

"Nothing important," she said cheerfully. "Is Allen coming this evening?"

It took me a moment to recall. "M-m-m, yes he is. Sue Partridge is having a soirée, and we've been invited to attend." I took her small hand in mine. "Why don't you go with us, Aunt Mina? We would love to have you, and I know Sue would be delighted to see you. Don't you get lonesome staying home alone so often?"

"Oh, dear me, no! You young people go out all you like. At my age, I look forward to solitude and rest."

"And I have kept your home in constant agitation since I arrived," I said contritely. "I should return to my guardians, I know, Aunt Mina."

"No, no, no, my dear!" She slipped her arm around my waist. "You are as dear to me as a daughter, and I would be happy to have you live here forever. Allen buried himself in that old office until he met you. Now he's become much happier." Her bright eyes studied me. "You don't intend to marry him do you? Are you in love with that handsome young scamp who was here today?"

I was at a loss for words. I was accustomed to her direct questions, but this one confused me and I wasn't sure how to answer. "Oh, no . . ." I stammered.

She patted my arm. "Never mind, dear. I know I'm a meddlesome busybody, and I'm foolishly fond of my nephew. But much as I would dearly love for you to marry Allen, you must do as your heart tells you."

While I dressed for the soirée, Aunt Mina's words returned to me. What *did* my heart tell me? I loved David, but why hadn't he sent some sort of message to me to let me know he still loved me? It was much too soon after Julia's death for him to declare himself openly, but surely it was cruel of him to leave me in such an uncertain state. Why couldn't I be sensible and fall in love with Allen? Then my life would be secure and comfortable.

Love was such a nuisance—look how unhappy it had made my childhood. Why hadn't I stayed with my resolution to do without it? What made a person fall in love anyway? No sensible reason, that was sure.

At the Partridge soirée the usual group was assembled, discussing the same old subjects, tittering at the same old jokes, and as always, drinking too much wine. It suddenly struck me that my life was quite boring—not secure, as I had thought. Was it because the man I loved was absent? Did love lend spice to an otherwise dull meal? I glanced at Allen standing beside me. He was dear, but unless I loved him, a life with him would be an eternal dullness.

"Are you going with us tomorrow, Allen?"

He shook his head, not questioning who the "us" was, nor our destination. "I'm about to wind up my father's old records, Shadow. Another day will get me through them, and I intend to finish tomorrow."

I looked at him imploringly. "Have you seen him since he was hurt?"

Again he didn't question the "him," but slowly shook his head. "Monterro asked me to arrange a meeting with you, so I brought him to my aunt's home so you and he could be together. I guess he knows you want to see who you want to see." He shook his head helplessly. "See the effect you have on us?"

"Don't be angry with me, Allen," I said quickly. "Perhaps tomorrow will cure me of my obsession."

"I hope it does, Shadow," he said. "A quick hurt now might not be as difficult to survive as a lifetime of endless misery."

Perhaps he was right, but if David no longer loved me, would it be a *quick* hurt? Or would it be a long, drawn-out series of hurts, such as my father had inflicted on me?

I hadn't thought about Edward St. George lately, although Carmelita always seemed quite near. Perhaps love kept you close even after death. My mother had probably loved me from the time of my conception and as I was nurtured in her womb—and my father not at all. The thought that he just hadn't known he loved me was a childhood delusion I had used to comfort myself.

The next afternoon Johnny Monterro arrived in a handsome light buggy drawn by a pair of restless black horses that chewed nosily on their bits while he escorted me from Aunt Mina's house.

"Toffs usually have coachmen," I observed.

He clucked the horses into a fast walk before he looked at me. "I'll never have servants . . . at least not for something I can do myself."

"Why not?"

"Oh, I suppose because I've been one most of my life. There's a lack of personal dignity involved in a servant and master relationship, on both sides."

I looked at him with new respect. Although San Francisco's aristocracy was built on young fortunes, most newly rich people were shunned because of their pretentious gaucheries and overbearing manners. Johnny was different. Aunt Mina had liked him instantly when they met. If the rest of the world regarded him in the same way, he would have no difficulty rising to the top.

He had grown into a handsome man, with suave manners he hadn't possessed when we were companions in New York. A year had wrought many changes in him.

"Johnny . . . where did you go after we rescued you from the vigilantes?"

His grin was companionable. "I like the way my name sounds when you say it, Shadow. Do you really mind my changing it?"

"Well, I'm not sure. It makes you seem like a different person from the Juan who was my friend for so long, but it does seem to fit your new status."

Then I realized he had avoided my question. "But where did you go? And how did you make so much money? Surely, not entirely by gambling." I flushed at my own curiosity.

He just shrugged. "I only made a stake gambling. Then I bought into a silver mine that turned out rather well. Now I don't have to work, so I gamble to pass the time and because I enjoy it." He urged the horses into a trot. "Besides, I'm good at it."

He was bragging like any small boy, I thought, but then didn't all men?

"It might keep you from being accepted in the best circles," I said primly. "As I told you, gamblers aren't well received."

He laughed out loud. "Best circles? You mean the dull little crowd who tosses soirées and parties from which we common folk are excluded. Ah, Shadow, if you were the same girl who slipped out of school to play with me, I would show you a whole new world where you'd have more fun than you ever dreamed of having."

"We have fun!"

"Snobs," he muttered, "most of them, anyway."

"You're somewhat of a snob yourself."

"Perhaps," he conceded. "At least I'm enough of a snob to think you are much too good for Roberts. What do you see in him? Does his appeal hinge on the fact that he resembles your father so greatly?"

I stared at him in astonishment. "How did you know that? You never saw my father. I never told anybody but Al . . . oh." They'd been talking about me again, and my anger rose. "Well! It certainly is lowbrow for two men to gossip about a woman!'"

"Is my brow low?" he asked innocently. "I hadn't noticed any change."

I sat seething, wondering how men managed to twist everything to suit themselves.

Then I looked around and saw we were in open country, although I had been too engrossed to note leaving the city behind. The team of black horses had covered the ground with a smoother gait than horses usually did, so fast were we approaching David's ranch.

When we stopped in front of the hacienda, Chico came running to meet us.

"Señor Monterro!" he exclaimed. "You have come

back! It is good to see you again, only Señor Roberts . . . he is in bad humor these days."

Johnny nodded as he handed the reins to Chico. "He isn't angry with me anymore, Chico. Walk the horses until they are cool, then bring them to water, eh, *niño*?"

My eyes were drawn to the low hacienda. If David was here, why didn't he come to meet us? Apprehension filled me when I remembered my conduct at the duel. Perhaps he might even refuse to see me!

Shawohanee opened the door when we reached the veranda. She motioned us inside and led the way to a room opening off the large center quarters. My heart beat so madly it seemed a certainty that everyone would hear.

Then I stepped into the room, and a gasp rose unbidden to my lips. David lay in bed, his bandaged arm showing above covers that concealed the rest of him. His eyes were closed in a face that was unnaturally white. Was he dead?

Chapter Twenty-one

"David!" I cried, running to the bed.

The eyelids above his sandy mustache slowly opened. His blue eyes had trouble focusing on me as a weak smile tugged at his mouth.

"Hello, Shadow," he said, trying to push himself higher on the pillows.

Shawohanee capably propped pillows behind him so he could sit up.

"What has happened to you?" I asked in dismay. "Have you been ill?"

"You might say that," he answered in a breathy whisper. "I think it's called steel poisoning."

"From the wound on your arm?"

He glanced at the bandage. "Oh, no, that's all right now. It's healing fine."

"Then what . . . ?"

He winced and light perspiration popped out on his forehead. "It's nothing."

"What did my uncle do to you?" I demanded. "Was there more fighting after I left?"

"Calm down, Shadow. Please don't get so excited.

I've had a fever for several days, and it's left me weak as a cat."

Shawohanee handed him a glass of water. He took a sip and then a wry grin showed on his face.

"Your spectacular entrance distracted me enough to let Count Chauvanne get in an extra lick or two. He punctured my side, and I didn't even notice it in the general confusion over my bloody arm."

"Oh, David, I'm so sorry," I said contritely. "I was an awful fool to come screeching in as I did. Can you forgive me?"

"You're forgiven, my dear." Then a weak grin showed as he said, "At least you didn't cause as much commotion as you did rescuing your sun-grinner."

"You *were* with the vigilantes!" I said indignantly. "You would have let them hang Juan! Oh, David, how could you be a part of such a thing?"

He groaned. "My weakened condition must be affecting my mouth. Yes, I was there. Having you see me knocked about made me so angry I was ready to kill. After I cooled off, I would have been glad to cancel the whole episode, but your uncle wouldn't hear of it."

A sinking sensation made my knees wobble, and I stared at him aghast. "You mean Count Chauvanne was there with the vigilantes, too? Why has he never mentioned it?"

"He's just biding his time, Shadow," David answered. "I warned you once about him, and I'll say it again. There's evil surrounding him . . . perhaps a sort of madness. He revels in misery and gore and thrives on killing."

"Then why do you go along with him?" Bewilder-

285

ment filled me as I watched David panting from his exertions.

He rallied to say, "Count Chauvanne is the head honcho of the vigilantes, and most of them are maniacs like him. We go along with him . . . after we've had enough to drink and after he's ranted us into a state of madness like his own. But I'm through with the whole bunch. No more . . . no more . . ."

Shawohanee tried to mop his forehead, but he impatiently shrugged away.

"How did you get out here, Shadow?" he asked. "Has your uncle treated you all right? He was like a crazy man the day of the duel after you left."

"I rode out with Johnny Monterro, David," I said evenly. "I've been staying with Allen's aunt, so I really don't know how things are going at the mansion."

"Monterro!" David exclaimed, mouthing the name as though it had a bad taste. "So the great master of all he surveys is now allowed to call on you just as though he were a regular gentleman!"

"You needn't be so ugly, David," I said angrily. "You should be grateful that Juan saved your ranch for you." Then I added more quietly, "Juan has always been a gentleman with me."

Shawohanee poured a spoonful of liquid from a small bottle and offered it to David. After he swallowed the potion, she nodded her satisfaction and left the room.

"Why doesn't she ever say anything?" I asked pettishly, miffed over David's sarcasm.

"She's mute—I thought you knew."

"No, I didn't. I'm sorry," I said vaguely. "Has a

doctor been to see you?"

"No, and I don't need a doctor. Shawohanee is better than any of the quacks I know."

"Oh, David, let's not quarrel. You look so weak . . . and to think of your being out here alone with somebody who can't even talk!" Tears welled to my eyes at the thought.

"Don't cry, Shadow. And please forgive my rudeness. It's just . . ." He shook the covers in a puny fit of rage. "It's just that I hate having to lie flat on my back like this. I hate it! I hate being wounded! I hate hurting!" He lay back gasping, while perspiration in fresh supply threatened his eyes.

I sat on the edge of the bed and used my kerchief to keep the salty fluid from running into his eyes, then smoothed his sandy hair back from his forehead.

"I know," I said soothingly, then, "David, do you still love me?" The question seemed to come from someone outside myself.

He looked surprised. "Of course, I still love you! But I'm not going to wait forever to marry you. As soon as I can sit a horse I intend to pay a visit to your guardian. I'm going to have it out with him, and this time he won't have a sword in his hand! No matter what he says or does, we'll get married and put this whole mess behind us."

He pulled me roughly against him with his good arm, wincing when my weight touched his body. I felt again the silky mustache as his lips covered mine. Then I was back in the clouds of happiness, with all the uncertainty and misery behind, and I reveled in the feeling.

When David at last freed my lips, I sat up. "David,

we'll get married right away! That way I can help Shawohanee take care of you."

"But it's so soon . . . you know . . . since Julia died," he said uncertainly. "If we don't wait, you know what a scandal it will cause. I thought I would go talk to him and either convince him to let you marry or take the case to court. Just the threat of that might make him reconsider, for it would cause talk he wouldn't like. We can't just elope for you're still his legal ward."

Restlessly, I rose. "We can't help it if people want to talk. You need me now, David, and you know it. Julia is dead, and nothing can hurt her anymore."

I walked to the window and looked at the sky. "I'm afraid of my uncle, David. I don't want to live in his house anymore. Allen said he's been using my inheritance for his own purposes, and I want it stopped. There must be a legal way to force him to an accounting. Perhaps I can use the threat of it to force his permission for our marriage."

"You'd better not threaten him, Shadow. He's capable of anything if he gets angry enough." Again he flapped the covers. "Damn! I'm going to get up!" He raised his voice to shout, "Shawohanee!"

Johnny appeared in the doorway. "She left, Roberts. Anything I can help you with?"

David glared angrily at him, then a glance at me made him take a deep breath, and his voice was lower when he spoke. "No, thanks, Monterro." Then a speculative look crossed his face. "Wait," he said slowly, "perhaps there is something you can do for me."

Johnny's eyebrows rose in a question.

"Keep Shadow from getting herself killed until I'm back on my feet. She's set on tackling her uncle, and he's a dangerous man, my friend, so don't let her do it."

Then he looked at me. "Wait until I can speak for us. Please, Shadow?"

"Don't worry about anything," I said softly.

My happiness at knowing we would soon be together for all time made me certain I could handle anything. Already I was planning to end my visit with Aunt Mina and return to the manor to face my uncle.

"Lie back now," I said, removing the extra pillows so he would. "I'll be back as soon as I can, David."

On the return trip I sat immersed in my thoughts until Johnny interrupted them. "He's right, you know—about your uncle's being dangerous when crossed."

"How do you know? You have never met him, have you?"

He clucked soothingly at the nervous team he was holding to a walk before he answered. "I couldn't help overhearing your conversation with Roberts. If Count Chauvanne is head of the gang of killers you rescued me from, I know him. He put the rope around my neck."

Trees were giving way to scattered buildings as we neared the city, but I paid them scant heed. My thoughts were of my uncle and the things I had learned about him, and they were not pleasant thoughts. He had tried to kill Juan and he had tried to poison me. Poor Carlie had nearly died from drinking wine meant for me. I had told David I was afraid of him, and I was, but it would not keep me from facing him. One way or another, I would force him to give permission for me to marry the man I loved, and soon.

Suddenly Johnny continued speaking, as though there'd been no interval of silence since his last words. "And Allen told me about his attempt on your life. We were lowbrow enough to discuss it in detail. I told him if you said you had been drugged, then it was so."

I tossed my head at the reference to being lowbrow. As usual, he was making fun of me.

"Count Chauvanne won't dare to harm me now," I said emphatically. "He could pooh-pooh my accusation the first time, making people believe I was delirious from a fever, but it wouldn't work again."

Johnny's look was skeptical, but he said nothing.

"Did you know his mother has been confined in the attic of the mansion for a long time?" I asked, but before he could answer, I continued, "Nobody has ever investigated whether or not she is actually insane. She is so drugged with opium she can't speak for herself anymore. Isn't that dreadful?"

Johnny nodded.

I raised my head defiantly. "Well, he isn't about to do that to me!"

"Why not?" Johnny asked, and suddenly the air seemed to grow colder.

Dr. Dijon's needle came to mind as I remembered the weeks I had lain delirious in what he'd called a bout of pneumonia. I had been helpless to stop him then, but now Allen knew about it, and David would surely investigate any disappearance or sudden illness on my part. And Johnny—he was still enough Juan to keep harm away from me, wasn't he?

"Because you wouldn't let him," I said in answer to his question. "You said you wouldn't let anyone harm me."

He glanced my way and his eyes were serious. "That's right, Shadow. But just so Count Chauvanne doesn't have the chance, why don't you stay at Miss DeJung's house until Roberts is up and around?"

"David needs me now," I said frankly. "I want to get Carlie and my things and return to the mansion this evening. Will you take me?"

"No."

I sat seething with anger. How dare he? No explanation, regrets, or pleas of another engagement. Just no to my request. Never in the past would he have refused me anything I asked. Why were things so different now? Where was the Juan I had known?

I sneaked a glance. He was serenely guiding the blacks through the city traffic, apparently unaware of me. It gave me a strangely forlorn and lonesome feeling, almost as though it were only recently that I had been orphaned. Had I lost my old companion now that he was rich and powerful? Pride forbade my asking an explanation.

We arrived at Aunt Mina's home and I allowed Johnny to assist me from the carriage and accompany me to the door. Then I turned to him, saying in my most haughty manner, "Thank you for the drive, Mr. Monterro. It's been a lovely day," before I sailed inside the opened door.

The housekeeper looked from me to where Johnny stood on the porch, patently uncertain as to what she should do. He bowed elaborately in my direction, then returned to the carriage as the door closed between us.

"Who is it?" Aunt Mina asked as she came into the hall. "Shadow, I'm so glad you're back. It's teatime. Didn't that young man stay?"

"I'm afraid not," I answered. "Perhaps I had better run up to my room before we have tea, Aunt Mina. I want Carlie to pack our things."

"Oh, dear me, are you going home already? I do wish you would stay longer. It will be quite late when you get there, won't it? Why not wait until morning? Oh, dear me! Young people are so impetuous," she said, fluttering in her dismay.

"You've been a dear," I said gently. "So dear I'm afraid I've stayed much longer than I intended. I'll only be a moment, and then we can have tea and a nice, long chat."

After telling Carlie my plans, I changed quickly to a tea gown before returning to the parlor. Allen was to call this evening, and I knew I could coax him to take me home.

I shuddered—calling the big, scary mansion home didn't make it any less fearsome. After the showdown with my uncle I would marry David—and then the word home would truly have meaning.

Chapter Twenty-two

Allen didn't come to see me that evening. Instead, a messenger brought a large box of flowers. The note inside read, "Shadow, my dear, please forgive me. Something of the greatest importance has arisen that I must attend to, and it concerns you more than anyone. I'll come to Aunt Mina's first thing in the morning to discuss it with you. All my love, Allen."

Oh, drat, I thought fretfully. Just when you need a man the most, he isn't there. Now I would have to change my plans for the evening.

"Allen isn't coming to call this evening, Aunt Mina," I said, and I tried to smile so she would think everything was all right. "However, I must return to my guardian's home at once."

I didn't understand Allen's note. But David was lying wounded, with only a mute Indian to care for him, and I wanted to change that as soon as I could.

Aunt Mina looked alarmed. "Oh, my dear, are you sure you wouldn't rather wait until morning? It's so late in the day, perhaps you should reconsider."

"There is something I must discuss with my uncle

tonight, Aunt Mina, and it's really quite urgent. If I stay here, I won't sleep a wink, I know."

"Oh, dear . . ." She glanced at her housekeeper. "Have my carriage brought round," she said, and then to me, "I'll get my bonnet and cloak, child."

"No, wait!" I put my hand on her arm to keep her from fluttering up the stairs. "You needn't go with me."

"You can't go out alone at this time of night," she said indignantly.

"I won't be alone. Carlie will be with me, and also your coachman, Aunt Mina."

Her quivering hand went uncertainly to her bosom. Impetuously, she hugged me. "You are so rash, my dear. Are you sure you'll be all right with just a maid in attendance?"

"Aunt Mina, I'm not a child," I said, returning her hug. "Of course, I'll be fine. We'll send your coachman right back when we arrive at Chauvanne manor. Oh, thank you, Aunt Mina. Thank you for everything."

She fluttered around until Carlie and I were safely settled in the big old carriage with our luggage in the boot. Amid flurried farewells we began our journey to the house I had come to dread.

"Wouldn't it be nice to live here in San Francisco, Miss Shadow?" Carlie asked wistfully. "I mean, all the time."

"I suppose," I answered absently. It would be nicer still to live with the man you loved.

David's hacienda was rather small, of course, but it could be made much nicer than it was now. New furniture and carpets would do wonders. And we would have to have servants. We could build a cottage or two for them to live in after we staffed our home as it should be.

Better still, as soon as David was well we could order a mansion built while we traveled on a belated honeymoon. I was a wealthy woman, I reminded myself. As soon as my guardian consented to our marriage, we could do anything and everything we wished.

Darkness was closing around the carriage. The smell of the ocean drifted into my nostrils as the night fog crept over the land. Sounds from the horses' hooves grew muffled and the air grew cooler. Shivering, I wrapped my cloak more tightly around me, but my chill wasn't only from the fog.

Was Count Chauvanne really mad, as David said? The thought was a terrifying one. When I had first arrived from New York, I had thought my aunt had him firmly under her thumb, but that had been disproved. She hadn't known of his refusal to allow me to marry, so she wasn't part of whatever plot he had to keep my money. Now that I was no longer a threat to Julia, perhaps my aunt would become my ally. Sadness filled me at the thought of my poor cousin's unhappiness. I wished again we had been better friends.

Another thought made the nape of my neck prickle. Had Count Chauvanne killed Julia? Had he stabbed his own daughter? Surely, it couldn't be—what reason made any sense? For that matter why would anybody kill her? There was no motive, no sensible reason.

Only David gained something by Julia's dying, and he had convinced me his freedom from the marriage would have occurred anyway.

The carriage stopped and I realized we were at the iron gates. We had to wait for them to be opened, since the fog had muffled our approach. We passed through and went up the drive, rattling to a stop at the veranda. The coachman helped us alight, bringing part of our luggage as he escorted us to the door. Chung ran to bring what the coachman hadn't carried as Bertha welcomed us.

"It's glad I am the both of you are back," she said happily. "This house has been a tomb without you."

"Is my aunt still up, Bertha?" I asked. I wanted her to be there when I confronted my uncle. I needed her support, for surely a blood relative wouldn't allow even her husband to harm me.

"Madam Countess is in the salon with Count Chauvanne. Will you be joining them, Miss Shadow?" Bertha asked.

I nodded, handing Carlie my hat and gloves and allowing her to remove my cloak. After smoothing my hair in front of the hall mirror, I raised my chin and walked into the golden salon to confront my guardians.

"Good evening, Aunt Elizabeth . . . uncle," I said quietly.

"Shadow! Oh, my dear, I am so glad you have returned," my aunt said, rising to meet me. "I've been so dreadful about so many things! My dear child, I have wronged you so terribly since your arrival. How can I make it up to you?"

Her abrupt change startled me before relief pushed my surprise away. "Oh, Aunt Elizabeth, it's all right. I think I understand."

"Yes, yes, my dear niece," Count Chauvanne said smoothly. "I'm afraid we've both been somewhat abrupt with you. However, things will be different from now on."

"Oh?" I asked, facing him. "Well, I would like your permission to marry David Roberts immediately. He is ill from the wound you inflicted and needs me to help care for him now, not sometime in the future."

My aunt gasped. "So soon?" she asked. "What will people say?"

"That's impossible!" the count said curtly. "I told you there would be no marriage to anybody for several years yet, and especially not to David Roberts!"

I raised my chin in defiance. "I don't care what people say, Aunt Elizabeth. And as for you, uncle, just why don't you want me to marry?"

"David Roberts is a cad!" he said angrily. "My daughter was in love with him, poor silly fool that she was. Even though I knew it was a mistake, I allowed the bounder to court her, and he didn't even stay true! I will not allow the same thing to recur."

"Julia broke their engagement," I said. "When she changed her mind and wanted David back, he preferred not to resume the arrangement. You forced him to agree to the marriage in the first place by threatening to take away his ranch. Do you think you can buy love?"

Our eyes locked until he broke away to pace the room. My aunt sank into a chair, sniffling into a kerchief, and she looked so forlorn that my heart went out to her.

"Please, Aunt Elizabeth, don't cry. I didn't tell David not to go through with the wedding, and as it happened, Julia never knew she was being jilted."

"My poor baby," the countess sobbed. "My poor, dead child." Then she looked up through reddened eyes. "Who killed her? Oh, why can't they find out? We are under a cloud of suspicion and scandal already, and if you and David marry so soon . . . oh-h-h," she wailed.

"Julia can't be hurt anymore, Aunt Elizabeth," I said gently. "She's at peace and not troubled by anything in this world."

Then I looked accusingly at my uncle. "David is wounded and ill. You nearly killed him."

"It's a great pity I didn't," Count Chauvanne said slowly. "You can forget about marrying him, however, or anyone else for that matter." He stared at me icily. "I will never allow it."

"Perhaps if the court calls you to account for the funds of my inheritance, you'll change your mind, sir. I'm sure Mr. DeJung can arrange to have an audit made."

Angry red suffused his face. "How dare you!" he thundered. Then, surprisingly, he began to laugh. It was such laughter as I had never heard—high and shrill, almost hysterical, and it seemed to go on forever. Cold chills ran up my spine.

My aunt ceased sniffling and stared at him, her mouth slightly open in amazement.

At last the eerie laughter was replaced by a sneer of deviltry. "What funds?" he asked scornfully. "You have no money, my dear. Your inheritance is gone!"

My aunt was the first to speak after the outburst. "What do you mean? Ferd . . . what have you done?"

"What have *I* done?" he asked scornfully. "What

have *you* done might be a better question. Where do you think the money came from to feed your insatiable appetite for clothing and jewelry? Did you and Julia have to parade like walking jewelers' cases, continually changing the display? You both have enough gowns in your closets to clothe every female in San Francisco. Did you ever think about the cost?"

Aunt Elizabeth looked bewildered. "But I thought we had plenty of money," she said uncertainly. "Why didn't you tell me I was spending too much?"

"Tell you! Before your brother died I told you I lost a great deal of money in a business deal that went sour, but you wouldn't listen," he said. "Have you even the remotest idea how much it costs to keep a houseful of servants and a stable of horses? Bah! You didn't care!"

I listened to their bickering with half an ear. Mr. Arbuthnot had said I was wealthy, but how much money that meant, I had no idea. However, surely it was a great deal. How could my uncle have spent it all in such a short time? Was this my father's final bitter joke—to leave me penniless in the world?

Raising my voice to be heard over the quarrel in progress, I asked, "Since my money has disappeared, now will you allow me to marry? After all, what further use am I to you?"

My guardians stared at me in horror.

"Oh, my dear . . ." my aunt began.

The count interrupted. "I'll take care of this, Elizabeth." His eyes seemed to bore into me. "I'll be perfectly frank with you, my dear. A husband—*any* husband—will demand an accounting, and that I cannot afford. You will remain in our household and say nothing to anyone. Do you understand?"

"I will not be held prisoner," I said defiantly. "You can't treat me as you do your mother, Count Chauvanne. I have friends!"

"What can friends do?" he asked. "I'm still your guardian. I need time to replace the money I lost, and with or without your cooperation, I shall have it. Now go to your room and stay there."

His voice lowered menacingly as he said, "I'm afraid Dr. Dijon will diagnose a relapse of your old illness and be forced to treat you again, my dear niece."

The blood drained from my face.

"Ferd . . ." my aunt pleaded.

"I will brook no interference from you in this matter, Elizabeth," he said. "Do you want to be forever disgraced by having the world know your husband is an embezzler?"

He grasped my arm. "This time I shall escort you to your room myself to make sure you're there. There will be no running away again."

I struggled furiously to free myself. When I would not go willingly, Count Chauvanne carried me up the stairs to my room. Without another word, he tossed me onto the bed and left. I heard the key turn in the lock and then his footsteps receding down the hall.

While I lay catching my breath, my mind frantically tested first this method of escape, then that, but there was no practical solution. I knew I had to find a way. If I remained until Dr. Dijon came, there would be no escape from his needle.

Questions would be asked, of course, but what could anyone prove? As Allen had said, Dr. Dijon was a respected member of his profession and above suspicion.

Rising, I went to look out the high window. The fog was solid and heavy. Even were I to shout for help, my voice wouldn't carry far enough through the muffling blanket to do any good. Probably no one was even out there in weather like this. If the servants heard me, it would do no good, for they would believe whatever Count Chauvanne told them.

All the servants, save Carlie, and surely she would come to tend me. She would unlock the door and we could go down the back stairway and escape. My spirits revived.

"Miss Shadow!" An urgent whisper came through the door with a scratching fingernail against wood.

I ran to the door. "Carlie! I'm so glad you came. Unlock the door and let me out."

"Sh-h-h, Miss Shadow. Count Chauvanne forbade my coming, but I had to see if you're all right. I can't unlock the door. There's no key."

"Go get help, Carlie," I said urgently. "Tell Tom the count is going to drug me again. Tell him to go fetch Mr. DeJung. Quickly!"

There was no answer. I put my ear to the door and heard faint scufflings outside. The beginning of a scream was cut short by a gurgling noise and then there was silence.

"Who's out there?" I called frantically, beating on the door with both fists. "Let me out!"

There was no answer. It was as though I were alone in the mansion, with only the creakings to keep me company. Panic surged through me.

Chapter Twenty-three

I screamed at the top of my lungs until my voice grew hoarse and my throat dry as dust. My fists beat against the door of their own accord until their soreness made me stop. Why didn't one of the servants come? They must surely hear the noise I was making. Where was my aunt? After her speech of repentance she would come to my aid, wouldn't she? Oh, why didn't someone come to help me?

I realized I was panting like a caged animal and paused to take stock. While I caught my breath I decided I would not be a craven coward and submit to whatever Count Chauvanne had in store for me. Conquistodore trumpets thundered a challenge of war as I looked around the room for a weapon.

Despairingly, I realized there was nothing I could use effectively against a man with more strength than I, and one who was probably armed with a weapon. Unless . . .

The chair at the dressing table caught my eye. Tipping it on its side, I pulled at the legs, hoping one was loose enough to remove. It was a sturdy piece of furniture, put together by a craftsman who had intended it to last. Tug as I would, the chair remained intact. At last I gave up, sobbing in frustration as I angrily thumped it erect.

Impatiently, I brushed at my tears, disgusted with this evidence of feminine weakness. At least I could make it more difficult for anyone to get into my room. Propped under the doorknob, the chair provided what I hoped was an effective barrier to entrance. To make it even firmer, I pushed and shoved the washstand until it provided a wall to hold the chair in place.

Satisfied I had done all I could to remain alone in my prison, I looked down at my traveling outfit. It was much too warm for inside. My efforts had caused rivulets of perspiration under its heavy folds. I selected a morning gown from my wardrobe, one light enough to run in if I were given a chance to escape.

Drearily, I wondered if Carlie was badly hurt as I settled on low-heeled slippers for my feet. Had she been punished for attempting to befriend me?

My fists clenched as I contemplated the possibility. If Count Chauvanne had harmed Carlie, he had one more sin I would make sure he paid for!

Hastily, I undressed. Removing the corset gave more room to breathe, so I omitted it under the loose gown, and also the long stockings that might hamper my movements. I thought longingly of the freedom I had experienced in Chico's garments, but they were unattainable now.

It would be well if I were rested, so I placed the slippers beside my bed and lay atop the green coverlet to compose myself. As usually happened in the silence of night, the house made strange sounds as it groaned and grumbled while damp, cold air swirled around its corners. Distant fog horns moaned warnings to a sleeping world that rocks and reefs were hidden in the waters of the harbor. It was an eerie cry that made me feel even more lonesome than before.

I glanced around the room, and the light from the lamp made corner shadows sway rhythmically as it flared and subsided. Perhaps it would be better if the room were in darkness. If the door were forced open, at least I could see better than someone coming in from the light. I turned off the lamp. Pitch blackness was unnerving, and the usual sounds grew louder as I strained my eyes looking fearfully around.

Once I thought I heard stealthy footsteps outside the door, but a shaky, "Who's there?" brought no response. No brisk footsteps heralded a passing servant, no door slammed to signal someone's retiring for the night, and no voices could be heard in the usual idle chatter the Chauvannes carried on when they were retiring. Was I alone in the house? Where had everyone gone?

The night crept on as though on the back of a snail, while I shivered on the soft coverlet. "Help me, Mother," I whispered. "Oh, Carmelita, tell me what to do."

Did Edward St. George know what he had done to me? His face floated before me, eyes devoid of expression, so there was no way of telling.

David . . . David, if you love me, why can't you sense I need you now? But what could he do? He was weak from his wound and unable to get out of bed. And most likely drowsy from Shawohanee's potions. David . . . my love . . .

I remembered our first meeting when I tripped over the rope on the ferry. How startled I'd been when I removed the hat from my eyes and saw how very much he resembled my father! His impudence in stealing a kiss before Sarah reached us made me smile. Even with Julia, David had been somewhat like a mischievous small boy, pliable and dependent on her whim to make plans for their future.

Our first ride together had not been his doing, but only because Julia had preferred a shopping trip and had carelessly turned her fiance over to her cousin as a sort of sop to both. Still, my pulse quickened as I relived the freedom and delight of that day with David.

He'd been so kind and attentive, much as I had always longed for Edward St. George to be. The warmth of his arms as he helped me alight had filled me with a lovely feeling of being cared for and cherished. Strange that David so closely resembled my father in looks. His actions were very different.

Juan's voice echoed in my mind. "Does his appeal hinge on the fact that he looks so much like your father?" Was that the basis of my love for him? I thought about it as the hours dragged on their interminable way. Perhaps I had been drawn to him at first because he was so like my father, but that didn't mean I had fallen in love with him for the same reason.

There had been mutual attraction between us from our first meeting. His eyes had lit up when he saw me, as though in recognition of someone he'd been seeking for a long time. Was that how love came to you?

If only I knew what real love was. My mother could have taught me, had she lived. Carmelita had surely been in love with Edward and he with her, else my father could not have hated her dying enough to estrange a child that was part of her. She and I looked much alike, and perhaps that was the reason he could hardly bear to look at me.

My thoughts jerked back to the present when I heard the creak of a slowly turning key in the lock of my door. I held my breath, straining to hear each sound in the pitch blackness. Goose bumps broke out on my arms, and a chill of fear went racing up my spine.

The doorknob squeaked slightly. I knew a hand was turning it while its owner wondered why the door wouldn't open. I slipped out of bed, kneeling on the far side from the door. The thudding of my heart was louder than any covert action outside as I strained to hear over its wild drumming.

Wood rasped against wood as the door was pressed inward against the chair propped beneath the knob. I wanted to go push my weight against the washstand to help hold it in place, but terror held me paralyzed. Would my barrier hold against the intruder?

A thud against the heavy paneling told me a shoulder had hit it in an attempt to open the door by force. Another followed, and then a thin streamer of light penetrated the darkness of my room. Now I could see the looming hulk of the washstand outlined in the light from the hall. It rocked back and forth as another blow landed against the door.

Blow after blow followed. They were accompanied by guttural grunts, as though an animal threw himself madly against a barrier between itself and its prey. Between blows I heard hoarse breathing, as though my attacker were in a blood rage. Panic made me whimper as the washstand swayed, each time in a wider arc than before.

With a screech as from a soul in hell, the door shoved the chair against the stand and toppled it with a deafening crash. A dark figure stood panting in the doorway, straining to see into the darkness beyond the circle of light coming from behind him.

It was Count Chauvanne, but not the suave gentleman of the mansion. This was a creature spewed from some lower region, slavering at the mouth as growlings came from deep within him.

The light glinted on steel, and my heart missed a beat when I saw the knife in his hand.

As his eyes grew accustomed to the dim light, he moved forward, still snarling and testing the scent of the air like a hound on the trail. His hair hung disheveled in front of his face, swinging from side to side as he swung his head first this way, then that.

I crouched, frozen, watching while terror threatened to strangle me. When he was far enough into the room to leave a clear path out the door, I leaped to my feet and ran.

But I wasn't fast enough. With a maniacal howl, he stretched out his arm and flung me backward. My head hit the window, shattering the pane into a thousand pieces. Dazed, I watched him come forward in an exaggerated slow motion, holding the knife high like a priest about to sacrifice an offering on the altar of his god.

I closed my eyes, waiting for the end of my life. Carmelita, oh, Carmelita . . . Mother, help me!

Suddenly an animal howl of pain broke the night. I

opened my eyes to see my tormentor clawing at his back, dancing in agony as he tried to evade a dark shadow behind him. He screamed again as he turned toward his fate, then fell backward at my feet, clawing weakly at the knife sticking from the center of his chest.

"Bad blood! Bad blood!" the old countess chanted, bending over him as she watched the twitchings accompanying his death. "Bad blood must end, my son. The Chauvanne line is tainted with madness. Let this be the last of it!"

She swayed, apparently mesmerized by the sight before her. She was still talking, but now the words were too soft to hear. Suddenly I knew who had killed Julia. On her granddaughter's wedding morn, she had made certain Julia would never bear children. The Chauvanne bloodline was ended.

Count Chauvanne's head lay on my bare feet while his lifeblood pumped out. I stood like a statue, wondering if I would be next, but the old woman took no notice of me. She straightened, watching her son until his movements ceased. Blood oozed more slowly from the wound in his chest, then stopped when his guttural breathing came to a halt.

The old countess nodded, as though satisfied. "It is over, my son, over." She crooned as though singing to a baby. "Now we will rest, you and I."

She picked up the lamp, crashing the chimney against the bedpost to remove it. Deliberately, she splashed the contents over herself and her son. A humming sound accompanied her actions, and she looked like a contented old witch watering her garden of death. When the lamp was empty, she dropped it amidst the wreckage and then hurried into the hall. Before I could move, she was back with a burning paper in her hand.

"It is time to go, my son . . . *mon petite*," she chanted. "It is over, it is over at last." She touched the fire to his clothing and to herself, all the while chanting a wordless mumble of sound as the flames took hold.

I stared in horror as the fire grew to encompass her face and body, hardly noting the fire at my feet. Something inside me snapped, and I screamed and screamed and screamed. Diedre's face appeared where the face of the old countess had been, her golden locks in flames around her head. Her bow-shaped mouth writhed in agony as she beat at the fire.

A burning I remembered spread over my hands and arms while I watched Diedre crumple and char in the devouring flames. The pyre at my feet ignited my flimsy gown, crackling its delight at new fuel, and my shrieking continued until there was nothing else in the world.

Chapter Twenty-four

Rough hands wrapped a blanket around me, smothering wicked tongues of fire. I fought in a frenzy of fear, still screaming because I couldn't seem to stop.

"Open your eyes, Shadow, open your eyes!" an urgent voice said close to my ear.

I felt myself lifted from the floor and held in a strangling embrace, but I was part of endless shrieking and it was part of me and would never cease.

"Stop your bawling," the voice commanded, and somehow I was forced to obey.

Through teary eyes I saw Juan's face as he carried me through the smoke and fire surrounding us. The flames had traveled from my room to the hall and blossomed like an evil spreading flower of hell. Fire was claiming the walls and ceiling and everything in its path. Juan dodged sparks as best he could, loosening one hand to beat out any that landed on one of us.

A babble of voices rose from below. The clang of a fire truck sounded faintly in the distance. Juan carried me to the stairway, backing away when sheets of searing flame shot upward in the draft. He whirled to retrace his steps, pausing when the door of a linen closet blew off in an explosion of heat.

Carlie toppled out at our feet and lay with her head at an odd angle to her body. Her poor face was splotched with bruises and her eyes stared unseeingly. I whimpered as I realized she was dead.

"Don't start howling again," Juan warned, shaking me gently to get my attention. "We have to get out of here. Is there another way down?"

I gulped back my horror as I tore my eyes away from the sight of my maid. "The back stairs are straight ahead," I said. "I can walk if you'll put me down."

"Shut up and lie still," he ordered. He clutched me tighter as his long strides took us to the back stairs.

Flames nibbled at the railings, but the steps were still clear as Juan raced down them with me in his arms. The hungry fire licked lovingly at the curtains on the door, then flared in anger when Juan kicked the door flat and walked across it and out into the night.

Once outside he broke into a lope, carrying me into the safety of the foggy garden. When we were well away from the holocaust behind us he stopped, then sank to the ground, still holding me tight.

"Shadow . . ." he said, and his voice broke as he lowered his head against the blanket I was wrapped in. His body shook against mine while he held me even closer, almost squeezing my breath away.

"I can't breathe," I gasped.

He raised his head and there were tears in his eyes. "Shadow . . . Shadow . . . you stubborn little mule!

311

You almost got yourself killed."

I moaned with pain when the burning sensation in my hands and feet turned to vicious smarting.

"What's wrong?" he asked. He gently examined my hands, exclaiming, "Dear God!"

"My feet hurt, too," I wailed.

He opened the blanket, spreading it over the ground in careless haste as he lifted my feet to the light. "They're blistered, Shadow. I'd better get something to put on them," he said.

My glance followed his when he looked through the fog toward the mansion. Fire shot through the roof at the front of the house, but hadn't yet devoured the kitchen. He sprang up and raced for the back doorway he'd kicked free.

Fear filled me as I remembered Diedre's face in the flames. But it hadn't been Diedre—she had died in the fire at Miss Brigham's school.

Then Carlie's staring eyes came to mind. Carlie was real! Carlie had given her life for me! Sobs shook me as I cried for her and for me and for a world that was burning. Burying my face in the blanket, I sobbed a never-ending stream of woe.

Cooling grease enveloped my feet as Juan applied lard from the bucket he'd found. My hands were soon covered with melting balm that removed some of the dreadful smarting. But despite the relief, I continued to sob.

"Stop your bawling," Juan said softly, pulling me into his arms while he tucked the blanket around my flimsy scorched dress. "Oh, Shadow, I love you so much!"

The words penetrated my grief, and at last I could

control my sobbing. "W-what?" I asked, hiccupping.

He dabbed at my dripping face with his handkerchief, tenderly stemming the torrent of moisture. "I said I love you," he repeated.

We stared at each other, and his brown eyes softened before he lowered his head and kissed me. His lips touched mine, gently at first, soft and coaxing lips, spreading warmth through my body to dispel the chill of terror that was part of me.

Then his mouth grew more demanding. My heart pounded, but not with fear. A pulse beat in my throat like a tiny tom-tom of ecstasy. I settled into the bliss of his embrace, and there was no more terror, no more uncertainty. This was Juan, and his arms were my home.

Carmelita's laughter tinkled in my ears. "Now you know true love, my daughter."

I pushed away from Juan, wincing at the pain in my hands. "What?"

"I didn't say anything."

"I know you didn't, Juan. My mother spoke to me."

"You're delirious, my poor darling," he said.

Then his lips claimed mine again, and I drifted on warm clouds of euphoria, for the first time experiencing the magic of pure and perfect love.

A rending crash as part of the mansion collapsed in on itself brought me from my dream.

"Oh, Juan, look at the fire!" I exclaimed.

We stared through the drifting fog at the scene before us. The fire truck pumped valiantly, while men ran here and there tossing ineffectual buckets of water into the inferno of the once proud mansion. At times the water seemed to do more harm than good, for wherever it landed flames shot skyward in defiance.

I came back to earth with a crash. "My aunt! The servants! Oh, Juan, did everyone get out?"

"I saw only you as I came up the stairs, Shadow. If anyone else was in the house, they'll stay," Juan answered.

I tried to rise, gasping as my feet protested.

"Don't try to walk," Juan said, gathering me into his arms. "Where do you want to go?"

"We have to help the others."

"There are enough firemen and people swarming around to give help where it's needed. I won't leave you, my darling, and I doubt I'd be much help with you in my arms. Besides, Allen is headed this way now, I think. Isn't that him supporting your faltering lover?" Juan asked, smiling at me as I blushed in dismay.

"You needn't be vulgar," I said tartly. "Just how did *you* happen to be here when I needed help? You wouldn't even escort me home!"

He grinned and kissed the tip of my nose. "Knowing your determination to have your way about everything, I just stationed myself on the grounds and waited."

"Well, you didn't give me a reason for refusing my request," I said indignantly. "How did you know I'd be here?"

"You were so blamed pig-headed about it, I knew you'd get here some way. You have poor old Allen obeying your command at a snap of your fingers," he said with another grin.

"You needn't laugh at me," I said huffily, then

relented. "Oh, Juan . . . I'm so very glad you were here!"

"When I heard that glass shatter I knew you were in trouble. I had to break my way in, which is why it took me so long to reach you."

He glanced at the approaching pair. "Say it before they get here," he demanded.

"Say what?"

"You must know."

I did know. "I love you, Juan."

"I just had to hear you say so before I was sure," he said softly.

"Are you two all right?" Allen asked, helping David to a seat on a nearby bench. He saw the blanket wrapped around me and my greasy feet protruding from the bottom. "Good Lord, Shadow, were you burned?"

I looked beyond him to David. "David? Are you sure you're able to be up and around?"

"I'm sorry I wasn't here when you needed me," he said wearily. "I did ask you to wait until I was well before you tackled your guardian."

"I know." I glanced at Juan. "There's something I had better tell you, David."

"There is something I had better tell everybody," Allen interrupted. "My note asked you to wait at my aunt's home, Shadow. If you had done that, all of this might have been avoided."

I scowled at him. "Where was everybody tonight? Why weren't there any servants in the house? Except Carlie, that is," I said sadly.

"Count Chauvanne ordered a midnight mass for Julia in the cathedral and ordered the servants to attend," Allen said.

"And my aunt?"

"She went with them," he said shortly.

"I'm so glad," I said; then, "Don't you want to know what happened in there tonight?"

A crash split the night as the remaining part of the mansion fell in on itself. We stared horrified at the wreckage of a once beautiful home.

"What did happen, Shadow?" Allen asked.

"Count Chauvanne tried to kill me . . . *again*," I said, emphasizing the word. "He locked me in my room, so I locked him out, or tried to. I put a chair under the doorknob and the washstand against it, but he pushed the whole pile aside and came in like some rabid animal."

Allen groaned. "I didn't think he would go that far. Oh, Shadow, forgive me for not stepping in the first time he tried to kill you."

"Count Chauvanne was insane," I said bluntly. "His mother knew it, for it was she who rescued me." I related the events of the night until I reached the part where Carlie fell from the linen closet. Then I began to cry.

Juan rose, still holding me in his arms. "She has had enough for now. Her hands and feet need medical attention, and not from Dr. Dijon. I'd like to borrow your carriage, Allen. Is it here?"

David rose clumsily. "You had better wait up, Monterro. There's something Shadow must know." His eyes locked defiantly with Juan's. "You, too," he said grimly.

"Not tonight, my friend," Juan said. He whistled into the night, and the black stallion trotted up. "I'll trade my horse for your rig, Allen. Hurry it up! You ride ahead and have a doctor waiting at your aunt's home. It will be all right to take Shadow there, won't it?"

"Of course, of course," Allen said impatiently. "Wait here, David. I'll get the carriages."

He mounted the black stallion and galloped toward the fire. Soon he returned with two carriages rattling along behind him.

Juan shushed me as he tried to stop my flow of tears. Weariness overwhelmed me to a point where nothing mattered. My burnt skin was on fire, and the pain would have been enough to make me wail to the skies if I weren't so tired.

The coachman nodded at Juan's orders and clucked up the horses. We rode in silence, except for the groans I couldn't suppress when we hit an unusually deep rut. Juan brushed endless kisses into my hair, murmuring words of consolation and love. Despite my pain, a comfortable feeling of security filled me as he held me in his arms.

Allen was waiting when we reached Aunt Mina's home. He opened the carriage door and held out his arms, but Juan shook his head and stepped out still holding me close.

Aunt Mina fluttered around us while Juan carried me up the stairs. "Oh, dear, oh, dear, oh, dear," she said tearfully. "What a dreadful thing to happen!"

The doctor stood beside a bed that had been prepared for me. His black bag was open in readiness and his eyes swiftly took in my appearance.

Juan laid me gently on the bed, his worried eyes never leaving my face. "Shall I stay, Shadow?"

"I'm afraid you can't, young man," the doctor said. "It looks as though my patient needs rest, as well as treatment for burns. Perhaps you can see her tomorrow."

Juan ignored him, waiting for my reply.

"I'll be all right," I said wearily. I tried to smile, but don't think I did.

He stooped to kiss my forehead. "I'll be back first thing in the morning," he said huskily.

I watched him leave, then gave myself up to the doctor's ministrations.

Chapter Twenty-five

Fever followed my exposure and shock accompanied the burns on my hands and feet. I entered a nightmare of delirium. Creatures from another stratum chased me through empty mansions, threatening me with slimy claws. Sheets of fire tried to surround me, but always I was able to break through the searing ring just before I caught fire. Then I would have to evade the claws again, and so it went, endlessly.

At last I was rescued. I was tossing in an uneasy sleep when the sound of Juan's deep voice woke me.

"Open your eyes, Shadow," he said urgently. "Please wake up, my darling."

His face wavered above me when I opened sleep-drenched eyes.

"You've slept four days through!" he exclaimed.

The doctor was beside Juan, and he nodded approvingly. "Sometimes it take more than medicine to heal," he said. "You seem to have the needed ingredient, young man."

"Oh, dear me, is she awake?" Aunt Mina asked. She was carrying an armload of pillows to prop me up.

"Hello," I said to Juan, but it came out in a sort of a croak.

He knelt beside the bed so our eyes were on the same level. Then he just looked at me, ignoring the movements of the other people in the room.

"Ahem," the doctor said, clearing his throat to get my attention.

Reluctantly, I glanced at him.

"Are you ready to take nourishment, Miss St. George? It is my prescription for your return to health," he said jovially.

"I brought some soup, dear," Aunt Mina added.

Weak tears oozed from my eyes as I closed them against the brightness of the room. I heard Juan's voice in low conversation, and when I opened my eyes again we were alone.

He lifted me higher against the pillows and sat on the edge of the bed. "I've been so worried about you," he said with a sigh. "Do your hands and feet feel better?"

I looked stupidly at my bandaged hands, until memory of the fire returned to my addled brain. "Oh, yes," I said vaguely. "Please . . . may I have a drink? I'm so dry. . . ."

"Of course." He held a glass of water to my lips while I sipped. "Now eat some soup," he said firmly.

Obediently, I opened my mouth each time he put the spoon to my lips. The warm liquid filled my stomach and gave me more strength with each spoonful.

At last I turned away from the spoon. "Enough
. . ."

Juan rose. "I had better get Miss DeJung before we
cause a gigantic scandal being alone in your boudoir."
His face was thoughtful as he looked down at me.
"You do remember saying you love me, don't you?"

I nodded, smiling so he would smile in return. His
answering grin brought relief to my troubled mind.
With him to take care of me, everything could be
righted in my shaken world.

He shook his head. "Here I stand smirking like an
idiot when there are things to be done. If Miss Mina
helps you dress, do you think you can come downstairs? There's a whole delegation waiting to see you."

"Who?"

"Allen, of course . . . and David Roberts."

"Oh, Juan, have you told him about us?"

He shook his head. "I didn't have to, Shadow. But
I don't want to tell you things in bits and pieces. If
you're able, please come down. Allen says he is your
attorney, and perhaps you had better hear it from
him."

"Carlie will . . ." Then I stopped, appalled. Carlie
was dead! My eyes filled with tears.

Juan pulled out his handkerchief, shaking his head
in despair. "Don't cry, my darling. The past is over.
You mustn't mourn any longer for things that can't be
helped."

He gathered me into his arms. "Shadow, I love you
so very much—since I first found you bawling in the
tack room. Now I'll finally have a chance to make
sure you never cry again."

I sniffled, but a chuckle made me sit up straight. "What are you laughing at?" I demanded.

"Those bandages make you look as though you're wearing boxing gloves," he said, still smiling. "Are you back in fighting trim already?"

"Well, I don't think they're so funny!"

"I don't either," he said softly. "I just wanted you to stop crying, and you have. Now I'll go ask Miss Mina to come up here."

He was right, of course. His teasing had brought me out of a crying session. It would be nice to be married to a man who could keep me from weeping. Then my eyes opened wide at an astonishing thought. Juan hadn't asked me to marry him!

Oh, dear me, I thought, much like fluttering Aunt Mina. Now that he's rich Johnny Monterro could he possibly think . . . no, of course not! He loves me. He said so many times. But he *hadn't* proposed marriage.

"So we're going to get up, are we?" Aunt Mina asked as she bustled into the room with a maid in attendance. "Edith will help you, my dear. Oh, I'm so glad you're out of that dreadful delirium! Allen has been out of his mind with worry. And that other young man! Oh, dear me!"

The maid helped me wash and dress. My feet were unbandaged but still tender, and I winced when shoes touched them. However, it felt good to wear a pretty frock instead of the nightwear I had worn through my scary nightmares. When my toilette was complete, Aunt Mina nodded her satisfaction.

"Now I had better fetch that nice young man to help you down the steps," she said. "You are in need of a much better prop than my feeble arm."

I expected Juan to appear, but it was Allen who presented himself, offering me his arm to lean on.

"It's wonderful to see you up, Shadow. You look absolutely beautiful," he said gallantly.

My reflection in the mirror showed a wan face much the worse for wear, but I was grateful for his chivalrous lie. The stairs seemed to waver before me as we started down, but I clung to Allen's arm and willed my feet to move properly.

When we reached the parlor, Juan and David were waiting. Allen led me to a deep chair and pulled another around so he could look at me.

"While you were ill, my dear, I took it on myself to assume the role of your attorney. Now that you're well, of course you may choose another, if you wish."

"Oh, Allen, you're one of the best friends I have," I said. "I'm very grateful you have concerned yourself with my affairs . . . and I certainly hope you will continue to do so."

I glanced at the others, wondering why David looked so sheepish. "Has your wound healed, David?" I asked.

He nodded. "Shadow . . ." He looked toward Allen. "If you don't tell her, I'm going to!"

"Tell me what?" I looked around in bewilderment. "What is this all about?"

"Shadow, there is something I've been trying to tell you ever since the night you insisted on returning to the Chauvanne home alone," Allen said. "However, I think it should be told in an orderly fashion."

Juan and David pulled chairs beside Allen's, and I thought how handsome the three of them were. Although he'd said nothing, Juan's eyes had met mine at each opportunity, and I knew there was love shining from them, but there was speculation in my mind. Did he intend to propose marriage . . . or something else?

Allen interrupted my speculations when he said, "Now, Shadow, I don't want to shock you, but there is something you must know."

Dear Allen, I thought, so pedantic and solemn and so very official. Was he going to tell me I had a diminished fortune?

"When I had almost finished reading through my father's records, I found an account of the bestowal of money on David Roberts when he was nineteen years of age." He glanced at David apologetically. "Attorneys don't usually divulge private matters, but I have your permission to tell Shadow the facts I have discovered."

David nodded.

"Oh, David, have you found out who your parents were?" I asked eagerly. "I know you wanted to so very much."

Allen cleared his throat. "We think so, my dear," he said, "at least one of them."

"Well, who is it?"

He glanced at David again before his eyes returned to me. "The donor of the money was Edward St. George," he said gently.

"My father?" I asked uncertainly.

Allen looked down at his hands, and when I glanced at Juan and David, they also studiously avoided my eyes. Realization came slowly. Edward St. George wouldn't give money to a stranger, so therefore he had known David. And more than just known him.

A blush of embarrassment crept up my face as knowledge of what that meant came to me.

"I told you I was a bastard," David growled.

"Watch your language, Roberts," Juan said curtly.

"Sorry," he muttered.

"Oh, David . . ." I said, and then realized I didn't know what to say.

Allen cleared his throat again. "Look, Shadow, this isn't exactly a rare happening. Your father must have been in love with a woman before he met your mother, that's all."

His eyes focused on David. "If he hadn't been in love with your mother, David, he wouldn't have cared a whit about you, would he? You must admit you had the best care and schooling a child could hope for."

"Oh, sure," David said ironically.

"Well, your father must have thought a great deal of you to go to the trouble to trace where you'd run to and arrange for you to have ten thousand dollars," Allen continued. "Perhaps your mother died before they could get married. All sorts of catastrophes happen to people, and it's no fault of theirs."

He paused, then turned to me. "And you, Shadow, you must not think any the less of your father because of this. I thought it extremely necessary that you know David is your half-brother."

My brother! Well that, of course, explained David's uncanny resemblance to Edward St. George.

David came to kneel beside me. "I'm terribly sorry about all this, Shadow. I had no idea."

I smiled at him. "I should have guessed there was a blood connection when I saw how very like my father you looked."

The worried frown disappeared and David smiled. "I knew there was something that drew me to you from the first," he said. "If you will acknowledge me as your brother, you'll be the only family I've known."

"Acknowledge you! David, I love you!"

Three pairs of startled eyes focused on me.

"Like a brother," I said hastily. "I also felt a tie drawing us together, and for a while I thought I wanted to be your wife. Then I found out otherwise. And now I think it's wonderful to have a brother!"

Relief showed on his face. "It's wonderful to have a sister, especially when it's you." He rose and brushed the knees of his trousers. "Well, I'm glad that's over, my dear sister. Bet I've aged to old manhood since Allen first told me about this."

Aunt Mina peeked around the door jamb. "May I interrupt this meeting to serve tea?" she asked.

Allen jumped to his feet. "Can you wait just a little longer, Aunt Mina? We aren't quite through. That is, Shadow, if you can stand a little more business. . . ."

A foreboding of bad news filled me when I saw his serious face. "Of course, I can," I said, and hoped my words were true.

"You must not tire Shadow too much," Aunt Mina warned. "Tea will be served in half an hour."

"Is it about my aunt, Allen?" I asked. "Is she all right? What's happened to her?"

"She's all right," Allen said. "She is taking everything better than expected. However, she has decided to enter a convent for the remainder of her life."

A convent! My worldly aunt a nun? Then I recalled her sorrow and remorse over Julia. With the horror of her husband's death added to the knowledge that Julia's grandmother had killed them both, she needed solace and a chance to pull her shaken world together. Perhaps in a convent she would find what she needed.

"Are you all right, Shadow?" Allen asked.

"Yes, of course," I said, then more impatiently I added, "If it wasn't my aunt you wanted to discuss, what is it? My inheritance? How much is left?"

David started backing toward the door. "Look . . . before you go into matters that are really none of my business, perhaps I'd better excuse myself."

"It's all right, David," I said. "After all, a brother should know what's happening to his sister."

He returned to kiss my cheek. "Only if his sister needs help. Right now I think you have able assistance at your beck and call, so I'll say good day." He nodded at Juan and Allen and left.

"Now, what is it you want to tell me, Allen?" I asked.

Once more came throat clearing before he said, "I'm afraid I have *very* bad news, my dear. Count Chauvanne used your entire inheritance for himself, and it still wasn't enough, for he left debts, too."

"You mean he spent all of it?" I asked, aghast.

"What about the money I paid him for the mortgage on Roberts's ranch?" Juan asked.

"It's gone. His affairs were in a much worse state than I suspected," Allen said glumly. "But don't look so frightened, Shadow. After the estate is sold—at least what there is left of it—there will surely be something left, and I'll make sure you get it."

I sat stunned by his words. How could such a thing have happened? I had feared my fortune had been diminished to some extent, but this was much worse.

Allen rose to bow over my hand. "Now, my dear, that is enough business for today. You mustn't worry about money. I am forever your slave, you know, and whatever is mine is also yours."

"Thank you," I murmured. It would take some time, I knew, before the full import of his words was borne in on me. What was it like not to have money? A fleeting image of the immigrants on the train that brought me to California flashed through my mind and I felt a chill. That was not having money. And Juan—stranded in a remote village while he tried to earn passage money. Was I to learn how it was to be poor?

I realized I was alone with Juan when he came to smile down at me. "Now that's over, we can relax, my darling." Without a by-your-leave, he bent and scooped me out of the chair.

"Kick off your shoes," he said cheerfully. "Bet your feet are still tender."

His nearness made my pulse quicken, but I tossed my head in pretended pique. "Must you always laugh at me?"

"I'm not laughing at you, my darling," he said with a sober face. "I just want happiness in your life instead of sadness from now on."

He deposited me on the sofa, then knelt before me. "I am going to propose," he announced. "Is this the correct position?"

In spite of myself, I laughed.

"Well, I want to do it right," he insisted. "Is it?"

"I believe kneeling is recommended."

He looked at me for a long moment, then said,

"Will you do me the honor of becoming my wife, Miss Shadow St. George?"

My heart seemed to stop in the flood of love that swept over me. This was Juan, my always beloved, and he was all I needed to be happy for the rest of my life.

"Oh, yes, my darling Juan, I'll marry you."

He gathered me into his arms and kissed me. Heaven opened wide its gates while I melted into his embrace. Happiness erased all worries and memories from my mind as ecstasy filled me with dreamy contentment.

Then a sudden realization made me push away and look at him with horror-stricken eyes.

"What is it, Shadow? What's wrong?" he asked in alarm.

"I have no money! I'm poor!"

Mirth began to fill his eyes while he stared at me, and the corners of his mouth quirked. Then he threw back his head and laughed aloud.

When at last he could speak, he gasped, "Oh, Shadow! Oh, sweet Shadow!"

Indignation seeped in while I watched his performance.

Then he rose and jingled the change in his pocket. "Remember?" he asked. "I'm Johnny Monterro . . . and I have money. Now can we go?"

The scene in Miss Brigham's stable when I had first met Juan returned to my mind. He'd asked me to ride the horse cars with him, and I hadn't even had pocket money.

"I remember," I said, and amusement at his small-boy posturing brought a smile and then laughter.

We giggled together like small children.

"Well?" he demanded, after we'd sobered and caught our breaths. "Now can we go?"

At last I had Johnny. I was no longer merely a shadow someone had left behind. My soon-to-be husband had promised me love and laughter, and I knew he would keep his promise.

I smiled contentedly when he lifted me from the sofa.

"Yes, Johnny . . . now we can go."

CAPTIVATING ROMANCE FROM ZEBRA

MIDNIGHT DESIRE   (1573, $3.50)
by Linda Benjamin

Looking into the handsome gunslinger's blazing blue eyes, innocent Kate felt dizzy. His husky voice, so warm and inviting, sent a river of fire cascading through her flesh. But she knew she'd never willingly give her heart to the arrogant rogue!

PASSION'S GAMBLE   (1477, $3.50)
by Linda Benjamin

Jade-eyed Jessica was too shocked to protest when the riverboat cardsharp offered *her* as the stakes in a poker game. Then she met the smouldering glance of his opponent as he stared at her satiny cheeks and the tantalizing fullness of her bodice—and she found herself hoping he would hold the winning hand!

FORBIDDEN FIRES   (1295, $3.50)
by Bobbi Smith

When Ellyn Douglas rescued the handsome Union officer from the raging river, she had no choice but to surrender to the sensuous stranger as he pulled her against his hard muscular body. Forgetting they were enemies in a senseless war, they were destined to share a life of unbridled ecstasy and glorious love!

WANTON SPLENDOR   (1461, $3.50)
by Bobbi Smith

Kathleen had every intention of keeping her distance from Christopher Fletcher. But in the midst of a devastating hurricane, she crept into his arms. As she felt the heat of his lean body pressed against hers, she wondered breathlessly what it would be like to kiss those cynical lips—to turn that cool arrogance to fiery passion!

Available wherever paperbacks are sold, or order direct from the Publisher. Send cover price plus 50¢ per copy for mailing and handling to Zebra Books, Dept. 1727, 475 Park Avenue South, New York, N.Y. 10016. DO NOT SEND CASH.

THESE ZEBRA MYSTERIES
ARE SURE TO KEEP
YOU GUESSING

By Sax Rohmer

THE DRUMS OF FU MANCHU	(1617, $3.50)
THE TRAIL OF FU MANCHU	(1619, $3.50)
THE INSIDIOUS DR. FU MANCHU	(1668, $3.50)

By Mary Roberts Rinehart

THE HAUNTED LADY	(1685, $3.50)
THE SWIMMING POOL	(1686, $3.50)

By Ellery Queen

WHAT'S IN THE DARK	(1648, $2.95)

Available wherever paperbacks are sold, or order direct from the Publisher. Send cover price plus 50¢ per copy for mailing and handling to Zebra Books, Dept. 1727, 475 Park Avenue South, New York, N.Y. 10016. DO NOT SEND CASH.

TRIVIA MANIA: TV GREATS